THE
TRUTH
COMMISSION

Books by Susan Juby

THE ALICE TRILOGY

Alice, I Think
Miss Smithers
Alice MacLeod: Realist at Last

Another Kind of Cowboy
Getting the Girl: A Guide to Private Investigation,
Surveillance and Cookery
Bright's Light
The Truth Commission

FOR ADULTS

Nice Recovery (memoir)
Home to Woefield (Canada: *The Woefield Poultry Collective*)
Republic of Dirt: Return to Woefield

THE TRUTH COMMISSION

A NOVEL

Susan Juby

illustrations by Trevor Cooper

razOr
bill

RAZORBILL
an imprint of Penguin Canada Books Inc., a Penguin Random House Company

Published by the Penguin Group
Penguin Canada Books Inc., 90 Eglinton Avenue East, Suite 700, Toronto, Ontario, Canada M4P 2Y3

Penguin Group (USA) LLC, 375 Hudson Street, New York, New York 10014, U.S.A.
Penguin Books Ltd, 80 Strand, London WC2R 0RL, England
Penguin Ireland, 25 St Stephen's Green, Dublin 2, Ireland (a division of Penguin Books Ltd)
Penguin Group (Australia), 707 Collins Street, Melbourne, Victoria 3008, Australia
(a division of Pearson Australia Group Pty Ltd)
Penguin Books India Pvt Ltd, 11 Community Centre, Panchsheel Park, New Delhi – 110 017, India
Penguin Group (NZ), 67 Apollo Drive, Rosedale, Auckland 0632, New Zealand
(a division of Pearson New Zealand Ltd)
Penguin Books (South Africa) (Pty) Ltd, 24 Sturdee Avenue, Rosebank, Johannesburg 2196, South Africa

Penguin Books Ltd, Registered Offices: 80 Strand, London WC2R 0RL, England

Published in Razorbill hardcover by Penguin Canada Books Inc., 2015
Simultaneously published in the United States by Viking, an imprint of Penguin Group (USA) LLC

1 2 3 4 5 6 7 8 9 10 (RRD)

Manufactured in the U.S.A.

LIBRARY AND ARCHIVES CANADA CATALOGUING IN PUBLICATION

Juby, Susan, 1969-, author
The Truth Commission / Susan Juby.

ISBN 978-0-670-06759-6 (bound)

I. Title.

PS8569.U324T78 2015   jC813'.6   C2014-904172-1

eBook ISBN 978-0-14-319445-3

American Library of Congress Cataloging in Publication data available

Visit the Penguin Canada website at **www.penguin.ca**

Special and corporate bulk purchase rates available; please see
www.penguin.ca/corporatesales or call 1-800-810-3104.

For my mother, Wendy

SUSTAINABILITY &
CREATIVITY IN ALL THINGS

GREEN PASTURES ACADEMY

OF ART & APPLIED DESIGN

Est. 2007

First let me say that this will not be an easy tale to tell, so I'll warm up with an author's note. That's one of the great things about creative nonfiction. You can write forewords and author's notes, prologues and prefaces before you start the actual story. They are the writing equivalent of jumping jacks and shadow boxing. Fiction writers are supposed to get right to it. Visual artists have it even worse. Most assume no one will read their artist statements before looking at their art. Michelangelo didn't write a preface about where he got the stone for David or an author's note about why he decided to make David's hands so big and his . . . well, never mind.

But authors expect responsible nonfiction readers to read every word. They get to tell the reader what she's going to read, as well as why and how it was written. So here goes:

This is my Spring Special Project for the second term of grade eleven.

The story that follows covers the period from September until November of last term. I can't believe all this happened so recently. It feels like a thousand years have passed.

Here's how this project is supposed to work: Each week I will write and submit chapters of my story to my excellent creative writing teacher.[1] She will give me feedback on those chapters the following week. I will write as if I do not know what will happen next—as if I'm a reporter, which is a device used in classic works of creative nonfiction.[2] When the whole manuscript is done, my teacher will share it with the project's second reader, Mr. Wells, Prince Among English Teachers. When those two arbiters of taste, style, and content sign off on what I've written, I will have my mark for the Spring Special Project. *Et voilà!* as we've been taught to say in French class.

What else do I need to say in order to begin? This might be the time to bring up my use of footnotes.[3] I know not everyone loves them. When we read that heavily footnoted David Foster Wallace essay about going on a cruise,[4] students were divided. Some of us loved the footnotes because they were funny and informative and demonstrated DFW's virtuosic vocabulary. Some of us thought they distracted from the main text and were annoying. Still others of us never do the class readings and so really shouldn't get to

---

1. That would be you, Ms. Fowler!

2. Such as *Fear and Loathing in Las Vegas* by Hunter S. Thompson and *The Electric Kool-Aid Acid Test* by Tom Wolfe.

3.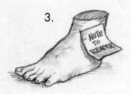

4. "A Supposedly Fun Thing I'll Never Do Again," first published in *Harper's Magazine* as "Shipping Out" (1996). Interesting fact: at first you think the essay's going to be about how wonderful it is to go on a luxurious cruise, but it turns out to be about death. Highly recommended for depressive readers as well as those who like bitter humor, lists, and footnotes.

have an opinion.[5] I don't want to test the reader's patience too much, so here's what I propose.

I will use footnotes to address my editor. I may also use them to include things that a) are interesting, and b) don't really fit in the main text, but nevertheless seem important. I may decide to stop using them partway through the story. Who knows what will happen? My random approach to footnotes might help build tension, which is a very big deal in fiction and in nonfiction. I might also decide to add illustrations and doodles in or near the footnotes. (Readers who are not giving feedback and assigning marks to this project can skip the footnotes, but those readers will be missing interestingness, diversity, and art, and those are things no one should ever miss.)

Finally, and even though this is an author's note and not acknowledgments,[6] I would like to take this opportunity to thank the powers that be at Green Pastures Academy of Art and Applied Design for allowing me to write a nonfiction manuscript for my Spring Special Project. I know other students here at Green Pastures are doing things like creating life-sized replicas of NASA's *Opportunity* rover out of circuit boards, old washing-machine parts, and antique fish tanks, and weaving huge wall hangings featuring images of our prime minister clinging to Parliament's

---

5. Ms. Fowler, may I compliment you on how patient you are with the nonreaders in our class?

6. I can't wait to write my acknowledgments for this project! It's going to be like writing an Academy Awards speech for an award that I gave *to myself!*

Peace Tower like King Kong in a sweater vest, so a regular old written story, especially a true one, seems a little prosaic and uninspired.

My best friend Dusk is doing a tabletop installation featuring a taxidermied shrew in a shrew-sized mobile home. My other best friend, Neil, is doing uncanny paintings of beautiful women. Just when you think you understand how attractiveness works, Neil's oil paintings will make you reconsider.

Their work is so physical and concrete. So *art*-y. It makes me doubt myself as I sit here at a computer, typing out words onto an electronic page. Sure, I do fine art or I wouldn't have been admitted into this school, no matter who my sister is.[7] I draw, I make stuff, and I'm a stitching fanatic (current obsession—embroideries that look like paintings), but I believe that writing is as much an art as any other. Some might fight me on this point, and they would probably win, because I'm not very tough—physically I could stand to work out more—still, I remain sort of convinced.

This story, which my creative writing teacher tells me falls into the "much maligned category of creative nonfiction,"[8] is complicated but it wants to come out. It *needs* to come out.

---

7. More about her later.

8. Just to show I've been paying attention in class, creative nonfiction refers to stories that employ the techniques of fiction, such as being interesting and fun to read, as opposed to fiction that has a few true bits. Notable contemporary practitioners include Jon Krakauer, Annie Dillard, and John Vaillant. Problematic practitioners include James Frey and Greg Mortenson.

Warning: Sometimes when I write, I find myself lapsing into what Mr. Wells calls "high turgid English." That happens when I'm not quite warmed up enough. My hope is, the further I get into this story, the more I'll move into "plain English" or, as Mr. W. styles it, "effective writing." I'm extremely nervous about telling all this stuff. That's the plain truth. Maybe I should write a preface or some other front matter next.[9]

---

9. Front matter is things like tables of contents, author's notes, prologues, prefaces, and copyright pages.

EPIGRAPH[10]

☐ *Tell all the truth but tell it slant.*
—EMILY DICKINSON

☐ *All I know is what I have words for.*
—*PHILOSOPHICAL INVESTIGATIONS,*
LUDWIG WITTGENSTEIN

☐ *Tell the truth, or someone will tell it for you.*
—*STRAIGHT UP AND DIRTY: A MEMOIR,*
STEPHANIE KLEIN

--- --- --- --- --- --- ---

10. Please tick your top choice for epigraph. I can't decide.

PREFACE

In the beginning, I had a mother, a father, a sister, and two real friends. My friends' names were Neil and Dusk. (Her real name is actually Dawn, but she prefers Dusk for reasons having to do with her essential nature and temperament, which is less morning, more evening.) Together, my friends and I formed the Truth Commission. We went on a search for truth and, to our surprise and my chagrin, we found it.

When all this started, the three of us had modest ambitions. We didn't set out to change lives. You will have noticed that there is no "reconciliation" in our title, as with other, more famous and important, truth commissions.[12]

-- -- -- -- -- -- -- -- -- -- -- -- --

11. I wasn't sure whether this should be called a prologue or a preface. As far as I can tell, a preface is more common in nonfiction. Feel free to advise. Would it sound like sucking up to say that I'm really enjoying this creative writing project so far?

12. For the gentle reader who has no knowledge of the subject, a truth commission (also known as a truth and reconciliation commission) is established to help a country's citizens find out the truth about abuses of human rights (such as genocide and torture and false imprisonment)

By the time you finish this story, you will agree that adding a bit of reconciliation to truth-seeking endeavors is a smart move. Neglecting it was an oversight on our part. A bad one.

As you know, there are several classes of truth. There are the truths that pour out on confessional blogs and YouTube channels. There are the supposed truths exposed in gossip magazines and on reality television, which everyone knows are just lies in truth clothing. Then there are the truths that show themselves only under ideal circumstances: like when you are talking deep into the night with a friend and you tell each other things you would never say if your defenses weren't broken down by salty snacks, sugary beverages, darkness, and a flood of words. There are the truths found in books or films when some writer puts exactly the right words together and it's like their pen turned sword and pierced you right through the heart. Truths like those are rare and getting rarer. But there are other truths lying around, half exposed in the street, like drunken cheerleaders trying to speak. For some reason, hardly anyone leans

----

and make recommendations—that's the "reconciliation"—about how to go forward. Think apartheid. Think Canadian residential schools for First Nations peoples. Dusk, Neil, and I were working on a completely different scale, obviously, but we didn't give much thought to reconciling ourselves or anyone else to the truths we found. Why is this a problem? Consider, if you will, the Oxford Dictionary definition of reconciliation: 1. The restoration of friendly relations; 2. The action of making one view or belief compatible with another. I think we can agree that we may have screwed up by leaving that part out.

down to listen to them. Well, Neil, Dusk, and I did. And it turns out those drunken cheerleaders had some shocking things to say.

This is a story about easy truths, hard truths, and those things best left unsaid.

A Vest-Induced Optical Illusion

On the first day of grade eleven, Neil, Dusk, and I were sitting on the benches outside our fair institution of moderate learning, the Green Pastures Academy of Art and Applied Design[13] pretending to smoke candy cigarettes and comparing our running shoes. We have this hobby where we try to see how long our shoes can hold out. In a culture that places undue emphasis on new footwear, we are passive resistors. Dusk has been wearing the hell out of her grandfather's New Balance (size 9, extra wide) for two years. They are disgusting, and Neil and I are envious and wish our grandfathers were still alive so they could give us some old man shoes.

Neil whispered, "Sweet Mother Mary."

"I know. I wore them all summer. I even swam in them. I think they actually rotted onto my feet. Practically had to have surgery to get them off," said Dusk, proudly lifting a wretched shoe the shade and texture of a badly used oyster. Dusk is one of the few people on the planet who can get away with disgusting shoes, because she's chronically attractive. When she has a blemish and hasn't brushed her

----

13. Serving oddballs in grades ten through twelve since 2007.

hair or teeth, she's a fifteen out of ten. On a good day, she's up in the twenties, looks-wise.

"Shhh," said Neil. "Look." He sounded like a bird-watcher who'd just spotted a blue-gray gnatcatcher. Gorgeous women are Neil's subjects, which makes him sound pervy. He's not. He's just very interested. In his drawings and paintings, he seems to be trying to get to the heart of what draws everyone's eye to one woman and not to another. Most of his paintings show a lone beautiful female avoiding the gaze of a crowd. Sometimes she's slipping off the edge of the canvas. Sometimes she's staring, exasperated, into the middle distance, as everything else in the picture seems to lean in toward her. Last summer Neil started a series of paintings of Dusk. He took Polaroids of her in various situations and then created his peculiar, uncomfortable scenarios around her. Dusk is perfect for Neil's paintings because few people can muster such sour facial expressions while remaining devastatingly attractive. Dusk is Neil's muse. Our instructors all think Neil has an extremely mature perspective and an "uncommonly sympathetic eye."[14]

Here's something else I can tell you about Neil: he has an adorably seedy vibe, thanks to his habit of dressing like characters from some of the grittier movies of the late 1960s and early 1970s, and thanks to his father, who leads a life of near-total leisure. For our first day of school Neil had on a too-large, formerly white, large-collared dress shirt over a V-necked T-shirt and brown polyester dress pants. This

---

14. A direct quote from Ms. Dubinsky, who teaches Women and Art: A Wild History at G. P. Academy.

outfit was an homage to Al Pacino's character in *Dog Day Afternoon*, which, according to Neil, is about an incompetent bank robber with a lot of secrets. Of course, no one picks up on the reference. They just think Neil is a super-bad dresser. Which is great.

Dusk and I followed his gaze past our candy cigarettes and spotted Aimee Danes, who'd just gotten out of her claret-colored BMW.

As we watched, Aimee stretched her nose up to catch passing scents and held out her arms to draw the sun's rays to her chest. But what a nose! And what a chest!

Aimee had had some renovations done over the summer.

At the close of grade ten, just three months before, Aimee Danes had an insistent nose. Long and gracefully curved, it was a nose that was sure of itself and its opinions. It was a bit Meryl Streep-ish, and I was a great admirer of its confidence. Her chest never registered with me, which means that it probably wasn't as impressive as her nose, but neither was it nonexistent, because I probably would have noticed that because I am relatively observant. Dusk, for example, is not well endowed. Neil says Dusk has a "runway bust." She replies that it better run on back before she reports it to the authorities. Anyway, back to Aimee and the alterations. Here it was, the first day of grade eleven, and she showed up sporting a shrunken nose and a rampart of a bosom tucked into a white leather vest. You think I kid about the vest. I do not. It appeared soft and made of the rarest hide. Baby unicorn, maybe.

The vest contrasted strangely with the new nose, which appeared to be huddling on Aimee's face, hoping not to be noticed. It was not a nose that would put up its hand and venture a guess. It was not a nose that belonged anywhere near a unicorn-hide vest.

You have to understand that G. P. Academy is not the sort of school where one expects to see plastic surgery. Maybe some of the students who are into the new primitivism have had radical and wince-inducing body modifications like forehead studs or whatever. But no one gets *cosmetic* procedures. We're about self-expression here, but not *that* kind of self-expression.

"Last year all she got was that car," said Dusk as we watched Aimee continue to sniff the air with her tiny nose and expose the Mariana Trench of her cleavage to the warming rays.

"Is all that new?" I whispered, making a windshield wiper gesture with my hand and wondering, as always, if I was seeing the situation clearly.

"Nose or chest?" asked Neil.

"Both, I guess. I mean, I can tell the nose is new. That's too bad. I *loved* her old nose."

"The girls," said Neil, making a vague double-handful gesture, "are definitely new."

"Maybe they just look really big because the nose is so small," I suggested. "And because that vest is so . . . white."

"So you're saying it could be a vest-induced optical illusion?" asked Dusk.

"Maybe. We shouldn't assume."

"I'm pretty sure those kinds of changes are meant to be noticed," said Neil. "They are part of Aimee's self-presentation. My guess is that she'd be devastated if no one noticed. It's like if you spent two days Photoshopping your

Facebook profile picture and no liked it or commented on how good you look."

"So we're supposed to notice but not ask?" said Dusk.

By this time Aimee had begun a series of attention-getting stretches. She looked as though she'd been gardening or bricklaying for eight hard hours and had a crick in her spine.

A lot of her posturing seemed directed at us. Which made sense, because we were the only people around. We had arrived thirty minutes early because we came in my truck, which has a tendency to flood and stall, so we build extra time into every trip.

"We should say something," Dusk whispered.

"Like what?" I asked.

"Tell her she looks nice. She's probably nervous. She's made all these changes and we're the first ones on-site for inspection."

"It's not an inspection," I said. "It's school."

"Same thing," said Dusk.

"We need to be more specific," said Neil, ignoring me. "We should tell her we think the work is excellent. Top-notch and first-rate. Madonna-caliber work."

"People don't want their fakery exposed," I said.

"I think a lot of the time, they do," said Neil.

"We live in an age of unparalleled falseness," said Dusk. Her voice had taken on that rebar quality it gets when she's about to take a stand on some issue. "And I for one have had enough. I'm going to say something." She stood, and her rotted shoes made a squelching sound.

"I don't think this is a good idea," I said.

Dusk repositioned the candy cigarette in the corner of her mouth.

"Dusk, you're the wrong person for the job," I whispered. "You're too perfect." My gaze slid over to Neil.

"Are you suggesting that I'm less than a total Adonis?" said Neil. Then he laughed softly to himself. Neil has longish hair that he slicks back with just a hint too much product. He'd unbuttoned his dress shirt, and the T-shirt was cut low so it showed just a touch too much chest. There are days when Neil wears a silk scarf. Neil kills me, but in a good way. He acts like he has Teflon self-esteem, even though he's one of the most sensitive people I know. His father is a local developer with a shady reputation and a relaxed approach to everything, including parenting his only child.

The first time Dusk and I went over to his house, right after he moved to town last September, Neil greeted us at the front door in a white terry après-swim robe. He'd laid out a tray of pickled onions and pimento-stuffed olives skewered with toothpicks. He asked if we'd like gin and tonics. We said we were driving our bikes, so he gave us cucumber water instead. Neil, Dusk, and I have been inseparable ever since. It's only been a year, but it feels comfortingly like forever. Anyway, back to that first truth telling.

"There are dynamics to consider here," I said.

That was my role in our little threesome. Dynamics considerer. Consequence worrier. Diplomat. Dusk was in charge of our moral compass, passing snap judgments, peer pressuring, and making bold pronouncements. Neil dealt in unconditional acceptance and appreciation of everyone, as well as unpredictable areas of expertise and jokes, mostly aimed at himself.

"Fine," said Neil, completely unflustered. "I'll do it."

By this point, I was no longer certain what we were doing or why, but Aimee was preening so hard that I was concerned she'd damage the vest that a unicorn baby had probably died for.

"Go!" whispered Dusk.

And so Neil got up, adjusted the enormous collar of his dress shirt, and shoved his entire candy cigarette into his mouth. We watched him stride over to Aimee. When he spoke, he was too far away for us to hear what he said.

Aimee's head reared back. Her posture stiffened.

More words from Neil, whose hands were shoved deep in the pockets of his polyester pants. His tan was terrific, because this summer, in addition to painting a series of pictures featuring Dusk, he'd decided to revive what he called the "lost art of sunbathing." He's also working on what he calls a "disturbing hint of a mustache." Disturbing on anyone else. Endearing on him.

As we watched, Aimee's shoulders relaxed. She leaned toward Neil. Touched his shoulder. She laughed and started to talk. Words, indistinguishable words, poured out of her. At the end of the conversation, she put her hand on his shoulder again and she *kissed him*. I swear it's true. Neil had confronted a girl about her new rhinoplasty and freshly installed breast implants and in return he received a kiss on the cheek.

He sauntered back, reverentially holding a hand to the cheek Aimee had kissed.

"She had the procedures done in July because it's her dream to become a broadcast journalist on a major network. She's always wanted a nose job, even though her mother told her that a nose job ruined someone named Jennifer Grey's career. It took some doing for her parents to agree to the implants because there was concern her chest was still growing but she talked them into it and she feels terrific and is glad we live in a time when God's mistakes can be fixed."

"You're a one-man truth commission," said Dusk, admiring.

"The truth shall set us free," said Neil.

"Will it?" I asked. But no one was listening.

"My refreshing directness startled her at first. But it also allowed her to talk about the most important news in her life right now. We're going for coffee later and she's going to give me more details." Neil was immensely pleased with himself. "Aimee and I are now on a different plane, relationship-wise."

"You have no secrets between you," I said, ignoring the twinge of jealousy I felt; Aimee would probably end up being his next muse. Not that I'm keen to be featured in anyone's art. I've had more than enough of that.

"I want to ask someone the truth," said Dusk. "I think truth is what has been missing in my life. Well, it's one of the things that has been missing, along with a sense of purpose and positive self-esteem."

Neil faced us.

"I believe this could be our new spiritual practice," he said. "Each week, each of us will ask someone else the truth."

"It is our destiny to bring some much-needed truth into this world of lies," said Dusk.

And so the Truth Commission was born.

A Word About My Sister

[15]I'm not that keen to get into it, but this story would be incomplete without one major piece of background. As many people already know, I have a sister. She's a famous graphic novelist and, to make a long story extremely short, she made me and my parents famous without our permission. The end.

Ha. Just kidding.

My sister, Keira Pale, is one of those people who seems

- - - - - - - - - - - - - - - -

15. Ms. Fowler, I just got your feedback on my first submission. The timing couldn't be better! You suggested I stop beating around the bush about my personal history and lo! This submission just happens to be about my personal history, specifically as it pertains to my sister. It's like we're reading each other's minds!

Also you are probably drawing some conclusions about me, Dusk, and Neil, conclusions that may be shared by other readers. After all, in addition to your extensive collection of "how to write and feel good about it" books by Anne Lamott and Co., you are a highly trained guidance professional with your own copy of the DSM-V. You have probably diagnosed Dusk as an angry depressive, me as a neurotic, and Neil as a young man overcompensating for self-esteem issues with excessive focus on hot girls, sun tanning, early 1970s films and fashion, and poor boundaries. You wouldn't be wrong. But there's more to us than that, as I think this story will prove. Anyway, carry on! (Aren't you glad you're only a *part-time* guidance counselor? Could you imagine listening to stuff like this full-time?)

to exist on a different plane. Maybe it's an artistic genius thing. G. P. Academy is full of people like Keira. People who go so deep inside themselves, especially when they're working, that they seem like sleepwalkers when they emerge. Traces of unconsciousness seem to cling to them, lending them an otherworldly sheen.

I can't tell you how many times I was sent to find Keira when it was time to eat/go to bed/graduate from high school only to find her deep in conversation with the neighborhood can collector, or out in the backyard staring intently at the moon at 3:30 in the morning, or watching some drama unfold between warring ants in the school parking lot twenty minutes after the bell rang. I believe the technical term is "space cadet."

But she is the kind of space cadet many people aspire to be. My sister is fully alive to each moment and each observation.

When I was younger, living with Keira was like living with a fairy. It was never her intention to be hurtful or destructive. She was just doing what came naturally to her. Telling stories and turning the lives around her into fantastical creations. It wasn't personal. Or so I kept telling myself, even after my sister started publishing her books.

Backstory Alert![16]

My sister's complicated, so I think the only way to help you understand her is through what we learned in class is

---

16. According to what we learned in class, backstory, flashbacks, digressions, and on-the-page musing are all welcome in creative nonfiction. I plan to take full advantage of that fact.

called an infodump. Dear Reader: steel yourself for a taste of death by exposition.[17]

My sister was part of the first group of kids who went through the Green Pastures Academy of Art and Applied Design. As a tenth grader, she'd already begun to write, illustrate, and self-publish installments of her graphic novel series, the Diana Chronicles.

The first volume is called *Diana: Queen of Two Worlds*. Diana, the protagonist, is a suburban girl who lives with her "painfully average" family, which includes her high-strung, easily overwhelmed mother, her ineffectual father, and her dull-witted, staring lump of a sister. Diana, who looks a lot like my sister, also happens to be the queen of Vermeer, a more beautiful or at least more melodramatic alternate universe named after my sister's favorite painter. Vermeer can only be accessed through a closet.[18]

In Vermeer, everything is the same as on Earth but amplified a hundredfold. In Vermeer, Diana's mother is politically and emotionally manipulative and *Game of Thrones* all over the place to keep the family in power. Diana's father is still unaccomplished, but he's also unscrupulous and has a passion for exotic foodstuffs and inappropriate relationships with half the household staff (male and female), as well as

---

17. If you don't know what exposition is, you have not been paying attention in your creative writing class! If you have been away due to a legitimate case of mono or mumps, exposition gives important background information about characters and setting and what happened before the story starts. Exposition can be useful. It can also stall a story deader than my truck on a hill.

18. Yes, the connection to the Chronicles of Narnia is intentional.

several of his first cousins. In Vermeer, as on Earth, Diana is burdened with a flaccid and enormous blob of a sister who is the target of every villain who passes through town. The sister (Flanders) is the especial favorite of cads and rakes who want to align themselves with the House of Vermeer.

In Vermeer, Diana has to keep her family from imploding due to their own stupidity, avarice, and laziness. It's a matter of multiverse importance. If the House of Vermeer falls, Vermeer will descend into war (always likely). Vermeer is Earth's twin, which means that as Vermeer goes, so does the Earth. Or something. I've always gotten a little tripped up on that part of the story.

The Diana Chronicles are funny and complicated and ironic. Diana's a bit of a bitch in both universes. She's rude to her family and half checked out, partly because she's so exhausted by the demands placed on her in Vermeer, where she spends half her time. She needs to be left alone to recuperate when she's in the Earth realm, but her mundane Earth family keeps interrupting. They sense her specialness and want a part of it.

The first chapters of the Diana Chronicles were photocopied and sold online and stocked in a few specialty stores. It gained an instant and devoted following. The combination of extremely personal stuff about Diana's life on Earth and the over-the-top violence and politicking in Vermeer made it hugely compelling to a lot of people. Her agent, Sylvia Kalfas, discovered her and got her a book deal with Viceroy, who put the chapters together into Volume 1. The money from that first book deal, which was serious, went into a trust administered by Sylvia and my parents until Keira turned twenty. The *Los Angeles Times* called the first

Chronicle "groundbreaking and hilarious." The *Globe and Mail* said the "combination of autobiography and fantasy make it an intoxicating entertainment." The *Guardian* said it was "wildly inventive." Readers couldn't get enough. People mentioned *Maus*, which is what people always talk about when they talk about massively popular graphic novels. (The Chronicles have less than nothing to do with *Maus*. Just to be clear.)

Keira had published three Chronicles by the time she left for college, which was the same year I entered Green Pastures. Each new Chronicle was more popular than the last.

This is probably the time to bring up the fact that Diana's family members look *a lot* like me and my mother and father. They are exaggerated versions, but identifiable. Of all of us, I'm the most deformed. The sister character is called Flanders (in a not-so-subtle reference to the fact that I was named after a famous World War battleground), and nicknamed the Flounder because she looks sort of like an obese, blank-faced flounder fish. I was a chubby kid, but I've lost most of my baby fat. I am not enormous and I am not dull-witted, not unless I'm really tired. In other words, we are ordinary people who have been made to look extraordinary, and not in a good way.

You cannot imagine how embarrassing it is to be in those books, especially when all the Earth plotlines are taken from minor and usually un-excellent incidents in our real life. The plots hit Vermeer and go so over the top, it's almost impossible to remember where they started.

Man, this chapter is getting long. And exhausting. Possibly also boring. But I'm not quite done.

Further background fact: I have never before spoken

to anyone outside my family about how I feel about our depiction in my sister's books. To be honest, we've never really discussed it *inside* my family, either. Breaking that long-standing silence is really taking it out of me.

My parents have always treated Keira like a rare and delicate houseplant they aren't quite sure how to care for. There's a good reason for that. She's like a rare and delicate houseplant they aren't sure how to care for.

End of backstory! Finally!

XXXXX

At the time I'm writing about, things had gotten strange at home. *Strange* is the wrong word. *Bad.* That's better.

After she graduated from Green Pastures, Keira took a year and a half off to write and draw the third Chronicle and bask in her ever-growing success. Then she went off to the most prestigious art and animation school in North America, CIAD—the California Institute of Art and Design.

Meanwhile, I, Keira's younger sister, Normandy Pale, started grade ten at G. P. on a partial scholarship. Keira had said she wanted to help out our parents by paying off the mortgage and covering some of my tuition, but things hadn't worked out on that front so far.

When I first got to school, I was semi-famous thanks to my sister's books. Everyone assumed that I was the staring blob from the Chronicles, the hapless target of pervs and leeches, even though I wasn't particularly big and didn't stare much more than anyone else.

Soon people realized I was deadly average, and I settled in and met my two friends—who just happened to be my first friends, really. With Keira away, life at home got simpler. She had always required a lot of quiet when she was working, so my parents and I had to tiptoe around. Strangers threw her off, so we didn't invite anyone over. Now we could do potentially embarrassing things and not have them end up in a book. It was pretty much a halcyon time.

Then, without warning, Keira came home at the beginning of April, not long after she turned twenty. She arrived in her white 1987 Crown Victoria, which looks disconcertingly like an unmarked police car.

She wouldn't tell us what happened, and when my parents asked if everything was okay, Keira got mad and said she'd leave if they asked again. So they dropped it. We're not really discussers in my family. After all, who wants to rip open a bunch of scar tissue to expose the abscess beneath? Not that I mean to compare my sister to an abscess. She is more like an inheritance.

Imagine someone gives you an incredibly valuable and famous gem. You can't sell it. Your only job is to look after it. Now imagine your behavior can ruin the value of that gem. If you talk too loud or watch TV, you can tarnish it or crack it. Finally, take the next step and imagine that the gem you inherited likes to tell stories about what happens in the house where you are already trying to be extra careful so you won't wreck the gem. Okay. That's enough. The gem analogy has officially fallen apart.

Anyway, in September, at the time our story begins, my sister was even less right than usual. She rarely left her room or our closet. When she did leave, she stayed out for days and we had no idea where she went. My mother turned nearly catatonic with concern, and my dad fussed around trying to distract himself. I concentrated on not making things worse. In other words, I made myself an extra unobtrusive presence. Caused no waves. Went to school. Did my work. When Keira was home, we tried not to upset her.

We were all just waiting for her to tell us what was wrong and what had happened at school.

The afternoon of the first truth telling, I went home and found Keira in our closet. For those who follow her career, it's true: she actually does work in a closet that we share. We each have a door to it, but she's the only one who uses the space.

You probably want a visual of her, to help you digest all this dry, dusty exposition. So here goes:

Keira has wild, two-toned hair (dark brown and silvery blonde) and dark circles under her eyes. There are photos of her as a toddler that show that, even then, she had dark circles under her eyes. She is a wisp of a person, and after she started making money and visiting New York on publishing business, she started buying all of her clothes from a store in

SoHo called 45 RPM. They specialize in handwoven fabrics cut into simple shapes that make anyone over a hundred pounds look frumpy and anyone under a hundred pounds look like she stepped out of a clamshell on an enchanted beach. Keira owns about fifteen garments in total. Her look is based on white cotton smocks and eleven-hundred-dollar jeans made from Zimbabwean cotton and hand-dyed by Japanese arti-sans. Her feet are almost always bare or encased in delicate ballet slippers.

These clothes are not very warm, so I often open my closet to find her wearing one of my sweaters. Sometimes two. It's funny that she sometimes borrows my clothes, since I'm not noted for the excellence of my wardrobe.

In another story, this closet dwelling would be a heavy-handed sign that my sister has repressed sexual urges. She does not.[19] She says she likes to situate herself at the "por-tal." She's turned that portal, AKA our shared closet, into a beautifully appointed art studio. She had excellent lighting installed, and she sits cross-legged on a special meditation seat, at a custom drafting lap desk she designed and built.

When she first started working in our closet, I asked if she wanted me to keep the door on my side locked, so she could have it all to herself. She said no. She said she found it comforting to have me close-by. I was ten, and my hero worship of my sister was at an all-time high. Now I'm stuck with no closet, which means that I have to keep my clothes in a cupboard in my room.

When I walked into my bedroom that afternoon, I could hear her humming as she worked. Having Keira at work in the closet meant I'd have to be very quiet all night, but having her at home meant my mom would be less worried. So that was good.

"Keira," I said after I gently knocked, then opened the door. "How's it going?"

---

19. At least, I don't think she does.

"I'm fine," she said. "Working."

So I quietly closed the door, picked up my needlework and schoolbag, and left. I would do homework for an hour or two, followed by a little writing, and then work on my embroidery until it was time for bed. There are few arts quieter than writing and stitching.

And that, folks, is a glimpse at life with my sister.

I would end this too-long chapter there, except I can't.

Because at midnight that same night, Keira left the closet and came into my room.

I was awoken by her soft voice.

"Normandy? Are you asleep?"

I raised my head. The room was dark. Keira had turned out the lights in the closet. She was just a shape in the darkness.

"No," I croaked.

"Can I come up?" she said.

"Sure." My sister hadn't gotten into bed with me since— well, since before she published the first Chronicle.

She shuffled up onto my bed. She'd wrapped herself in a puffy sleeping bag she keeps in the closet for when the "portal gets drafty" and my sweaters aren't protection enough. I have a queen-sized bed, which is one of the most luxurious things in my life. I got it from Neil when his dad decided to change all the mattresses in their house, which he does every two years. I sincerely hoped this mattress was Neil's or from a guest bedroom, and not his dad's. Anyway, there should have been plenty of room for me and my sister, but somehow it didn't seem like enough. She lay halfway down the bed, so she was talking to my knee.

"I think it's time for me to tell someone what happened."

Keira's voice is soft and raspy. It goes with her haunted eyes and distracted demeanor. I used to live for the times my sister would focus her blazing attention on me. Her focus was so total, it seemed to transform the entire world. Just talking to her used to turn me into someone special. That was before I got scared of talking to her. Scared of what she would do with our conversations. With my small secrets.

The key was to let her take the lead. Not react.

I could hear my heart thud in my chest. I wanted to know what was wrong, but I also felt unqualified. What if I listened badly and made things worse?

"I need to tell someone what happened at school," she said.

"Ponchohontas" and Other Problematic Tales

[20]I'm really not ready to go into what my sister said.[21] I mean, the details were fuzzy and she has this way of stretching stories out in a way that's almost painful,[22] so I'll move the narrative back to school. As we are so often reminded in creative writing class, this is referred to as a transition. These are the points in the writing that move the reader from one place and time to another. Without clear, brisk transitions, all books would be like *Under the Volcano*. I dare you to read twenty pages of that and tell me what happened. Nothing clear and brisk, I assure you. So, consider this your transition.

--- --- --- --- --- --- --- --- --- --- ---

20. P.S. Thank you for your editorial feedback on my last chapter. It was very encouraging! In other news, I saw you and Mr. Wells talking at the entrance to the Guidance Office. I'm going to tell myself that the fact that you had a copy of my last chapter in your hand is a coincidence. He's not supposed to read this until you've approved the first draft. Still, he got all blushy when I walked up, so that's interesting. Okay. Carry on.

21. I hope you approve of the cliff-hanger at the end of Chapter Two. It wasn't intentional. I was just tired out and couldn't continue. Maybe the cliff-hanger was invented by an exhausted writer.

22. As noted, there are other reasons her stories are painful, but there's no need to harp on that.

A week after the first truth, Dusk found us Candidate #2.[23] [24]

Mrs. Dekker. Office secretary.

Mrs. Dekker is right out of central casting. The unhappy secretary, with back-combed bangs, a sun-ravaged complexion, and a dyspeptic expression. And let's not forget the PONCHO! Worn for most of the school year, the poncho tends to suggest a certain lightness of spirit. After all, ponchos indicate a person is a funny sort who likes to surround herself with her own snuggly body heat.

Mrs. Dekker's poncho had pom-poms at the edges. It looked like it was from Peru or Bolivia or some other poncho-producing nation. In shades of red and orange, that poncho indicated oneness with the earth and possibly a side career in hillside potato farming.

But one only needed to raise one's eyes to Mrs. Dekker's face to see that the poncho was not the accurate character marker[25] it ought to have been. The poncho set up expecta-

---

23. Now I forge into that difficult territory in which I write about one of your colleagues and refer constantly to the class handout on libel and slander and how not to get sued for your work of creative nonfiction.

24. I think I'm overusing footnotes. I'll try to cut back. As for the correct placement of superscripts, let's worry about that later. I like little numbers popping up at random in the beginning or middle of a sentence! It keeps things lively. Action-packed, you might say!

25. Character markers being those smallish details that tell a bigger story about a person. Examples might include the school a person attends—Ivy League versus community college, art school versus technical; or the vehicle a person drives—Lexus versus *Firefly*; clothes—Hermès scarves versus ponchos. See? I pay attention in class!

tions and then destroyed them. It might even have been a red herring.

When you raised your eyes from the handwoven and hand-embroidered Bolivian/Peruvian joy of the poncho to see the thin-lipped mouth and slitted eyes, Mrs. Dekker went from gentle back-to-the-lander to Clint Eastwood at his least forgiven.

I happen to know that Mrs. Dekker scares not just students but also teachers, and even Principal Manhas walks softly ~~among~~[26] around her.

When a person or a person's parent calls Green Pastures Academy of Art and Applied Design to report that a person has a *legitimate* illness, Mrs. Dekker has decided it's her job to heap on the shame and scorn.

"Oh really," she rasps, sounding like she was exhaling smoke from an extra strong Cuban cigar. "And I'm supposed to believe that?"

All this makes her sound kind of salty and charming. It is not. She is not. Rumor has it that when George Chan was carried past the office on a stretcher by *uniformed paramedics* after he fell off some risers in the drama room, Mrs. Dekker hacked a cough into the poncho-covered crook of her arm and said, "Some people will do anything to get out of class." As we all know, George broke his arm *and* his

---

26. For some reason, "among her" sounds great here, but I know it's wrong. I'm going to keep it in place, with a line through it, so you see that your editorial feedback is getting through (and is probably having a negative impact on my sense of imaginative freedom).

neck and spent six months walking around school like an extra from season one of *The Walking Dead*, back when the series had a proper budget.

Mrs. Dekker hates students and teachers. She doesn't like her job or the education system. I personally know two students who have sustained bruises when they were knocked over by Mrs. Dekker in her 3:10 p.m. après-school race to reach her Dodge dually.[27]

Dusk, who has a soft spot for negative people, chose Mrs. Dekker to be the next target of the Truth Commission.

"You can't ask her about anything personal. It's not safe," I said.

"It really isn't," agreed Neil.

"You can't even report an absence to that woman, never mind ask her intimate, probing questions. She'll tear your guts out," I added.

Neil nodded. Sighed. Rallied his courage. "You know what? I think it's worth the risk. Just make sure you ask her in a safe place. *Not the office!*"

"Why not?" I asked. "Principal Manhas is there to keep order. The nurse's office is nearby. You know, in case it goes wrong."

Dusk shook her head. Her ponytail looked like it had

----

27. For readers who are not familiar with dual-lies, I offer you this enriched footnote with an illustration. It is a truck with four tires in the back and two in the front. It's a badass truck, though not usually known for fuel efficiency.

been slept on for three days straight and then a troll had spent an enjoyable hour poking at it with old branches and broken cutlery. Yet somehow, the ponytail still looked like it belonged on a Fashion Week catwalk.

"Can't ask her in the office. It's the scene of so many unhappy hours. I have to talk to her in neutral territory."

"You're going to follow her to the most hellish part of Peru?" I asked.

Dusk rested her chin on the back of her hand and stared at me.

I shrugged. "She always looks to me like she should be in Peru. The unhappy part of the country."

"Wasn't Paddington Bear something to do with Peru?" asked Neil, opening his lunch: a jar of olives, a box of ten-dollar crackers, and a block of cheese covered in Welsh thistle dust or similar.

"I'm going to speak to her near her truck," said Dusk. "That truck seems to be her happy place."

"Death wish," muttered Neil, breathing out a small cloud of cracker particles. He brushed the residue off the chest of his dark blue turtleneck (à la Steve McQueen in *Bullitt*) with the backs of his fingers.

We were sitting outside at the pitted picnic table in a small cul-de-sac between the office and the curved brick wall of the theatre. It was shaded by a gnarled, misshapen tree. Thanks to a fork in the trunk, the tree is a popular site for photo shoots and portrait paintings. More than once a naked or semi-naked student has been asked to get out of the tree by Mrs. Dekker or one of the teachers, due to safety concerns and regulations having to do with student nudity on school property. The Green Pastures Academy of Art and Applied Design is *that* kind of school.

A small brown wren had come along and was hopping toward a fallen morsel of cheese, an avid look in its round black eye.

"Don't eat that!" Dusk admonished it. "Your cholesterol levels will skyrocket. If you must scavenge, scavenge from me." She scattered a bit of her homemade granola on the dead grass.

"Let the bird live, woman," said Neil as he tucked the thistle-covered cheese into its wrapper and the rest of his lunch into a linen napkin and put it all away in the tackle box he uses to keep his paints and brushes. Then he shrugged on his brown suit jacket, another key component of McQueen's *Bullitt* look. He'd earlier asked if it would be "too much" to wear one of those shoulder pistol harnesses that look sort of like suspenders, and we assured him it would be quite a bit too much.

I tried to refocus us. "I'm just saying, Mrs. Dekker's truck has *six* fully inflated tires. On most days, Nancy has only three." Keira named the truck Nancy for reasons I can no longer remember. She gave her to me when I turned sixteen last year and got my learner's license. My sister is like that. She is prone to bursts of careless generosity. At least, she used to be.

"Well, I'm not going to follow Mrs. Dekker home," said Dusk. "We need to ask the truth on or near school property. We are not free-range truth seekers."

This is a fine illustration of how weird little rituals develop. One person says something is a rule, and then it is. Once in a while there's an argument and the rule is changed slightly, but mostly these things happen arbitrarily. Come to think of it, more argument might have been a good idea when we were establishing the Truth Commission.

Before we could ask Dusk any more questions, the bell rang and we had to go in for history. That would be followed by traditional arts (me), sculpture and installation (Dusk), and AP oil painting (Neil). Our school is the brainchild of a farmer named Ronald Green who, late in life, became a famous and wealthy international artist thanks to his uncannily powerful paintings of pastures, barns, and feedlots. (As our instructors like to say, with a discernible note of bitterness, "It's just plain amazing how much money some artists make.") Ronald Green was like the Grandpa Moses of Nanaimo. Our Founding Farmer.

No one thought a private high school for artistically inclined high school students would work in a town of less than 90,000. They were wrong. Green Pastures[28] has a long waitlist. Our students are a mix of the rich, the bullied, and the talented—usually some combination of all those things—plus those like me, who got a scholarship because my sister is a famous alumna and they probably hoped that I'd have some thin shreds of her ability.

I made sure I was ready to sprint out of class when the bell rang at 3:10. Neil must have done the same, because we met in the hallway at 3:11, but we weren't quite fast enough. When we reached the lobby outside the office, moving like a pair of power walkers—no running in the halls of Green

------

28. It is too bad the school sounds like a funeral home, but you can't have everything.

Pastures because there was too much chance of knocking over one of the many ethereal, artistic types wandering around in hip glasses with the wrong prescription—we were just in time to see Mrs. Dekker's poncho sweeping out the door. Dusk, in her vintage Adidas warm-up suit, was hot on her heels. Mrs. Dekker looked like a Dorito running away from a stoner.

"She's gone off the reservation," said Neil.

The two of us followed at a careful distance, pushing through the glass doors and past the Photoshoot Tree. The path led to the teacher and staff parking lot. Teachers didn't finish until 3:30, so Dusk and Mrs. Dekker were more or less alone out there.

"Excuse me," said Dusk. "Mrs. Dekker?"

Neil and I backed away and took our seats on the picnic table. We couldn't hear, but we sat sideways so we could watch the scene unfold out of the corners of our eyes. We were ready to run for help if Mrs. Dekker pulled a knife on Dusk or began to smother her with the poncho.

My heart thudded and I could hear Neil breathing quickly.

Dusk and Mrs. Dekker faced each other. Dusk spoke and Mrs. Dekker stood very still. Then she leaned in to listen more carefully.

"This is making me crave antianxiety meds," said Neil.

Then, astonishingly, Mrs. Dekker shook her head and leaned back against the gleaming rear wheel well, as though settling in for a chat. She began to speak. She pointed a thumb at an animal-shaped sticker in the back window of the truck's extended cab and shook her head again.

She put her hands on her hips, at least I think she did. That poncho hid a lot. She spoke some more.

Neil and I watched, fascinated. Dusk hadn't moved, but some of the tension had gone out of her body.

The two of them talked for fifteen minutes. Teachers passed on the way to their cars, staring in obvious amazement at the tête-à-tête. *No one ever* chatted with Mrs. Dekker. When they were done, Mrs. Dekker reached up and put a hand on Dusk's shoulder. Then she swept away in her poncho, climbed up into her truck, and drove away, leaving behind a cloud of diesel exhaust.

Dusk returned dreamily to us, coughing out small puffs of pollution.

"We're dying here," said Neil. "What did you talk about for *fifteen minutes?*"

Dusk smiled.

"Ostriches," she said.

We waited.

"Mrs. Dekker raises ostriches. She is, in fact, one of the foremost breeders in the region."

I was too busy reeling from the obvious symbolism to say anything,[29] but Neil responded without hesitation.

"So what does that have to do with the truth about Mrs. Dekker? Why she hates her job? Hates students?"

"She doesn't hate her job or the students. She even called me 'honey.' She said that she is often worried because ostriches are, and I quote, 'surprisingly tricky wee scunners.'

----

29. You know: ostriches are famous for putting their heads in the sand to avoid unpleasant realities. Maybe the connection with me isn't obvious at this point in the story, but I feel I must mention it in case I can get credit for noticing thematic connections, which are extremely important in works of creative nonfiction.

Mrs. Dekker is of Dutch-Scottish heritage, not Peruvian, as you'd speculated, Norm. She visited Scotland over the summer and picked up some of the lingo. Hence the term 'wee scunners.'

"She's saddened that her natural brusqueness, quite common among the Dutch and some Scots, is mistaken for ill temper. She started wearing the poncho so people would find her more approachable. It hasn't worked. However, the poncho *has* been useful for keeping infant ostriches warm. Orphaned ones."

"You should suggest she go the Aimee route," I said. "Get her face surgically adjusted to express her warm, sunny personality."

"Don't be mean, Norm," said Dusk. "Being a part-time ostrich farmer is not as lucrative as it used to be. In fact, over the past several years the bottom has fallen out of what is known as the Aves market. When Blaire—that's her first name—started, a breeding pair might go for fifty thousand dollars. Hatching eggs went for a thousand. But that was a long time ago. Things have changed in the ostrich-ranching world. At this point, she probably doesn't have the funds to get her face done."

"Blaire?" said Neil.

"Ostriches?" I added. But before I could bring up the whole "head in the sand" thing, Dusk went on.

"Blaire—Mrs. Dekker—*thanked me* for asking her how she felt about her job. She thanked me for asking her the truth about how she feels. We are sisters in truth. Or at least friendly acquaintances."

"Just like me and Aimee," said Neil. "We are really onto something here. I'm so in love with the three of us right now. Which reminds me, I'm getting together with Aimee tonight. We're doing coffee before her date with Joel Nordstrom. She just wants to touch base first."

"Doesn't she call you almost every day now?" I asked.

Neil sighed. "Yeah, I'm pretty much part of Aimee's inner circle."

I didn't point out that Aimee had yet to invite him out with her friends. She just took him aside and dumped all her problems on him. Neil, lover of female beauty, didn't seem to care that the relationship was unequal. He was probably getting ready to ask Aimee to pose for him. As I have already mentioned a time or ten, the last thing I wanted was to be featured in anyone else's art, but I couldn't help feeling slightly left out. I pushed my feelings aside.

Dusk barreled on. "I think Mrs. Dekker may have smiled at the end of our little talk. Also, she twice told me to call her Blaire and told me that she calls her truck Gervais. Isn't that funny? She loves Ricky Gervais. So you know she's okay, deep down, even if she is pretty upset about her ostrich troubles."

"Right," I said. "Well, I'm glad we have learned the not-so-dark truth about Mrs. Dekker. She's just Scottish and Dutch and has ostriches."

Dusk leaned her head back and breathed in deeply. "I feel so amazing right now. The truth is strong, Norm. Really strong. I can't wait until you ask someone the truth."

I smiled, but didn't tell her that I was already getting all the truth I could handle.

Represent![30]

A few days after Dusk broke truth with Mrs. Dekker and discovered ostriches, I came home to find Keira's former agent, Sylvia, sitting on our couch. Since Keira suddenly came home, Sylvia has made the trip from Los Angeles to Nanaimo every couple of months to see how Keira is doing and to check whether anything has changed, meaning

- - - - - - - - - - - - - -

30. It's funny how when you start a story you might not be sure what you want to say or how to say it, but the more you write, the clearer it becomes. I would not have expected that, had I not embarked on this project. Before I continue, I wanted to say that I noticed yesterday that you were wearing not just lipstick, but also, forgive me for pointing it out, a new scent. In English, I noticed that Mr. Wells also wore a new scent. He didn't over-shoot the mark into Axe Body Spray territory, but he definitely smelled of something effortful. Coincidence? Ha! Won't it be funny and charmingly awkward when you two confab over this chapter at the end of term! I know you told me not to make comments about you and Mr. Wells in the text, but footnotes aren't really the text, as you've pointed out when you say that they have a way of "pulling you out of the text." Anyway, it's like you always tell us in class: a writer must be brave and honest. Politeness is the death of good prose. God, I kill myself sometimes. Anyway, let me transition seamlessly back to the primary narrative . . .

  P.S. Thanks also for your comments on the last chapter. I know it had too much backstory but I appreciate that you think it's necessary and that it works. I promise to focus on action as much as possible from now on.

whether a) Keira has decided to rehire Sylvia and let her sell the film option for Diana; b) Keira has finished the new Chronicle, for which her publisher has been waiting; or c) some other agent has tried horning in on her ex-client.

Several major movie studios were interested in optioning the Diana Chronicles. For those who don't know, an option gives a producer the right to turn a property[31] into a film or TV series. The studios wanted to turn the Chronicles into one of those "tent pole" movies that would support the whole studio for a season. The producers said they wanted to make at least three movies based on the books.[32] But my sister wouldn't sell the rights. When Sylvia pushed, Keira fired her. That happened not long after Keira came home from college.

When I walked into the house, my mother was in the kitchen making coffee. Coffee is about the last thing my mother, who has the most threadbare nerves of anyone not currently being experimented upon in a lab, should have.

"Hello, Normandy," said Sylvia from the living room. She has black hair with red accents, and aggressive eyewear. She used to run the horror division of a publishing company before she started representing writers and artists.

As always, I was happy to see her. She's extremely

---

31. The word *property* should give you some idea about how the relationship between writers and film companies works. Yes, I am repeating something I heard my sister's agent say.

32. Since you are a dedicated creative writing teacher/guidance counselor, I won't tell you exactly how much money Keira's been offered. (Salt: stop looking at that wound!) Just know that it's an obscene amount.

un-suburban and charismatic and has this way of making you feel like you're the only thing standing between her and death due to boredom.

"Hi, Sylvia."

"Talk to me, Normandy. Tell me what you're reading. I need the freshness of your young mind to clear my own suffocating cynicism and despair."

Sylvia is in her forties. Now that I think about it, she's probably about the same age as my parents. It's odd. The difference between their forty and hers is the difference between a forty-year-old horse and a forty-year-old parrot. The horse is tottering around on its last legs, and the parrot looks the same as it ever did. My parents have this ground-down quality that is probably related to worrying about my sister. I also wonder if they're exhausted by their never-ending wait for Keira to appreciate them or at least for their investment in her career to pay off, financially or otherwise.[33] Sylvia, on the other hand, looks like she eats stress as an *amuse-bouche* and turns problems into cocktails. Or something like that.

The best thing about Sylvia is that she always asks my

_____

33. Poignant background detail: my parents both wanted to be artists and go to art school. My dad wanted to make models for architects, and my mom wanted to do some sort of graphic design. But right after high school, while they were working to save money, they got pregnant with Keira and they didn't have much family support and so they had to give up their dreams. They've mentioned about thirty thousand times how much they would have loved to attend a school like Green Pastures. It goes without saying that they are familiar with living vicariously through their kids. Mostly Keira.

opinions about books and movies and music. I pretty much love her. She makes me wish I had an agent.

I sighed, like I wasn't interested in being listened to.

"There's this book called *Auntie Mame*. I found it at McGrew's Second Hand."

"Oh, my God! To read *Auntie Mame* for the first time. You lucky, lucky thing."

I was disappointed she'd already read it, but trying to name a book Sylvia hadn't already read was part of the fun. Lots of people *say* they read everything, but Sylvia really does.

"Have you finished it?"

"No. Too busy in school right now."

"Ah," said Sylvia. "You call me when you're done with *Mame*. We'll talk about it. The author, Patrick Dennis, had an amazing life. After selling millions of books, he left the writing life and became a butler. His employers had no idea who he was. Apparently he loved buttling."

I made a mental note to look him up, and also to check whether buttling is a recognized verb.[34]

"What are you working on at the Art Farm?" she asked. The Art Farm is the name Keira gave to the G. P. Academy, with one part fondness to two parts disdain. I don't think it ever occurred to my sister that some people need extra creative nurturing. She would have had mind-blowing artistic output no matter how she was raised.

I debated whether to tell her. Sylvia, for all her coolness, was in our house because of Keira. She was only there to

- - - - - - - - - - - - - - -

34. It is.

see if Keira had snapped out of whatever state of suspended animation she'd fallen into.

I considered telling Sylvia about the Truth Commission. That was something that might catch her attention. It was just strange enough.

No, and no.

"Oh, you know. We're doing oils in painting. We're doing embroidery in traditional arts class. One of my friends is exploring small animal taxidermy."

"Taxidermy? Really. How cutting-edge. It's *the* hot thing in London right now, you know."

I did not, but I wasn't surprised. Dusk has a way of finding the edge of everything. She has some sort of trend-spotting instinct that I completely lack.

"English? Math? Computers? Science?" Sylvia asked. "What about those classes?"

"Oh, yeah, we're doing those, too. I'm just telling you about the ones where I'm getting over a B."

Of course, Keira never got a grade lower than an A and rarely lower than an A+, no matter what the subject.

"We're also doing a creative nonfiction module in creative writing. I'm enjoying it," I said, trying to keep Sylvia's attention. She'd begun craning her head to catch a glimpse of Keira.

My mother came into the living room carrying a tray. She still had on her blue postal uniform pants and limp waterproof jacket. She set down the tray with two mugs of coffee, a carton of half-and-half, and a dish of sugar.

"I'm sorry, Sylvia. I can't remember how you take your coffee."

My mother can't remember anything since Keira came

home. As noted, we'd slipped into a new, more open way of living while my sister was at CIAD, doing the kinds of things that would make us look pathetic if they were shown in the Chronicles. For instance, my parents started socializing again with their few friends, such as the nice gay couple from Dad's Diorama Club,[35] and Mom's only friend from work, a woman so glum, she makes my mom seem practically vivacious. And they'd started up with old hobbies that Keira had lampooned. My dad created reenactments of famous battle scenes using tiny, hand-painted models, and my mom handmade jigsaw puzzles. A few times I invited Dusk and Neil over, and even tried some minor alterations to my appearance, such as changing the direction of the part in my hair. No big deal to most people—daring in the extreme for someone who grew up under Keira's magnifying glass. We made more noise and resumed doing some normal, everyday things.

Let me give you a specific, concrete visual[36] example. As you know if you've read the Chronicles, the Earth mother's[37] hair looks like old rags. My real mother's hair *is* quite limp, and not just because she's a postal carrier and

----

35. Dad was president until the unfortunate incident (his extramarital affair) with the checkout girl. Whose uncle happened to be the secretary. The nice gay couple, Georges and Claude, are the only ones who still speak to him.

36. Because if there's anything creative writing teachers love, it's specific, concrete *visual* details.

37. By "Earth mother" I mean the mother who exists in the Earth realm of my sister's comics, not a hemp-trouser-wearing, quinoa-eating, downward-dog-doing mom.

out in the elements all day.[38] You see, Keira's sensitive to
noises, so no one in our house has ever used a hair dryer.
But some people, like my mother, have fine hair and need a
blowout for volume. About two months after Keira left for
CIAD, my mom started blow-drying her hair. All of a sud-
den it looked cute. Lively. Full of body. Practically a L'Oréal
commercial. The dryer disappeared the day Keira came
home, and not just because the noise would bother her. I
think my mom stopped blow-drying her hair because she
remembered the spread in one Diana Chronicle that showed
the Earth mother's tragic attempts to curl her bangs, which,
of course, was based on a real-life incident. My mom had
been new to curling irons and her first attempts left her
looking like she'd taped a sausage to her forehead.

The experiment should have been a fond family anec-
dote. Instead, it became a cruel joke in the Earth realm of
the Chronicle. It inspired a Vermeer plotline in which the
mother gets into a battle of the Grand Dames over who has
the highest hair. The competition to create the most impressive edifice ends with the Vermeer mother's enormous
coiffure catching fire and burning down half the castle.
Only Diana's quick thinking saves them all from dying.
The father is caught in a compromising position with some
oranges and a scullery maid. Getting Flounder off her divan
and down a staircase nearly cripples three knights.

All very funny, but I have to point out that it takes
time to learn to curl hair, and a certain amount of privacy.
That's something we don't have when my sister's home.

----

38. And because she had to give up her dreams to raise two kids.

End result: none of us have styled hair. Living in our house is like being a reality television star against your will and without the requisite narcissistic personality. What would you do? Answer: as close to nothing as possible.

Back to the awkward coffee visit in the living room with my sister's agent.

"This is perfect," said Sylvia, smiling her crooked city smile. She lifted a mug to her lips and sipped politely.

My mother finally shrugged off her jacket and went to the hall closet beside the front door.

"So how are things going?" asked Sylvia.

"I think they're going okay," said my mother, still facing the closet. "Don't you agree, Normandy?"

"Yeah," I said, trying not to think about what my sister had told me in the dark. "Things are good."

My mother sat down in the green chair, easily the nicest piece of furniture in our house. Keira bought it before she left for CIAD. The chair was created by a famous German designer whose name sounds like something a school-yard bully calls you before delivering a beating. It cost about the same amount as Mrs. Dekker's dually truck, and we probably shouldn't sit in it because it might end up forming the basis of my parents' retirement plan, but there are only so many seating options in the living room, which is pretty small.

My mother has a tendency to perch when she sits in the German chair, as though she's worried there's a hidden ejector button.

"Is Keira ready to speak to me yet?" asked Sylvia.

My mom and I exchanged glances. In another family, one of us might have gone to ask Keira if she'd like to come out and talk to Sylvia. But this was chez Pale.

"You know she loves you, Sylvia." My mother's hands clutched her knees. Her fingers looked raw. Her eczema had been acting up. "She just needs time."

Sylvia put down her mug. "I feel terrible about this, and I don't want to pressure her. But there is a financial issue at stake here. Keira's financial future. My financial future. Perhaps your financial future. As you know, Keira's main goal has always been to take care of you. She's right on the cusp of being able to do that with this film deal. I don't want to nag and I know I'm no longer Keira's agent, but I negotiated the deal for the new Chronicle. So I have to represent her interests. It's a year overdue. I know you've said she's working on it. That early burn phase of a new work is intense. I want to respect that and I know you do, too. I just need you all to know that I'm here for you and for her. If you ever want to discuss anything."

From anyone else this would have been four steps over the line, but Sylvia had been Keira's agent since my sister was sixteen. She had been the person closest to Keira right up until the time Keira came home and stopped talking to nearly everyone.

Sylvia turned to look at me.

"Has she said anything to you, Normandy? What happened at school?"

I willed my blood to stop moving in my veins and my facial muscles to freeze. I'd made a promise. I wouldn't repeat what she'd told me. It was a miracle that my older sister, after years of treating me like an inconvenience (or material), was opening up to me. Her trust made me feel respected, even if the "me" character in the Chronicles was a dud in every recognizable way. Discretion was all she'd asked. I had to show her that I was capable of that. Maybe she'd even redeem my character in the Chronicles if I proved myself worthy. I admit that part of me hoped she'd go back to school if I handled this situation right.

I shook my head. "No," I said, the lie coming out clear and steady.

"She has to start talking. If we don't know what happened, we can't help her."

My mother, her face even more drawn, said, "We *have* tried to talk to her, but she said she's not ready. We've asked if she'd like a counselor, but she said no. She just wants to be left alone while she finishes the new book. She's under a lot of pressure."

Despite what my sister's graphic novels may have insinuated, my parents are good people and hard workers. My mom, as I noted earlier, works for the Postal Service. In addition to carrying letters and packages, she carries all the weight and worries of the world. Okay, so in that regard the comics are true. She gives the impression that if one more letter-sized envelope is added to her sack, she'll fall right over and die.

When my aunt called to tell us my grandmother had been diagnosed with terminal cancer, my mom got up and went to bed. She didn't get up again for a week. My grandmother was sick for four months before she died, and I bet my mom spent half that time in bed. If she doesn't collapse at bad news, she goes lightly hysterical. *Then* she collapses. (Other than that, she's tops in a crisis.)

My dad works veg at Premium Foods. Again, that part of the Diana Chronicles is true. But he's *nothing* like the dad in Vermeer. Yes, a few years ago he did have a short-lived affair with a checkout girl. He and my mom nearly split up over it. But that was a long time ago and they worked things out, even though it resulted in his ouster from the Diorama Club. He would *never* get it on with his first cousins, and we have no household staff for him to molest. He's cheerful and wears an apron beautifully. He can help you pick the perfect pomegranate or pineapple, and his carrot arrangements are magazine quality.

Unfortunately, he's not so skilled in the areas of common sense or practicality. That's not me being critical. That's experience talking. We are the proud owners of four vacuums, thanks to the charms of hyper-persuasive salespeople. We also have every cutting device known to humanity. In fact, our combined vacuum and knife holdings are worth serious money. I don't even want to think what would happen to my dad if he had enough money to invest in a pyramid scheme.

One of my favorite writers is Flannery O'Connor—the way she turns the gimlet eye on various kinds of human frailty and stupidity and writes about scammers and serial killers and people with heads like cabbages. Flannery O'C didn't shy away from even the sharpest truths. She would have had a field day with my parents. That said, she probably would have been kinder about them than my sister is in the Diana Chronicles.

If anyone really pressed my mother and father to do some full-contact parenting of my sister, they'd get completely overwhelmed and probably just buy another vacuum. I think Sylvia knew that, because she looked to me for answers.

"I know Keira's working," I said. "She's in the closet practically every day." I didn't add that she also spent entire days MIA.

Sylvia's face brightened. "That's great news." She handed me her card, just like she did every time she visited.[39] "Where there's work, there's hope."

I wasn't so sure, but I smiled reassuringly anyway. It was the least I could do.

---

39. Sad, specific, concrete detail: I kept all of them.

Bedtime Stories

That night, hours after Sylvia left and I'd gone to bed, Keira woke me up again.

"Norm," whispered Keira. "Are you awake? You want to talk?"

She didn't wait for me to answer. She slipped out of the closet and into my room, a mummy-shaped lump moving on whispering nylon feet.

"Come in," I whispered, although she was already on my bed. My sister is very small.

"What did Sylvia say?" she asked.

I rolled onto my back and stared into the dark above my bed. "She just wanted to know how you are."

"That's so sweet. I just don't feel ready to talk to her. There's so much to deal with."

"Yeah," I whispered.

Keira lay down and I drew up my feet.

"Our last talk really helped me," said my sister. "It helped me to realize that what happened wasn't my fault."

"Of course not," I said. The mattress beneath me grew warmer. I read somewhere that if you put a frog in a hot pan, it will jump out. If you turn the heat up slowly, it will keep trying to adjust until it dies. As Keira resumed her story, my skin prickled in protest. I wondered how much heat I could stand.

My emotions turned end over end. Anxiety about what she was about to say got tangled up with happiness that she was talking to me, just like in the old days when she used to take me into her confidence. When I was a kid, I loved listening to my sister. Whenever I caught sight of her out in public, I felt a pride so sharp, it was painful. People paid attention to Keira, and she had this way of not noticing. Specialness was a particulate cloud that seemed to float around her.

One summer when we were both in grade school, my parents signed us up for an art camp. Keira was with the oldest kids. I was with the youngest. Our groups met in different rooms so I didn't get to see her very often, but news of the extraordinary girl in the Picasso Blues spread even to us little ones in the Da Vinci Squad. The other campers talked about her in hushed voices. The camp leaders did, too.

"Keira Pale is your sister?" asked the Da Vinci Squad's head counselor, a thin, faux-hawked college student home for the summer from Emily Carr University of Art and Design.

I nodded, feeling lucky that Keira was, in some way, mine.

"That must be intense," he said. "Living with a genuine prodigy."

I didn't know what a prodigy was, but I loved the sound of the word and whispered it over and over to myself.

I even got a little bit popular at camp, a completely new

experience, because everyone wanted to know all about my sister.

"Is it true she taught *herself* to draw like that?"

"Is it true that her first cartoon was published in the newspaper when she was only ten?"

"Yes," I said proudly. "It's all true."

"I love her hair," sighed one boy. "It's like a painting."

"I love her voice," said a girl with too many braids in her fine hair. "It's totally fascinating."

My sister's hair, which rose in a teeming mass, *did* look like a painting. As for her voice, people were always surprised that a body as small as hers could produce a voice with such a deep and intimate rasp. She always sounded like she was telling a secret. And her enormous brown eyes seemed to see things other eyes didn't.

The best was when she actually spoke to you. She would sidle up and say, "What's *your* favorite shade of green?" You'd want to give her the impression that you'd spent a lot of time considering the issue. No matter what your answer—the green of arbutus leaves, the green of your favorite gym shorts—she'd sigh and say, "Yes!" like she agreed with you absolutely. She made everyone feel like they'd just inspired her.

What a thing to inspire a real artist! A prodigy!

When Keira started working on the Chronicles, she was fourteen and I was eleven. I knew she'd been paying close attention to what went on at home. Even closer than before. I could not have been more excited. I told everyone that my sister was working on her own book-length comic, and that me and my parents were *in it*!

Then came the fateful day when I met myself in graphic novel form. Keira left neatly hand-bound photocopies of *Diana: Queen of Two Worlds* on each of our breakfast plates. My dad is very big on making us all a full breakfast—at least he was until that morning.

"Don't read it when I'm around," she told us. "It will make me feel funny." Then she wandered away.

My parents and I grinned at one another, waited until she'd left, and then opened our copies in unison.

It took about two pages for me to realize what I was reading and another page or two for the impact of it to sink in. We looked like idiots. It was like my sister had held up a hideousness magnifier to each of us and then drew what she saw.

She showed us doing silly things. Being shallow. And when the action moved to Vermeer, the alternate universe, we looked and acted like monsters.

Once I started breathing again, I looked at my parents. The color was gone from my mom's face, and my dad looked stricken, almost the same way he had when they told us they might be separating while they worked things out. Think: deer hit by an arrow from a crossbow.

I ran to the mirror to check to see whether I really did look like a flabby, dead-eyed fish with a mouth that hung open when I listened. I was so upset, I could barely see. I came back to the table and stared at the pages again, swamped with humiliation and shame at how I'd been por-trayed. Maybe the right word is *betrayed*.

I waited for one of my parents to object. Maybe my dad would say that he wasn't a failure or a creep. My mom would protest that she wasn't a neurotic basket case who called the suicide hotline over every piece of burnt toast and that in another universe she wouldn't be a psychopathic power-monger with the morals of a Norway rat.

But no.

"This is . . . remarkable," said my dad after a long, long pause.

At his words a little color came back into my mom's blanched face. "My goodness," she said. Then, never afraid to be repetitive, she added, "This is so good. She is just . . . so good."

I blinked as though someone had deliberately placed a piece of sawdust in my eye with a pair of tweezers.

"What?" I said.

"My God," said my father. "This is going to be a sensation. A comic set in two universes! Wow!"

"I always knew," said my mother, not bothering to say what, exactly, she always knew.

"I don't think . . ." My voice trailed off when I realized my parents were staring at me. "We look like that," I finished.

My father, Mr. Kindly from the Produce Section, nodded at me in a way that was the opposite of affirming. "It's art, Normandy," he said. "Those characters aren't us."

My sister was using her talent to turn us into a joke. My parents could see it, too, but they were going to make the best of the situation. Just like they always did. No matter what the cost. "But they look like us. They do the things we—"

"I only wish people had supported my creativity when I was younger," said my mother.

"Agreed," said my dad. "It's what parents do with talented kids."[40]

Before I could say anything else, the front door opened
and Keira reentered the house.

"Shhh," said my mother. "She's coming. This is a vulner-
able time for her. Just let her know how good it is."

And that morning, over cold pancakes, my mother and
father told Keira that she was brilliant. Keira seemed to take
in what they had to say. She accepted their effusive praise
and listened with a stillness that was hungry but strangely
detached.

When she was tired of their compliments, she turned
to me.

"Norm? What do you think?"

My copy of the comic lay in my lap. I was afraid to get
syrup on it.

"It's unbelievable," I said. "Are you going to show this
to people?"

Keira cocked her head a little. "Well, yeah."

"Of course," said my dad. "She's got to get it out there."

"*Everyone* has to see this," said my mother. "Talent runs
deep in this family."

I thought of the fun-house images of us heading into
the world. Our worst, ugliest, most ridiculous selves in our
smallest, weakest moments. But I couldn't say anything.

----

40. It goes without saying that my mom's parents hadn't exactly been sup-
portive of her teenage dreams, and my dad's mom couldn't afford to help
him, either.

The rest of the story is pretty much history. People loved the books. They thought my parents and I were "great sports" about the whole thing. With each new accolade my sister, once my idol, moved even further away. "Genius must be allowed to flower," said my parents. What they didn't say was that apparently the subjects of genius could only flop helplessly around and try not to look too stupid. And even with all that, I missed her.

So when Keira came into my room to pick up the story where it had left off as though no time had passed, how could I refuse?

"He was the best teacher I ever had. So talented."

She shifted in her mummy bag and I stayed still.

"Can we put on a lamp?" she asked. "This will be easier to talk about in the light."

I clicked on the lamp.

In the stretched-out silences between her sentences, our breathing was loud, out of sync.

Despite what I've told you, which I realize makes her seem completely cruel and insensitive, I will say again that I don't think my sister set out to do harm with the Chronicles. Her brain just naturally used what was near at hand and turned it into art. It's what artists do.

And, like other extraordinary artists, she's got the self-protection instincts of a freshly hatched robin. It sometimes pains me to think of her out in the world that way, open and exposed to every sensation, every experience.

"He was good to talk to. Really smart. Not much older than me. We started talking in the studio after class. Like, when everyone else was gone."

"Oh?" I said.

"Then we texted. Talked on the phone."

Part of what makes Keira's stories so popular is that she tells them in such a way that you always think something important is about to happen. They feel dramatic, even when they aren't. Her sense of timing works well on the page. In life, it's sort of painful.

The bed beneath me turned to quicksand.

I waited and listened and the details dripped out as though from a dislodged IV.

"He never treated me any different in class. But we had a strong connection. Our approach to our work was really similar," she said.

"And?"

"That was it, at first. He was so open and honest. Most people don't understand what it's like to be consumed by the artistic process."

My hands were clenched into fists under the light summer duvet.

"His art wasn't going great. I know how that feels."

I doubted that, but didn't say so.

"Your teacher was writing you personal messages?" I asked, hating how conventional I sounded. "Did you report him?"

"Of course not," she said. "We were just talking. But then he asked if I wanted to go hiking with him." She sighed and shifted, and her sleeping bag rustled in the dark. "I guess I shouldn't have said yes."

There was something in her voice. A vulnerability I hadn't heard for a long time. She sounded like the old Keira. The one who used to ask me about the color green.

Before I could figure out a response, my sister got up and took her excruciating timing back to her own room. She left the next morning and didn't come home for three days.

Winner of the Title of Biggest Disappointment Who Ever Lived

Dusk and Neil started in on me as soon as I picked them up the next day. My friends like to go to school in my truck, which, as I think I mentioned, is not one of your newer vehicles. Nancy is a 1970 Dodge Power Wagon with a paint job that demonstrates how badly red can fade in the sun. She's got some rust and a tendency to flood and to overheat. But she's also got character.

Dusk and Neil are both way wealthier than me, and they have late-model, reliable cars given to them by their parents. But a three-year-old Honda Civic (Dusk) and a brand-new Mazda something-or-other (Neil) doesn't have the cachet of a Nancy, who, after all, was formerly owned by the one and only Keira Pale.

"This truck makes me feel like Neil Young," said Neil when he pulled himself up onto the bench seat.

"It makes me feel like Fiona Apple," said Dusk, who actually does have a bit of an Apple-ish haunted-waif quality to her, but not as much as my sister.

"She needs some work," I said.

"Oh, Norm. Let her be. She's getting to be a local broken-down-on-the-side-of-the-road attraction," said Dusk.

"I have been keeping track of our breakdowns," said

Neil, shooting a cuff under his distinctly un-Neil-Young-ish light blue Dacron suit. "We have broken down at every main intersection. Next, I'd like to see us stall out on every major artery."

I pulled into the turning lane heading off Uplands Drive onto Rutherford, and as we slowed, Nancy hesitated. I revved her engine and kept my foot on the brake. Five months has made me a skilled and resourceful driver, at least according to me. I'm much better than those people who just assume their vehicles will accelerate when they hit the gas.

The engine roared, and in the rearview I saw white smoke pour out of the exhaust. The driver behind us frantically waved a hand in front of her face and leaned over to adjust her car's air intake.

"Go, go, *go!*" chanted Neil and Dusk as we crept into the intersection to make our left-hand turn.

Nancy obliged like an exhausted and overburdened cart horse in a Dickens novel.

"None of us should have kids," said Dusk. "It's the only way to atone for the air pollution produced by this truck."

"Fine with me," said Neil. "I hate the way kids want all the attention. It's like I'm not even there when there's a baby in the room."

I concentrated on my driving, but as we crawled toward the school, Nancy slowed down. I'd misjudged the gas going through the intersection. She was flooding.

"Damn," I said as Nancy's engine coughed, and we sputtered

to a halt. I eased her over to the side of the road. We were nearly at school. "Folks, we'll be here for about five minutes. Talk amongst yourselves."

Neil and Dusk both pulled out their candy cigarette packs and removed candy smokes. Neil, who sat between us, handed me one.

"So, Norm. You ready?" he asked.

"Sure," I said, agreeable but entirely clued out.

"So who's it going to be?" asked Dusk.

I found myself wishing I had a real cigarette. Then I could blow a meditative smoke ring or contemplate one of the horrific medical warnings on the package.

"Oh," I said. "I thought you were talking about the essay on the history of poetics. I've got mine ready to go."

"We're not talking about schoolwork," said Dusk. "To discuss schoolwork voluntarily would violate the agreement I have with my parents that I will be the biggest disappointment who ever lived."

Neil nodded sagely.

Dusk's battles with her family are ongoing. She comes from what she refers to as a two-Tiger family: physician parents—Mother a Korean-Canadian neurosurgeon! Father a Jewish-Canadian emergency room specialist!; a brother in his early twenties already halfway through med school; and a younger brother at age eleven headed along the same steep and well-lighted path. Dusk says that her parents find her used- (and not by anyone with taste) clothing aesthetic baffling. They find her low-B average upsetting and her interest in things artistic disconcerting and impractical. They find her friends off-putting, but before we came along, Dusk didn't have any friends. She had only her looks and her acid remarks to keep her company. So they haven't banished us, even though we are overtly unaccomplished in their eyes. At least I have a famous sister, and Neil's dad has a lot of money.

"I believe she's referring to the Truth Commission," said Neil. "We don't want to keep all this goodness for ourselves. Seriously, Norm. You won't believe how it feels to cut through the bullshit. To go right to the heart of the matter."

"It's exhilarating," said Dusk. "And I don't even *get* exhilarated."

"I'm still thinking." I checked my watch. In two more minutes Nancy would be ready to go, at least long enough to stall in the school parking lot where she belonged.

"You're a retiring person. We understand that. But I think"—Neil corrected himself—"*we* think that this will be good for your confidence."

They'd been discussing my confidence? Since when was my confidence any worse than theirs? I suppose their concern might have been based on Volume 2 of the Diana Chronicles, the one that shows Flanders having tragically ill-attended eighth birthday parties in two universes. This episode was closely modeled on my own eighth birthday party, which was not, shall we say, a huge success, thanks to some kids spreading a rumor about me misusing another kid's underpants. I will say no more.[41] I'm not sure whether Dusk and Neil have read the Chronicles. Out of respect for

---

41. If you really want to know, the Chronicle spells out a version of the whole sordid affair in unsparing detail. And no, the story about the underpants *was not true.*

me they don't really talk about them, but occasionally they let something slip that suggests they are familiar with my other life as a semi-fictional character.

God, I hate it when people talk about me. Or look at me.

"We've even come up with the perfect person for you to ask," said Dusk.

"Because we care," said Neil. He flipped the candy cigarette into his mouth and began to chew.

"Tyler Jones," said Dusk.

That was all they needed to say.

Tyler Jones is a gifted sculptor who works in stone and metal. He's tall, muscular, and has that sculptor-y bass voice and a half-asleep demeanor that makes toes tingle. He also has awesome dreads and listens to underground hip-hop mixes and electronic dance tracks that his brother sends him from Baltimore, which gives him instant credibility in Nanaimo. He's also one of only six black kids in a school that wishes it was more diverse.

Everyone at school wonders whether he is gay for the following reason: he has no girlfriend, in spite of the fact that every straight girl in school has thrown herself in front of him like an insurance scammer in a Walmart parking lot.

If Tyler Jones turns out to be a gorgeous gay sculptor, it will be a credit to the whole G. P. Academy and a disappointment to all the females (including terrifying Mrs. Dekker) who stare longingly after him when he walks languidly down the hallway. But he's not saying one way or another.

"You're not serious," I said.

"Of course we're serious. He's probably just waiting for someone to ask."

"He probably wants to bring his boyfriend to prom," added Neil. "The right question at the right time will open the door."

"Can you imagine what kind of guy Tyler goes out with?" said Dusk. "I bet he's ridiculously gorgeous. *Too* hot, even."

"Maybe he just goes out with a regular guy who's nice and funny," said Neil.

"Yeah," she agreed. "That would be even cooler. Thinking about it makes me wish I was a regular-looking but smart and funny gay guy."

"Me too," said Neil cheerfully. Neil may the straightest, most girl-focused guy imaginable, but he's not afraid to acknowledge that dash of gay that makes life fun.

I looked at my friends. "In case you haven't noticed, Tyler Jones is the most together guy in our school and maybe on Vancouver Island. He's extremely self-possessed. He doesn't need me to ask him anything. People get to make their own schedules for things like coming out."

"That's where you're wrong," said Dusk. "Everyone assumes that because Tyler is so handsome and talented and quietly confident and everything, he doesn't need to be nurtured. *Everyone* needs to be nurtured and encouraged."

"Asking people their private business isn't nurturing them."

"I think it is," said Dusk. "It shows you care." She pointed her index and middle finger at her own eyes and then at mine. "'I see you.' That's what we're saying to people with the Truth Commission."

"He's too cool," I said. "I can't do it. I can't even look at him."

"Oh, Normandy. Don't be so easily intimidated," said Dusk.

Easy for her to say. She was the only person at school in Tyler Jones's league, looks-wise.

"You're part of this thing, Norm. We just don't want you to miss what is turning out to be one of the most valuable life experiences we might ever have," said Neil.

I turned the key. Nancy's engine whirred, coughed. She backfired a couple of times, causing a startled deer to burst out of the trees and bound across the road in two gravity-defying leaps. It narrowly avoided being hit by a car coming the other way. The north end of town is lousy with deer, thanks to all the new subdivisions.

I pulled the truck back onto the road. When I flipped on the turn signal to go right, Neil couldn't stand the suspense anymore.

"So?" he asked. "Are you going to do it?"

We rolled into the gravel parking lot, which merged beautifully with the xeriscaped grounds of Academy.[42] Art kids loitered everywhere, many of them looking vaguely French.[43]

----

42. School motto: Sustainability and Creativity in All Things. Of course, Green Pastures being Green Pastures, our school motto is always written in multiple languages, including Island Hul'q'umin'um' (the living language of the Snuneymuxw traditional territories, of which Nanaimo is a part), French, Spanish, Mandarin, Cantonese, Latin, and Braille.

43. Parisian French. French-Canadian. Either/or. (I have never been to Quebec or to France. I'm just impressed by Frenchness in all forms.)

"I'm not ready," I said, staring at three hipsters singing an a cappella version of Public Enemy's "He Got Game" near the front doors.

"Fine," said Dusk. "We'll do it. By which I mean Neil will do it. Then I'll do another one. You'll see how important this work is and be ready to join us."

Neil put a hand on my shoulder. He mimicked Dusk's finger-eye thing. "The truth, Norm. Powerful."

"Set you free," added Dusk.

Monday, September 17

Game of Benches

As we hung out in the vicinity of Tyler Jones, I felt a strong desire to disappear. Or to pull out my embroidery and go sit in a tucked-away place to work on it. My friends didn't share my reluctance to sneak around.

"I think I might have a talent for this," said Neil.

"Lurking?" I said.

"Please. That's such a harsh word. I mean blending in. Going unnoticed while remaining extremely observant. I feel like a character from *Dune.*"

"One of those big sandworms maybe?" said Dusk.

"Please don't start speaking in convoluted riddles, the way you did when you were reading those books," I said.

"If you would read the series, too, you would be aware that I was doing an uncannily accurate impression of a Mentat. A human supercomputer, if you will, able to think and feel in multiple dimensions. My ability to—"

"There he is," said Dusk before Neil could go full-Mentat on us.

We turned and watched Tyler Jones walk out of Pod 3, where he was working on his Senior Year Major Project. In grade eleven, every student at G. P. does a Spring Special

Project.[44] In grade twelve, the Major Project runs the full school year and forms the basis of your graduating portfolio.

Tyler Jones was one of the few students who got his own studio pod. There are twelve small studios and three large spaces arranged in a sort of honeycomb in the Fine Art Hall, which is essentially a dome, because our Founding Farmer was a big fan of Buckminster Fuller, the theorist and designer who was popular with hippies and radicals and people who had a thing for domes. Most of the students— painters, sculptors, potters, etc.—share space and work on their major projects in shifts. Tyler's year-end sculpture was deemed so outstanding, so groundbreaking, that no one, including janitorial staff, was allowed into his pod.

Naturally, the rest of us would have run over Joss Whedon[45] to get a look at what Tyler was doing in there.

When Tyler emerged from Pod 3, he looked like he always does—distracted and handsome with a double help- ing of hot-artist sauce. At risk of sounding pervy, I will describe him. About six feet tall, broad-shouldered, loose jeans hanging just so from narrow hips, denim work shirt, hair tied back with a random piece of twine.

"Damn," whispered Dusk.

Neil and I nodded mutely while we watched Tyler lock up his studio.

--- --- --- --- --- --- --- --- --- --- --- ---

44. Like this here work of creative nonfiction.

45. You work in an art-focused high school, so I'm sure you understand the significance of this. It's a bit like saying you'd run over God in a Christian high school.

"You can't do this," I said as the three of us sat, turned to stone by the perfection of Tyler Jones.

"That's just your fear talking," said Neil. His voice was slightly strangled, and I could tell he no longer felt so nonchalant.

"But you hate labels," I said.

Neil ignored me. In truth, Neil quite likes labels, as long as they are interesting to him. He has a strong preference for 1970s brands and culture, and has been known to point out the signature buttons on his vintage Halston blazer.

We were sitting on a handmade bench in the round atrium between the studios. The ceiling was made of glass panels, and the space was brilliant from the sun blazing directly overhead.

"Okay," said Neil. He got to his feet, shot his cuffs, and straightened the permanent polyester crease in his dress pants. Then he was up and walking his light-blue-suited self toward Tyler Jones.

As Neil approached, Tyler gave him a little jerk of the chin by way of greeting. It's a gesture predicated on the notion that people are paying such close attention that even one's smallest movement will be noticed.

"Hi, Tyler," said Neil. "Could I speak with you for a moment?"

I wanted to shout "Stop!" This was completely different from Aimee, who'd obviously been dying to tell someone about her operations. This was different from Mrs. Dekker, whose issues were acute. Tyler Jones had a delicious mystery about him. He should be allowed to remain a private person.

He looked at Neil and smiled, and I felt myself sag onto

the bench, which was made of concrete and had an assort-
ment of old silverware and utensils such as spatulas and
wire whisks sticking out the back and sides. The title *Game
of Benches* was hand-carved into the seat. Art school humor.

Tyler Jones was DEFCON 4 on the charisma scale.
Maybe the reason he didn't seem to hook up with anyone,
female or male, was because his sexual magnetism was so
strong, he'd kill the person. Maybe it was an artistic genius
thing. My sister has never really dated, as far as I know. All
her energy goes into creating the Chronicles.

Dusk, who was apparently thinking something similar,
whispered, "Wow," over and over again.

Neil pulled his sunglasses from their resting place on his
head and put them on, perhaps to dim the effect of Tyler's
gorgeousness. "I want to ask you a private question."

Tyler's smile faded. I thought I saw dismay flit across his
face, but that might have been projection on my part.

"Okay," he said.

Then Neil ushered him into an unoccupied studio, and
Dusk and I were left on the bench to wonder.

We were silent for at least two minutes. That's one of the
great things about Dusk. She knows how to be quiet. In fact,
she's one of my favorite people to be quiet with. I feel closer
to her when we're not talking than when we are.

I spoke first. "I hope they're okay in there."

"They'll be fine."

"Yeah," I said. As I spoke, I realized that I hoped that
Tyler Jones would tell Neil to mind his own business. Then
maybe all this Truth Commissioning would just go away.

But Neil and Tyler had been in the studio for too long.
They were obviously talking about something.

"Do you know why people overshare online?" asked Dusk, surprising me.

"Because they're attention whores?" I said.

"Because they want people to know them. To know the truth about them."

"Isn't it enough that we know the truth about ourselves?" I asked. But as I spoke, I realized that I *didn't* really know myself, never mind the people in my life.

"I think we learn the truth about ourselves by telling it to someone else," said Dusk.

That observation was followed by another five minutes of silence. During that time, it came to me that I should find out more about my sister's story. She'd gotten involved with a teacher. That was bad. But was there something else going on?

Tyler Jones and Neil stayed in the empty studio for another ten minutes. In those minutes, I made a plan. I would find out more about what happened to Keira at school. Just in case . . . just in case what? I had no idea. Even if I found out her teacher was sleeping with every girl in his classes, my sister had sworn me to secrecy.

I was so caught up in my thoughts that I was only half paying attention when Neil emerged from the studio.

Dusk and I stood and watched him come.

Tyler Jones followed him out, looking thoughtful. Not worried or angry. Just thoughtful. He chin-nodded us and left the atrium.

"Well?" said Dusk, rubbing her hands together, visions of dating opportunities with the possibly heterosexual Tyler Jones dancing in her head.

"He said it was a fascinating question. He appreciates

us being interested. He's going to give the matter some thought."

"That's it?" said Dusk. "Ten minutes to get three sentences?"

"I feel lucky that he didn't punch me in the face. He's a big guy. I think he works out. And the minute I asked him, I realized that the question was . . ."

"Inappropriate?" I offered.

"Brave," said Dusk.

"He's going to get back to me."

"It's much more satisfying when they just answer our questions," muttered Dusk.

"He will. He just needs to think about it."

I saw a flash of orange and red out of the corner of my eye.

"Hi!" Dusk offered Mrs. Dekker a sunny and open smile.

"You kids get to class," rasped Mrs. Dekker in a voice that sounded like the result of a back-alley tracheotomy.

Dusk recoiled. I could see that she wanted to say something, but Neil grabbed her by the leather-patched elbow of her old tweed jacket.

Mrs. Dekker, as unfriendly and unpleasant as ever, flapped out of the atrium, and we retreated to our respective classes.

"I don't get it," muttered Dusk. "I thought we had an understanding."

"Maybe something happened to one of her ostriches," I said.

Pale Investigations

By the time I got home, I'd decided that since I was initiating a Pale Family Truth Commission comprised of me, myself, and I, the first order of business was to speak to Keira's friends. Maybe they knew something about her teacher. Of course, first I had to figure out whether she had any friends.

My sister has always been too consumed by her art to really nurture friendships. Still, everyone at the Art Farm paid attention to her, just like all the kids at camp had. At G. P. she mostly hung out with a girl named Constance, who went off to the Ontario College of Art and Design to study Industrial Design. Constance was one of those people who don't mind doing most of the work in a relationship. If I ever get married, I hope my first husband is like Constance.

I assumed things had been different at CIAD. I'd seen the website: tiny class sizes, low student-teacher ratios, acclaimed yet engaged professors. In addition to the Chronicles, Keira had submitted a superstar portfolio, and there's no way she'd have gone unnoticed by her peers. Even if she hadn't made any close friends, she must have had acquaintances. Someone must know something.

Unfortunately, the school had a privacy policy.

Enter Facebook: Slayer of all privacy policies!

It took me about three seconds to find a Facebook group for students taking the undergraduate animation program at CIAD. The program has a reputation for being harder to get into than Harvard or Yale, and being more expensive.

I switched my profile photo to one in which I was wearing an ironic chapeau. From what I could see in their profile pictures, the heads of CIAD students were festooned with berets, trucker hats, deerstalkers. To be honest, I briefly considered using a photo of Dusk and me together, in the hope that I'd be mistaken for her. Studies have confirmed that beautiful people get special treatment, and I needed some.

I sent a Facebook message to one Roberta Brown Heller II because, despite the regnal number after her name, she had a friendly, freckled face.

> Hi. My name is Normandy Pale.
>
> I think you went to school with my sister, Keira. We are planning a surprise party for her and wanted to ask a couple of questions about her time at CIAD. On the Q.T.
>
> Thanks,
> Normandy

The message would go into that "Other" message box that Facebook helpfully makes invisible, so I hoped that Roberta Brown Heller II would get it. Trying to friend her seemed too pushy. After all, we were supposedly just planning a surprise party. No need to get psycho about it.

Less than a minute later, I got a response.

> If you're some desperate fan, please go away. She doesn't even go to school here anymore, and we're all sick of getting Facebook messages about her. Same goes for Instagram, Twitter, etc.

How to respond?

> I really am her sister. I go to Green Pastures Academy. Ask me anything about her.

This was like a Jason Bourne moment, only not athletic and on the world's least secure privacy platform other than skywriting.

> Get lost.

Heller II's friendly, approachable profile picture was misleading. She was rude and off-putting. I was starting to like her.

> I am not a stalker. Seriously. I'm Keira's sister.

> Then you should ask her your questions. You people are really pathetic.

> That's just it. She's not talking much. Since she came home.

> Just go away.

You're very rude.

And you're annoying. I have a short film due in three hours. Our time is up.

Clearly, you have something against surprise parties. So what if I told you I'm not writing because of a surprise party? Also, I can't help but notice that you have time to check your Facebook messages.

My Facebook habit is none of your business. (I use it to relax.) Keep talking.

My sister hasn't been feeling well since she came home. We thought that if we could talk to her about her friends at CIAD it might cheer her up.

Still think you're probably a sadfan.

My sister never wears socks. A lot of her shirts are white and billowy. She drives a white 1987 Crown Vic. She looks *very* tired. Except for her hair. It looks like it's in mid-cartwheel.

Go on.

I tried to think of a detail I knew about Keira that a classmate might also know but that the people who obsessively followed her career wouldn't.

> She has this nervous habit of tapping her thumb on her chin when she thinks.

> Maybe you saw her at a signing.

> My sister doesn't do signings. Hasn't for a few years.

> Why don't you just go ask her whatever it is that you want to know?

> She's not talking.

I had to be careful here. Keira had made me promise not to tell what happened at school. Of course, she hadn't exactly told me what happened, either. It was all vague allusions. Looking into her story was a betrayal. But I felt compelled. She was finally talking to me again, and I had a terrible feeling that she was leaving things out. Important things.

What if I pretended she'd never said anything and she went out one day and never came home? She was disappearing more and more often. I knew it was connected to what had happened. What was my responsibility here?

I was about to close Facebook when another message popped up.

> No one knew your sister. She seemed cool, but she kept to herself. Sorry can't help. It's been pretty shitty around here since the spring.

I hesitated. Then I typed:

Why?

I don't want to get into it. I hope your sister feels better and that she comes back. She's got serious talent. We could use someone else to look up to.

Okay. Thanks. Good luck with your film.

There were no more messages after that.

Making the World Safe for Bad Judgment

"Got one," said Dusk.

Neil and I turned to her. We were in Acrylics 1, taught by the effervescent Cynthia Choo. Ms. Choo looked like a recent graduate from grade eight. She wore her medium-length black hair in two braids and shuffled around in cheap embroidered Chinese slippers and silk coats.

Ms. Choo had been my sister's favorite teacher, and she always asked after Keira in a way that was nicely friendly as opposed to overly interested, which I appreciated.

"Shouldn't you get the last candidate to cough up the facts before you move on to a new one?" I said.

"Don't worry about backlog," said Neil. "The truth is a river. We've got to let it flow."

He looked down at his cell phone. "Oops. It's Aimee. I have to get this."

"Aimee. Agony Queen," intoned Dusk.

It was true. Aimee, though popular and in demand even before the renovations, spent her time reeling from imaginary crisis to imaginary crisis. Her boyfriend of two days had looked at another woman. The guy she dated after that looked at a guy. She'd read in the *Los Angeles Times* (online edition) that broadcast television networks were only hiring men of color. Her best friend had had a vision board party and sent her an invitation a full two days after everyone else.[46] Other Aimee problems: The new sweater from that adorable store in Qualicum had been stolen out of her gym bag. Jo Malone discontinued her favorite cologne. She gained half a pound. And her perennial favorite: people were talking about her.

Aimee was paranoid, self-centered, and fear-based. She did not share much in the way of affection or support with Neil, at least not that I could see, but she sure had a free hand with the neediness. I was going to resent it very much if she became his new muse, even though I'd pretend I wasn't bothered.

Neil took it all in stride and even seemed to like it.

"No one is listening to me right now," said Dusk. "This Truth Commission is starting to feel like home."

"I'm listening," I told her.

"Not to me you're not," said Ms. Choo, sliding up to us on her tiny embroidered slippers. These ones were high-noon blue with plenty of metallic embroidery. Her robe, made of some papery material, was suburban lawn green. White cranes flapped their way across the fabric. "Is any of this getting through?"

"Ms. Choo," said Neil. "Those clothes look wonderful on you."

----

46. For those of us who never get invited to vision board parties, not even late, such events involve cutting out magazine images that represent your hopes and dreams and gluing them to a piece of cardboard. You use the resulting collage of lifestyle and product images to focus your aspirations.

"It's true," said Dusk. "They do."

"Allow me be the first one to say something that doesn't rhyme. I like your ensemble," I said.

"But do you like the brushstroke technique I just spent twenty minutes explaining and demonstrating? That's the big question."

"Love it," I assured her. I stabbed at a blob of paint on my canvas to show how much.

"Me too," said Neil. "It's so open and expansive."

"I don't think I'll be incorporating it in my next installation," said Dusk. "But I'm glad to know how it's done."

"Every person can benefit from brush skills," said the unflappable Ms. Choo.

"Touch!" said Dusk, who likes to mangle words because it drives her parents crazy. She held up a hand to be slapped. Ms. Choo stared at the offending appendage.

Dusk took her hand down.

Then Ms. Choo went to check on what the other painters were accomplishing.

We all got to work leaving brushstrokes in heavy globs of acrylic paint. It was quite satisfying, and I'd have been happy to work in silence and cozy togetherness, but Dusk would not be prevented from telling us about the new target.

"Zinnia McFarland," she said.

"That girl who puts on the Slut Walk?" I asked.

"That's the one."

"What are you going to ask her?"

"Whether it's true what they say."

"What do they say?" I found myself dreading the answer.

"Her sister did a little web-stripping. Then she got severely online bullied."

"Inter-tormented," said Neil. "That's the worst."

"She tried to kill herself," said Dusk. "Zinnia's been try-ing to make the world safe for bad judgment ever since."

My brush had frozen a foot away from the canvas. "Dusk, that's not funny."

"I don't mean it to be funny. Everyone knows that Zinnia puts on the Slut Walk for a reason. And it's not because she personally is sexing it up all over the place."

"Or sexting, presumably," added Neil.

"It's not your business why she puts on the walk. It's cool, and she's right. Women should be able to dress how they want."

"Here, here!" said Eleanor St. Pierre, who was at the easel behind me, clearly eavesdropping for all she was worth.

"Looking gorgeous, Els!" said Neil with a big smile.

Dusk shot me a look, and I lowered my voice. "It's one thing to ask people their private business. But this is about her sister. So it's not Zinnia's truth to tell."

Dusk added a few more brushstrokes to the small shrewish shapes on her canvas. Since she got the idea to taxidermy a shrew for her Spring Special Project, everything she makes is vaguely shrew shaped, and she's frequently in a bad mood because taxiderming, especially tiny creatures, is very hard. Or so she reports after each failed attempt.

"I'm just asking her about her motivation. She's putting it out there—how we should all be able to dress how we want. Get our revealing on. But at the same time, she keeps this very personal motivation private. I think it would be both healing for her and inspiring for others if she talked about what happened." Dusk turned to me and lowered her voice. "Norm, we all know you're kind of sensitive about family stuff. Because of your sister and everything."

I was about to protest, but Neil beat me to it.

"Everyone is sensitive about family," he said. "Not just Norm."

"That doesn't mean it's okay. Our families are often the thing that keep us stuck," said Dusk. "If I bought into my family's agenda, I would—"

"Be getting better than a C in biology right now," I said.

"C-minus," Dusk corrected. "Anyway, I think that if you want people to join you in a cause, you should be honest about where you're coming from."

"Why?" My voice was rising again. I couldn't help it, even if Eleanor was straining an eardrum trying to listen in. "It's not our business. The Slut Walk is to protest all the bullshit that girls have to deal with for how we dress."

Out of the corner of my eye I saw Ms. Choo's head come up and turn to us.

"If she doesn't want to talk about it, she won't," said Dusk. There was a stubborn set to her chin. "I'm allowed to ask."

"Let's all just relax and enjoy our brushstrokes," said Neil. "I think it's good to discuss these things openly. Like Tyler Jones might turn me down. I'm still waiting for him to get back to me. No harm, no foul."

"Do I need to separate your easels?" asked Ms. Choo, coming over to us.

"No, ma'am," said Neil. "We're just excited about the whole modern brushstrokes thing."[47]

- - - - - - - - - - - - -

47. It is a nice change from some of the more classically technical approaches.

The Truth Is a Daisy

Zinnia McFarland was a senior on a mission. Multiple missions, actually. Her specialty was protest art.

Zinnia is a skilled illustrator and a gifted painter, and she uses her talents to "undermine the system." Her words. She has been arrested multiple times for putting politically minded art—some backward thinkers call it graffiti—on public works, such as bridges, dams, and the steps of city hall. But she goes further than balloon letters rendered in dripping spray paint. She draws and paints hyperrealistic images as a commentary on political decisions, like Banksy, but in a style all her own.

When the mayor and city council gave their approval to cull the local rabbit population, Zinnia used chalk to create a devastating battle scene on the steps of City Hall. The picture showed bunnies with the faces of the mayor and members of the city council sprawled in a hideous death tableau. Before they could get a city worker in to wash it off, an art historian from the university saw it. He took several pictures that ended up being published in a special feature in *Art Tomorrow* about young radicals. The editors said it was as good as anything Petr Krivonogov, the Soviet battle painter, ever did. Someone else said they saw the influence of John Singer Sargent's *Gassed*. Dealers started contacting the school, asking if Zinnia had representation and whether she was interested in having a show. Rumor has it she told them all that she still needed time to develop her work. Now *that's* radical. Most of us would jump at the chance for a show, ready or not.

Anyway, quite a few other people were sure that Zinnia's chalk drawing was the best thing that ever happened at city hall. Period. Full stop. But the cull went ahead, and the drawing washed away in the next rain. Chalk art is only so-so at effecting political change.

When she wasn't making public protest art, Zinnia was protesting. Last year she started a local Slut Walk, which is ironic, because pretty much everyone dresses sluttier than Zinnia, including Queen Elizabeth II. (I overheard one of the catty girls in the fashion program, also known as the "Clothes Cult," say that Zinnia should really be organizing the Slob Walk.) Her fashion sense goes beyond can't-be-bothered art student into blind-gal-sent-into-badly-organized-thrift-store-and-told-to-dress-herself territory. She's a committed cyclist, never a good sign for fashion.

At the first annual Slut Walk, she appeared to have taken her cues about provocative clothing from a children's program made by people who've taken too much acid. She had on yellow tights, green felt boots with a stack heel, and some kind of shapeless red-and-brown-feathered tunic. Only a male robin would have found the outfit remotely slutty.

Neil, in his tightest skinny jeans, his best shiny dress shirt unbuttoned to his sternum, and patent leather ankle boots, looked way more risqué than Zinnia. In fact, everyone did, including the Jehovah's Witnesses who were handing out *The Watchtower* along our route.

Anyway, in spite of her tendency to throw herself into political commentary, she wasn't one to explain her motivations. Which made it that much more fascinating and awful when Dusk confronted her.

Dusk convinced us to wait for Zinnia at the bike racks before school. In addition to being disheveled, Zinnia's also chronically late. This is standard at G. P. Academy, where people think that being on time suggests that you are insufficiently creative.

She finally shambled along about ten minutes after the first bell. It might have been an optical illusion, but her old cruiser bike gave the impression of having two flat tires and severely bent rims. I think I saw dust bunnies blowing out of hidden air pockets in her enormous billowing sweater as she wheeled up to the bike rack.

She'd painted her helmet, the full-coverage kind skateboarders wear, to look like a beehive that had been split open, revealing a honeycomb inside. *pleasesavethebeesplease-savethebees* was written all around the bottom edge. It was possibly the greatest bike helmet in the world and, to be quite honest, I think Zinnia might have been one of my favorite people at school. I mean, I didn't really know her, but the *idea* of her is part of what makes the Art Farm great.

Dusk sauntered over, wearing a little K-pop-inspired number.

"Zinnia," she exclaimed. "Looking comfy as ever!"

Zinnia smiled under her shattered beehive, and I was reminded of daisies and other flowers that are sunny and unpretentious. No one would ask a daisy the truth. A daisy *is* the truth. If I'd been able to cope with confrontation in any form, I would have tackled Dusk just then.

Instead, I just muttered, "Aw, jeez," and stared at my feet.

"It's okay," whispered Neil. I heard uncertainty in his voice.

"Hi, Dusk," said Zinnia. "I love your jacket. When the sun hits it just the right way, that blue shades into indigo, which is an impossible color to find. Some eye shadows get close, but only near the right eyes."

"Yeah?" said Dusk. "Thanks. I hadn't noticed."

Zinnia stared expectantly at Dusk. Like my sister, she has this way of turning her full attention on you, like you are the only person in the world and she doesn't want to miss some excellent thing you might do or say. Part of me prayed the Dusk would notice that. Would realize that someone like Zinnia was dangerously open.

Dusk did not. Maybe because her family was the opposite of open, and in order to be herself, she had to be walled off. If that makes any sense.

"So, Zinnia, I was wondering. About the Slut Walk—"

"First week of May," said Zinnia. "And I'm getting some great speakers from the Women's Support Society. We might have a film night first. It's so great of you guys to take part. It's important to raise awareness."

"Why?" asked Dusk.

"What do you mean?" Zinnia seemed genuinely confused.

"Why do you care?"

Sarcasm was not in Zinnia's repertoire. When she gave painted rabbits the faces of politicians, it was because she was trying to communicate, not hurt anyone's feelings.

"Oh, Dusk," she said earnestly. "It's really serious. There was that police officer who said that women shouldn't dress like sluts if they don't want to be victimized.[48] Women all over the world are harassed, beaten, and even raped for how they dress."

"I get that," said Dusk. "But is there any personal connection for you? Does the issue hit close to home for some reason?"

Zinnia's earnest face crumpled in on itself. She stood motionless, holding the length of chain she used to lock her bike. It was so heavy, she tilted slightly sideways.

Finally, she said, "You probably know about my sister."

I could feel my eyes bulging. I wanted to scream at Dusk. Tell her to let Zinnia keep her motivations private. We had no right to them. This was not fair.

"I heard something," said Dusk noncommittally, like a cop interviewing a witness.

Zinnia sighed. "She had some trouble a few years ago. You know, online."

Dusk waited. She was getting pretty savvy with the silence. It was no longer companionable. Now it was an interrogation technique.

Neil and I were leaning against the gym, which is a half-hearted building, especially compared to the rest of Green Pastures's facilities. It's more often used for art installations and performance pieces than for sports. Other than an elite hopscotch team and a nearly unbeaten three-legged-race squad, we aren't really known for our athletics. Oh, and we have a pretty stellar badminton team, but I think they practice in one of the hallways.

---

48. This happened in 2010.

"She got a little too . . . comfortable on a webcam. She put up a few profile pictures that were kind of revealing." Something in Zinnia seemed to rouse as she spoke. She blinked rapidly and then leaned forward. "Would you listen to me?" she said. "This is incredible! I'm using the same language as that cop who said women have to cover up or risk getting harassed. Oh, man."

She turned in a circle, still holding on to the length of chain. When she was facing Dusk again, she spoke in a rush.

"The negativity just gets *in* a person. The sexism. The oppression. Why *don't* I talk about what happened to my sister? It was totally not her fault! She looked beautiful in those pictures. Because she *is* beautiful. That bra was, like, the most gorgeous color! It was mine. New. She snuck it from me and wore it for this guy she met in a chat room. She took it off when he asked. She's beautiful. Why not? Then everyone in her school found out. The kids in her school weren't cool about it. Oh, my God. This is unbelievable. I can't believe my language."

Dusk had taken a step back, perhaps alarmed at the flood she'd released.

"You know what else?" said Zinnia. "I had sex."

"Whoa!" said Neil.

"Oh, shit," I said.

"I did. Unprotected. When things were going so bad with Camelia, I got with this guy and we didn't use protection. Because I was tired of being careful. I could have gotten an STD. I could have gotten pregnant. I *never* talk about that at my Student Artists for Choice events."

"Oh," said Dusk. "Well—"

"You are absolutely right," said Zinnia, turning in a circle. "It's not enough to protest. You've got to stand up and be counted. It's got to be personal. No more secrets."

"Well," tried Dusk again. "You might want to keep *some* sec—"

"Absolutely not. Silence makes us part of the problem. No more silence."

Zinnia had begun swinging the fat chain like a cowboy who wanted to lasso a steer or maybe kill one.

Dusk took a step back.

"You know, I felt so bad about that bra. Camelia just, you know, developed and she loved that color. I felt like that stupid bra started it all. The kids were so awful. She ended up dropping out of school and moving to live with my dad in Edmonton. And we're hippies! Self-esteem to burn! Imagine what happens to kids with straight or mean parents."

She was jerking the chain back and forth so hard, I worried that she might dislocate her arm.

"This year Slut Walk is going to be personal. And it's going to be militant. It wasn't my fault or the bra's fault or Camelia's fault. A girl can get naked if she wants. Boy, I'm really mad right now."

"Okay," said Dusk. "I'd like to thank you for sharing your—"

"Every day is going to be Slut Day in my world," said Zinnia. She dropped the chain and it clunked to the ground. Then she began stripping off her big sweater.

"Oh, jeepers," said Neil.

"Do something," I told him.

"Can't," he said. "Too scared."

"We'll dress how we want or we won't dress at all!" cried

Zinnia nonsensically. This was an art school. It went without saying that we dressed how we wanted. And as anyone
who spent more than twenty minutes near the Photoshoot
Tree could attest, a lot of us barely dressed at all, at least
when the weather was fine.

"Well," said Dusk.

"Come on!" Zinnia peeled off her checked work shirt.
"Who's with me?"

"Oh, God," I said.

To her credit, Dusk looked at us. Then she took off her
shiny, in-certain-light-indigo K-pop bomber jacket.

I gave her the big eyes and a nod.

Zinnia was down to her boxer shorts and an undershirt.
I reviewed my underclothes. It was like that car accident
moment mothers are always warning kids about. Only it
was an impromptu Slut Walk through school. I decided my
bra and underpants were adequate. In fact, my briefs actually had a cool print of a robot on the front. I gave a silent
prayer of thanks and began to strip down.

A minute later, the four of us wore only our undergar-
ments.

"Come on!" said Zinnia, and marched off, leaving her
bike unlocked and her pile of clothing on the ground. Dusk
and I clutched our clothing to our chests. Neil picked up
Zinnia's clothes and added them to the neat pile of his own.
Together, we followed Zinnia past the gym and around to
the side door. There was no one in the Photoshoot Tree. As
we walked past the office, Mrs. Dekker rose up from behind
her desk.

There was something different about her.

No poncho!

Mrs. Dekker was dressed in a bright yellow sundress with spaghetti straps. The left one had slid off her massive sloping shoulder. She looked like a fridge in a dress, but the significance of the change was impossible to miss. Mrs. Dekker was opening up and we were in our best underpants and the truth was breaking out all over our school.

"What's going on?" asked Mrs. Dekker with only a fifth of the usual hostility in her voice.

Administrators came out of the office. Students and teachers came out of classrooms. Seniors emerged from studio pods.

"My sister dressed in a provocative way and she was tormented for it. I didn't talk about it because I was embarrassed and I felt guilty. No more!" cried Zinnia.

Our fellow students, never ones to miss an opportunity to make a statement, immediately and unquestioningly started taking off their clothes in solidarity.

"These three finally asked me why I put on the Slut Walk," brayed the formerly soft-spoken Zinnia McFarland in a voice like a labor riot. "And I finally told the truth. I feel *great!*"

A few of the more forward-thinking teachers fell into step with us. Some removed blazers and horn-rimmed glasses. Thankfully, none took off their clothes.

"We're all sluts!" said Zinnia.

"Sluts!" cried the students.

"Whores!" someone added.

"We're taking back those words!"

"We're taking back all the words they try to put on us!"

"Fag!"

"Loser!"

"I'm totally a fag!" said Aimee. "A whore, slut, fag."

"We all are! And we're wearing our underpants!" cried someone else.

And that's how the Truth Commission set off the first Slut Riot Parade.

Tuesday, September 25

An Acute Eye

The truth movement felt radical, at least until the following Sunday.[49] My sister hadn't disappeared for over a week. Nor had she come into my room to talk. She'd been in the closet all weekend, which gave me plenty of time to work quietly on my embroidery.

If you aren't familiar with the stitching world, I do embroidery that lets me make detailed images in thread.[50] Needlework is the perfect pastime for people who are obsessive and don't want to draw much attention to themselves. I can sit hunched over my embroidery frame for five or six hours, and people forget I'm there. As an added bonus, I don't disturb my sister by rattling around in my own room.

Almost as soon as my sister came home from college, I began a series of images I'm excited about. I often stayed late at school to stitch while Dusk worked on elements of her Spring Special Project. She was calling the piece *Taxiderming the Shrew*. I gave her plenty of space. My guess

---

49. Which reminds me, I saw you and Mr. Wells talking in the parking lot after the riot. You laugh nicely together. ☺ ☺

50. I use photographs as my guide. Think of Chuck Close's portrait tapestries. That's the effect I'm aiming for.

is that bad things can happen to beginning taxidermists. Dusk had posted a notice seeking shrews that died of natural causes on Craigslist Nanaimo and gotten an excellent response. She was always taking delivery of dead shrews people had found while they were out walking.

While I stitched and Dusk tried to mount shrews (so to speak), Neil made paintings of elusive beautiful women. Sometimes we all worked together in the same room in happy silence.

Still, stitching at home took the edge off, and it pleased my parents to see me busy doing things that wouldn't aggravate my sister.

The night after the Slut Riot, after I'd gone to bed, Keira came out of the closet and into my room again. Like a ghost or a bad dream.

"Norm?" she whispered. "Do you want to talk?"

My eyes snapped open.

Keira stretched and yawned, rising up on her tiptoes and reaching her thin white arms over her head.

"I get stiff from staying in one position so long. You too?"

She'd been working hard for the past several days. She even let my parents bring her some lunch in the closet. I knew because they had told me about it at least three times.

I nodded, my head half hidden by blankets.

"The needlepoint stuff you do is probably even worse for your back and neck than drawing. We should do yoga together. Go to a class."

"Yeah," I croaked, trying to imagine doing yoga with Keira. It would be such a normal thing to do. So unlike us. She'd done less and less socializing since the days when we'd gone to summer camp together. Now she rarely went out in public. That was part of her mystique. A couple of years ago, a few of the older comic artists and a couple of important critics had criticized her for how she used our family in the Chronicles. In response, she pulled a semi-Salinger and stopped going to Comic Cons or interacting with her fans, who accused the people who'd given her a hard time of driving her "underground." Apparently, if you don't "get" my sister, you're an uptight censor. At least, that's what I read on the Diana Chronicles blogs and message boards before I stopped reading them.

"Let me get my sleeping bag," said Keira. She retreated into the closet and I steeled myself for the next storytelling session. I had no idea what to do with the fact that Keira and one of her teachers had crossed the line. My Facebook exchange with Roberta Heller II hadn't cleared anything up. Also, I felt guilty about my motives. I listened to my sister because I wanted her respect. I listened because I hoped she'd realize that talking helped and that she should talk to someone better qualified than me. Those were not exactly noble reasons.

I lay frozen on my bed as the story wafted out like mustard gas.

"So we went hiking a couple of times. He had an acute eye for landscape," she said.

I wasn't sure what that meant but I didn't interrupt to ask.

"He was worried people would think it was strange, his spending so much time alone with a student. Me."

Long, poisonous pause.

"So he picked me up about a block away from the school. No one saw us together."

An alarm bell was going off in my head. I didn't mention it.

"The hikes were great. It was just nice to get off campus and move, you know? School could be such a hothouse—worse than the Art Farm, even. The third time we went out, he took me on this super-steep path with cliffs and these deep canyons. And at the top, a few hundred yards off the trail, there was this abandoned hiker's cabin."

My sheet was pulled over the lower half of my face, and my breath puffed warm against my own face.

"He asked if I wanted to check it out."

She paused.

"Can you turn on the light? This is hard to talk about. The dark makes it worse."

My arm felt like lead when I reached to switch on the desk light. When the light flickered on, I was surprised to see that my sister wasn't lying down anymore. She sat upright, tucked deep into her red sleeping bag, which she'd pulled up over her head like a hoodie. Her face was deep in shadows. Her eyes shone from inside the darkness.

I felt myself trapped by that gaze, which didn't seem to waver as she continued.

"That's where it happened. Between us. He . . ."

Even though her eyes were disconcertingly bright, her voice was quiet.

"I didn't mean for it to happen," she said at last. "He was married."

The room was absolutely silent and I struggled to unfreeze my face.

"I'm sorry," I said inadequately.

"You can't talk about it," she said in a faint voice teetering at the edge of tears.

"You didn't say anything?" I asked.

She shook her head, but somehow those big shining eyes seemed not to move.

"Should we tell someone? I mean, teachers can't just—"

"No!" The hesitation was gone. "I just needed to talk. You're the only one I trust. Promise me you won't tell."

In spite of the horror of my sister's story, I once again felt a little thrill at being the only person she trusted enough to talk to.

"I won't," I said.

"Okay. I guess I've said enough for one night."

And my sister got up and left. Her outline was deformed by the sleeping bag. She looked like a mermaid who'd swum through a toxic spill.

"I'm sorry," I repeated to the door as it closed behind her, though I wasn't sure exactly what I was sorry for.

I Heard It's Bad for Your Teeth

On Saturday, Dusk and Neil and I went to Tina's for lunch. Tina's is one of those retro diners with a Formica lunch counter and stools and red vinyl booths. I think the restaurant is actually old as opposed to pretend-old. Neil says Tina's serves the best eggs Benedict in the known universe. I have the Veggie Bennie and Neil has the Blackstone and we are full and happy for about two days afterward. Dusk has orange juice or coffee and sometimes, if she's in the right mood, something from the kid's menu. Dusk is one of those "eat to live" people, unlike Neil, who lives to eat. I'm sort of a let's-have-delicious-eats-until-the-gnawing-stress-of-my-home-life-makes-it-impossible-for-me-to-work-up-an-appetite person.

"What do you mean, you're not having a Benny?" said Neil to me. "That's a violation of protocol."

There are several protocols that have to be followed when we go for Saturday brunch. We have to arrive at precisely 9:15 a.m. Neil says the breakfasts don't taste as good if we don't get a booth, and Dusk won't wait in a line for anyone or anything. Dusk would have a lot of trouble in a Soviet-style economy, where apparently up to 80 percent of life was spent waiting in line for things like bread. Then again, Dusk doesn't really eat bread, so maybe she would have been fine.

If you are later than 9:20 or so, you will miss the booths. If you get there before 9:15, then you feel like a morning person or a farmer. Organizing Saturday brunch is my job. It requires considerable skill. Normally, the food makes the effort worth it, but not today.

"My stomach's already . . . got food."

Neil snorted. "That food is lonely."

"I'm going for orange juice," said Dusk. "I heard it's really bad for your teeth. My dad said that we all have 'compromised enamel.' It's some genetic trait, and he and my mom want us to be careful. So I'm going to hit the OJ super hard, and if that doesn't work, I might start doing meth."

"Still feeling hostile toward your parents?" asked Neil.

Dusk raised a perfectly arched eyebrow. "Being a disappointment is a lifelong practice, like meditation. You can't just disappoint in one or two areas. If you want to really disappoint, you need to apply yourself. Be well rounded. Take up art. Fail foundation courses. Let your teeth rot, and dress in ways that draw the wrong kind of attention."

As if to demonstrate, she looked like an eighteenth-century chimney sweep who had a second job as a stripper, circa 1984. Neon yellow tube top, suspenders, tweed gauchos. She wore oxfords because the sole had fallen off her grandfather's old New Balance. Patched tweed coat.

The waitress, Tina's daughter, came to the table.

"The usual?" she said.

Neil put a hand over his heart. "Kiki. You have no idea how touched I am when you remember what I like."

Kiki, slight and ever poised, smiled. "My pleasure."

Maybe *she* would be Neil's new muse. I fought back the flutter of something I hoped wasn't jealousy.

"We've been coming here for ages," Dusk told Neil. "And you have never changed your order."

Neil ignored Dusk and gazed adoringly at Kiki.

"Thank you," he said.

"You're welcome."

"No, really. Thank you. I feel special for the first time today."

Kiki smiled again, managing to seem friendly and just distant enough to make Neil stop talking.

"Nerd," said Dusk, but she said it fondly.

I ordered toast and coffee, and Dusk ordered the enamel-destroying orange juice.

"So. I think it's time to review. We're in the middle of a social movement here. Maybe even a revolution. We need to take stock," said Dusk. "You agree?" she asked me.

"Yes."

"So far we've performed four truthcavations."

"We're calling them truthcavations now?" said Neil.

"It's awkward," I said. "From a language perspective, I don't love it."

"Fine. We will come up with a suitable and specific noun soon. We need our own jargon."

Neil and I agreed. Jargon was good.

"Of those four truthsplorations, three were unqualified successes."

"I don't love truthsploration, either," I said. "Not to be negative."

"Oh, no, you could never be negative," said Dusk.

I recognized but did not comment on her sarcasm. Neil bumped me gently with his argyle cardigan-clad shoulder. "Maybe we should define success?" I said.

"That's easy. Success is when someone tells us the truth."

"What about when things get confusing? What about the effects of the truth? Like, if telling the truth makes a situation worse?"

Neil and Dusk stared at me.

"You're overthinking it," said Dusk.

"Truth is the goal," added Neil. "We can't control what comes from it."

I shrugged and sipped my coffee.

"Aimee tells me everything now. We have no secrets," said Neil. His phone buzzed and he looked at the screen. "See? This is the fourth text I've had from her this morning. She's worried there's a change in Number Two."

"Number Two" was what Aimee had named her left breast. She was starting to worry that there was an capsular contracture issue[51] developing; hence the near hourly

----

51. Meaning the body forms a fibrous shell around a foreign body, such as a breast implant. According to my online research, if this shell hardens, it can become quite painful—another reason I'm not going to spend the two hundred thirty dollars I have in my savings account on that particular upgrade.

updates. Neil was starting to look pained every time his phone sounded.[52]

"I can report that the truth has had lasting positive effects on Mrs. Dekker's wardrobe. I'm sure you all saw the sundress at the riot. I believe Mrs. Dekker is an unqualified success story."

"She's still kind of moody. She was back in her poncho the next day and she was kind of a bitch when I went in to tell her I had to go to the dentist," I said.

"Normandy, really, enough with the negative nellies," said Dusk.

Kiki dropped off our breakfasts. A plate of toast for me and a Blackstone for Neil. We applied our preferred condiments and began to eat in silence. It was all going well until Dusk spoke up again.

"Neil? Can you stop tearing into that meal like it's a gazelle you brought down with your bare hands and give us a report on Tyler Jones?"

It was my turn to bump Neil with my shoulder.

"We've been in contact four times. He's still processing the request."

"So not an unqualified success. Let's say that particular truth seeking is still in process."

Neil went back to his food, but with less enthusiasm.

"And of course, the Zinnia McFarland Truth Riot was amazing."

--- --- --- --- --- --- --- --- --- --- --- --- ---

52. I don't know if he looked pained because he was worried about the state of Number Two or because he realized how far Aimee's confession put him into the friend zone.

I wasn't sure. The day after the riot I saw Zinnia heading into the guidance office.[53] She looked like she'd been crying. But I'd been called "negative" enough times that morning, and I decided not to speak up.

"I think truth is spreading," said Dusk, swishing her orange juice around in her mouth so it could do as much enamel damage as possible.

"First, G. P. Academy. Next, the world," said Neil.

"Before the movement can reach a full flowering, all founders of the Commission must experience the power of asking the truth," said Dusk. "I know you're shy, Normandy, and so I've taken it upon myself to find you another target. One you'll feel more comfortable approaching."

My head snapped up, alarms going off.

"Lisette DeVries," said Dusk.

"Oh, shit!" said Neil. "That's genius!" He put down his knife and then put up a hand for Dusk to slap.

I put my head in my hands and stared at my untouched toast. Dusk was an evil genius. She was sending me up against the least truthy person in all of G. P. and, possibly, the world.

At this juncture, I feel it's important to point out that lying is not the same as not telling the truth. Leaving things unsaid is part of being a civilized person, at least according to me.

Lying is a different matter. It requires effort and creativity, rather than the ability to stand still and take it. There are also levels to consider.

----

53. I guess I don't need to tell you that, Ms. Fowler.

Scenario: A girl tries on a pair of jeans that make her appear to have only one long, flat butt cheek. She asks her frenemy, who is a liar, if the jeans look good.

Level-One Liar: "You look awesome in those. But I think I liked the other ones better."

Level-Two Liar: "You look awesome."

Super-Lying Liar: "I once had that exact pair of jeans. In fact, they were the jeans I was wearing when a modeling scout came up to me and wanted to take my picture. They really wanted to bring me to New York City. But instead I chose to go to the tryouts for *Canada's Next Top Model*. Which I would have gotten into and probably won, except for that thing I told you about that happened with my glands. I think you should wear those jeans on your next date."

Lisette DeVries is a Level-Three Compulsive Super-Lying Liar, minus the slight meanness given in the example. So far as I can tell, she lies because "there is no there there," if you know what I mean.[54] She's always seizing upon stray identities and running away with them, like an animal rescuer escaping from a stranger's backyard with a neglected dog. In grade nine, she joined the Gay-Straight Alliance. A week later, she declared she was a lesbian. All the pictures of cute boys in her locker were replaced

---

54. According to Wikipedia, this phrase was coined by Gertrude Stein in *Gertrude Stein, Everybody's Autobiography* (Random House, 1937) and is often applied to the city of her childhood, Oakland, California. She also said "Rose is a rose is a rose." I find that quote less compelling. Perhaps due to its repetitiveness.

by shots of Portia de Rossi and hot chicks on motorbikes. That would have been fine if she'd actually been gay or at least curious, but she wasn't. She just thought it would be cool for a while, or at least while she was a member of the Alliance.[55] The minute she left the GSA, which she did after an incident with another member's brother at a dance, she was ruler-straight again.

Down came Portia de Rossi, up went Justin Timberlake, because she'd joined Song and Dance Club.

DeVries is such a compulsive liar that she's kind of an icon around the Art Farm. Her lies are like little Fabergé eggs: unexpected, intricately detailed, and completely and utterly pointless.

When Dusk proposed that I confront Lisette DeVries, she was essentially asking me to take a ornate little egg of a person and smash her against the ground. I said as much.

"So narrow it down," Dusk said. "Pick one obvious lie. Right now the burning question is does she really think she's a member of the First Nations."

"I can't do that," I squawked. "She might be one-fortieth Aboriginal or something. What if that's the one thing about her that turns out to be true? It's not my place to ask. So what if she wants to be someone she's not."

"You know," said Neil, using his fork to drag a hash brown through a puddle of ketchup, "I'd like to be someone I'm not."

---

55. In prison, they call that sort of thing "going gay for the stay." Or so I hear.

"There's no one better than you," I told him. Because it was true.

"I'm doing you a favor by giving you a subject with so many points of entry," said Dusk.

"What?"

"She means that Lisette is constructed of eighty-five percent lies," said Neil. "You could ask her about just about anything and if she answered honestly, you'd have uncovered a truth."

"That reasoning is flawed."

Dusk leaned across the table and put a hand on mine. Neil, sitting beside me, did the same.

"Ugh!" I said, flinching. "Stop touching me! Both of you."

"Not until you promise," said Dusk.

"You are going to love dancing with the truth. Seriously," said Neil.

"I'm not ready."

"So spend some time with her first. Don't just dive in there."[56]

"You are both terrible people."

"We appreciate your honesty," said Dusk and Neil at the same time.

"Fine."

They let go of my hands and looked very pleased with themselves.

"But I'm not doing it right away. I have to warm up."[57]

---

56. The screech of metaphors crashing into each other was overwhelming. That probably added to my pain.

57. You, Ms. Fowler, may have noticed that I'm a big fan of warming up, or,

"Fine. We have other truths to discover while you conduct research and surveillance," said Dusk.

Research. There was only so much research I could conduct. At least researching Lisette DeVries would be easier than poking any further into my sister's recent past.

— — — — — — — — — — — — —

as you have sometimes called it: *repeating myself.* Which reminds me, you looked really nice in that blue dress you had on yesterday. Mr. Wells was totally staring at you when you walked by. How is me being a fan of warming up connected to you and Mr. Wells? I think you know. First it's scent. Next it's blue dresses. I smell long walks on a warm beach in someone's future!

The Opposite of a Starfish

The good news about Lisette from a tracking and monitoring perspective was that she was the opposite of unobtrusive. In fact, she was full-blown trusive.

At about the time the Truth Commission started, Lisette had thrown herself body, soul, and fashion sense into the Indigenous Art and Performance Program. In a move that I'm pretty sure violates every protocol there is, she had given herself a spirit name, which she said was given to her in a secret ceremony by a very powerful yet little-known elder from Haida Gwaii.[58] The elder was so little known that no one, including our school's First Nations elders, students, and teachers had ever heard of her. The spirit name was "Red Starfish," and she started using it in everyday conversation.[59]

----

58. Known for a time as the Queen Charlotte Islands. Haida Gwaii is on my list of places to visit at the first opportunity due to its culture and natural beauty.

59. I figure the starfish is probably a psychologically revealing choice on Lisette's part. Wikipedia says that because some starfish can digest food outside the body, they hunt prey much larger than their mouths, including clams and oysters, arthropods, small fish, and mollusks. Starfish may also supplement their diets with algae or organic detritus.

She had a temporary tattoo of a red starfish on her neck, where it looked like the worst melanoma dreamt up by an oncologist who ever ate spicy food late at night.

She started wearing Native-inspired clothing with madcap abandon and a complete disregard for coherence or accuracy. Her wardrobe included items significant to the peoples of the about twenty different nations, plus Pendleton Mills, Disney, and all points in between. She wore feathers in her hair, turquoise and jade jewelry, buckskin chaps, and a button blanket she'd made herself.[60] She went around telling everyone she was one-tenth Tla A'min and that her great-grandmother was part of the Sliammon First Nation of Powell River.

All of it was, of course, total fiction. Lisette DeVries's grandparents were from Prince George by way of Holland and before she came to Green Pastures she'd gone to the Dutch Reformed Christian School.

At first, Dusk and Neil joined me outside the Shed where the IAP programs are housed.[61] The Shed is much nicer than it sounds. It's a big open post-and-beam building attached to the rest of the school by a glass-and-cedar

---

60. Button blankets are used as ceremonial garments and gifts by the Northwest tribes. They're usually made of wool and show a family crest. Hers was a fleece blanket with the green, red, yellow, and black Hudson's Bay Company stripes on it and some random buttons attached hither and yon around . . . you guessed it: a red starfish.

61. Ms. Fowler, do you sometimes marvel at the budget this school has? I do, and I'm only sixteen. I've seen Season Four of The Wire, at Mr. Wells's suggestion. Not every school has studio pods, theaters, and roundhouses. Thanks be to our Founding Farmer!

walkway. Huge ceramic pots of ferns line the approach and are good for sitting on while pretending you are an elf or similar. Or maybe that's just me. On this day the double doors to the Shed were thrown wide open and we could see some students painting drums and others making a canoe out of a huge log. Our school is getting a reputation for producing some of the most promising young carvers in BC, aboriginal and nonaboriginal. The distinctive scents of tanned hide and cedar floated out.

Before Dusk could begin issuing orders and taking control of the situation, her cell phone buzzed.

"It's Zinnia," she said.

"Already time for another Slut Riot?" asked Neil.

"She wants me to meet her by the bike racks. We've been touching base regularly. We're becoming honest but not close friends."

And just like that, Dusk left, medical bag in hand. Since she started working on her Spring Special Project, she's begun carrying around an old-fashioned black medical bag everywhere. This thrilled her parents, who thought it was a sign of incipient medical-ness. Then they figured out it is stuffed with taxidermy tools like latex gloves, scalpels, a fleshing beam,[62] bondo, and fake eyeballs. It's basically the kit of a serial killer or Damien Hirst. I guess she wants to be ready in case she comes across a recently deceased small creature. She'll be able to preserve it at the side of the road, then build it a tiny trailer to live in.

- - - - - - - - - - - -

62. Here's a disturbing detail: a fleshing beam is used to scrape the extra flesh off the hide of an animal.

"Do you think—"

Before I could finish my sentence, Neil's phone buzzed.

"Aimee," he said. "She wants to talk. Something going on with her parents. Also, there's been a change in Number Two. See you, Norm. Good luck."

"I'm not talking to Lisette today!" I told his retreating back.

"No rush. We love you," he said.

"I don't feel the same," I said. Even though I totally did.

It was odd to sit by myself. Neil and Dusk and I did almost everything together when we weren't making stuff or at our separate houses. We were a unit, and I loved it. I became more and more aware of how lucky I was to have my two friends as I watched Lisette.

She wore her long blonde hair in two braids and had on a rawhide headband. She was carrying a drum and dancing from group to group.

The painters smiled tolerantly and said a few words to her, and the canoe carvers did the same. A boy working on a mask at the end of the hall didn't even look up when she came banging over to him, but another one gave her an indulgent high five.

She was like a butterfly that had no place to alight. In fact, she was basically the opposite of a starfish.

"Hey."

I looked up to see Mr. Thomas staring at me.

Mr. Thomas, AKA Randy, was G. P.'s visiting artist. We get two artists every year. In the fall, we always have a First Nations artist. In the spring, the artist is international. The visiting artists are always amazing, but Randy Thomas took it to the next level. Maybe because he sometimes worked in television. Or maybe in spite of the fact he worked in television.

He was at least six four and massive all around, but he had this light, dancer-y way about him. He was a choreographer, a writer, an artist, and a musician. He was the most popular teacher at G. P., maybe because he was the embodiment of what all the administrators and teachers wanted us to become: well-rounded artists and creative people.[63] He was also funny, which was my favorite thing about him, and he was deep.

"Can I help?" he asked. He stood near where I perched on the edge of the giant potted fern.

I felt a surge of guilt and wasn't sure why. "I'm just hanging out."

Randy smiled. His face was round, and when he smiled, he looked very young.

"You planning to start some more riots?" he said, settling down on the huge ceramic pot next to mine. He didn't look like an elf beside the fern. He looked like a giant who would flatten it if he shifted his weight the wrong way.

I gave a small, insincere laugh.

"That was interesting. You and your friends really started something, eh?"

"I guess."

"I just saw them leave. Where'd they go?"

One thing I've noticed about our visiting artists is that they're all very curious, and they notice everything.

----

63. "Contributing to the cultural life of this country." Yes, I know the whole mission statement for G. P. Academy.

"They went looking for the truth," I said before I could stop myself.

"So that's what you guys are doing."

I nodded glumly.

"How's that working out for you?"

I considered the question for a long moment.

"Mixed," I said. "We asked Mrs. Dekker why she's so . . . you know, grumpy."

"I hear she has ostriches," said Mr. Thomas, folding his arms over his broad chest and leaning back. The fern seemed to cringe behind him.

"Yeah."

"She's a moody one," he said.

"That hasn't changed. Even if she has taken to wearing sundresses from time to time."

"Not sure about that yellow color on her," said Mr. Thomas. "But you have to appreciate the effort."

After a longish pause, he spoke again. "So the truth has put a yellow sundress on an ostrich farmer and created an underwear riot. Powerful stuff. You got your eye on someone in here?" He nodded in the direction of the Shed.

I looked down at my old Chucks and felt ashamed. Dusk and Neil didn't feel this way about what we were doing. What was wrong with me?

"I'm supposed to ask Lisette something," I said.

"That right?" said Mr. Thomas. "Says who?"

"My friends."

"What are you going to ask her?"

"I was supposed to ask if she really thinks she's Native."

"Ah, the Indian question. That's dangerous territory right there."

I chanced a look into his face. It was as nonjudgmental as his voice, and full of the same gentle interest and amusement he brought to most things.

"I think I'm supposed to ask why she can't just be who she is."

Mr. Thomas nodded slowly. "Yeah, lot of trouble comes from not wanting to be who we are."

"But I'm actually pretty sick of asking the truth. I'm definitely sick of hearing it," I said. Not that he'd asked.

"You're pretty sick of everything."

Mr. Thomas and I had locked eyes.

"Yes, I am."

"Pretty angry, too," he said.

"Yeah."

Tears started to push their way up, but I refused to bring my hand to my face to brush them away. "Do you ever feel like you just need a break?" I asked.

"Hell, yeah. All the time."

"What do you do?"

"Used to be wine, women, and song. Now I act. I teach. I create." He put a pompous spin on the last word to let me know he didn't take himself too seriously.

"I already know why Lisette lies," I said.

"Course you do. You're a smart person." Mr. Thomas straightened his long, jean-clad legs. He wore fancy cowboy boots. There are about four people in the world who would not look ridiculous in those boots, and he was one of them.

"I once heard gossip defined as 'emotional speculation,'" he said. "I read it in a crime novel by Louise Penny. I can't remember which one. You can learn a lot from crime novels."

This was where I was supposed to admit that what we were doing was emotional speculation. That what we were doing was gossiping. Only we weren't. There really was more to it than that. We were going right to the source. We weren't even talking much about what we learned.

"We're not gossiping," I said. "Asking people the truth is a spiritual practice."

Mr. Thomas's broad face became serious. "I must have got that wrong. I thought that spiritual practice involved asking *yourself* the truth."

A Candid Q&A with Normandy Pale

I'm not one to sidestep a throwdown, especially a spiritual one. I can look myself in the eye. Ask myself the hard truths.

When I finished talking to Mr. Thomas, I went to one of my favorite corners and instead of working on my embroidery, I got out my journal. I wrote the following candid Q&A with myself.

> Q: What are you doing?
> A: I don't know.
>
> Q: Could you be more specific?
> A: I'm avoiding the truth about my sister.
>
> Q: What truth is that?
> A: The one she tells me when she sneaks into
>   my room at night. About her relationship with
>   the teacher.
>
> Q: Isn't the whole sneaking-into-your-room-at-
>   night thing a little creepy?
> A: Uh, yeah. It's a lot creepy. It's about as
>   creepy as working in our closet. The good

news is that a person can get used to
anything.

Q: So why do you listen?
A: Because she needs to tell someone. She
needs to get it out.

Q: Why can't she talk to someone else? A
professional.
A: Because she won't.

Q: Are you sure?
A: I'm the only one she trusts. Maybe if she tells
me, she'll feel strong enough to tell someone
else and if she tells someone else, she'll feel
better and go back to school. After someone
deals with her teacher, that is. Something
will probably have to be done about him.

Q: What about you? Are you sure you can
handle her truth?
A: No.

Never Kick Puppies. Or Let Them Buy Knives.

As much as I love my friends, I wasn't ready to involve them. My sister would never forgive me. Plus, my friends were turning into evangelists, ideologues, and full-fledged fanatics when it came to the truth. They had lost sight of the fact that the truth could be extremely complicated. They were the cops. I was the lawyer, but one without a financial incentive.

If I was going to get help, I needed to find it in-house. Literally.

I went home after my meeting with Mr. Thomas and found my dad in the kitchen. He had a couple of days off, and spent his time cooking produce that he got on markdown from Premium Price. We may not have a lot of material things other than vacuum cleaners and knives (and the German chair), but we have a superabundance of frozen vegetable concoctions. The more stressful things get, the more my dad cooks and freezes.

"Potato and cauliflower curry," he said.

"Smells amazing."

I did not point out that the six or seven containers of potato and cauliflower curry currently residing in the big freezer in the basement would probably smell equally delicious if defrosted. My dad's like puppies. You don't kick puppies when they make curry.[64]

"Going to make raita, too. And maybe naan bread if you're really, really good."

"When have I ever been anything but really, really good?" I asked. Which, sadly, was absolutely true. If you rock the boat in a fragile family, the concern is that everyone will drown.

"Hmmm," said my dad, his head buried in the cookbook. He is always coming home with cookbooks that didn't sell or that he got for the low, low price of $2.99. I've tried to explain the concept of a Google recipe search, but he insists that second- and third-rate cookbooks are the way to go. It's a mystery why he needs cookbooks at all, because he makes the same thing over and over.

"Your mom will be home in half an hour and I want the house to smell good."

I reached for the regular mismatched dishes, but my dad wouldn't hear of it. "Norm! Come on! It's a great day. Let's use the custom stuff."

When he said "custom," he wasn't kidding. I'm sad to report that the Diana franchise does a brisk business in unsettling kitchen and tableware. There is Diana cutlery (our faces embossed on the backs of spoons, and knives and forks with handles shaped like our bodies) and a Diana tablecloth (one side shows our house as it appears in real life—and in the Chronicles—and the other, the household in Vermeer).

---

64. Yes, yes, I know that metaphor doesn't hold up. But I do sort of like comparing my dad to puppies.

Each of us has two place mats with our deformed faces staring up at us. We also own all four sets of Diana salt- and pepper shakers. Seriously. I could not make this up.

"Normy? Why don't you put out the Vermeer place mats?" said my dad, who is always trying to get me to set the whole table with my sister's distorted versions of us in merch form.

I ignored him and put four non-Diana plates on the bare table. The fourth place setting was pointless, because Keira almost never eats with us.

"Did you see her today?" I asked.

"Her car was gone when I got home."

I felt my fists ball up and forced them to relax. "When did she go out?"

"I don't know. Your sister is a grown-up. Plus, she's working on something new. You know how she gets when she's in the zone. How I ended up in a house with three beautiful, artistic women I do not know," said my dad. "Who was that fellow married to the gal with the eyebrows? The one who painted a lot of pictures of herself?"

"Diego Rivera," I said. "He was married to Frida Kahlo."

"I have a lot of sympathy for that guy. I wonder if he spent half his life making potato curry." My dad chuckled nonsensically to himself and it occurred to me, not for the first time, that my dad is fairly demented. Example of his dementedness: he and my mom telling us about their marital troubles thanks to his little interlude with the nineteen-year-old checkout girl. I was only six at the time, but the memory is clear. If mine's fresh, my sister's is probably in HD. The only good thing that came out of it was my dad's extreme solicitousness toward us, which persists to this day.

"Luckily, I got this new knife. See? It's Swedish."

He held up a small, bright blue knife. It certainly looked Swedish.

Instead of giving him hell, I reminded myself that when a puppy buys a new Swedish knife, you don't yell at it.[65]

I needed to ask my question before my mother came home. "So, Dad," I said. "Have you asked or at least wondered about why Keira's home from school?"

"Your sister has her reasons."

"Sure, but shouldn't you know what the reasons are?"

"Have patience. She'll tell us when she's ready."

"Will she? She doesn't seem a little strange to you? Since she got home."

"Oh, Normandy. You know your sister. She goes her own way. It's an artistic genius thing. Can't be helped," he said.

"What about those letters from the school? Did you look at any of them?"

"They were addressed to Keira. How would you like it if your mother and I opened your mail?"

I didn't get much mail so it was a moot point. I wanted to tell him that she'd shared at least some of what happened with me, and I didn't know what to do with the information. But part of me thought he'd be even less able to handle the situation than I was. Some people are good at letting you know they can't cope. My parents had gotten that message across loud and clear. My mom and dad just got smaller and

---

65. The puppy or the knife.

sillier as they waited for . . . what? What were they waiting for? My sister's success to finally pay off for them? For her to turn around and tell everyone she respected them? Cash prizes? New cars? We don't have much in the way of an extended family. My grandparents are all dead. Dad has a few cousins, but they live in the Northwest Territories. My mom has a sister, but they don't really talk. No wise elder was going to swoop in and lay a little reality on our family situation.

"Don't you wonder where she goes for days at a time?" I asked.

"For goodness sake, Normandy. You're a teenager. You should understand your sister's need for privacy."

"Oh," I said. Wind? Say good-bye to sails.

"Why so many questions? You have always been a worrier. Your sister is fine. You've always been less intense than Keira. It doesn't mean you're any less talented."

I felt my mouth fall open in amazement.

"What?"

"Your mother and I know that Keira's intensity makes you question yourself. It shouldn't. You're very talented, but in a different way. A quieter way. You're going to do great things, kiddo."

"Are you serious?"

My dad stirred the pot of curry and then held the spoon to his lips to taste.

"Ohhh, that's good."

"This isn't about me," I said, trying to keep my voice level. "I think Keira needs help."

"You want to taste?"

"Are you hearing me? She doesn't leave the house for days. When she goes out, she's gone for days. As soon as she got control of her own business affairs, she came home from college, fired her agent, and never said a word about any of it. All that seems fine to you?"

"Now, Norm. I think that's enough." My dad was back in chief curry-stirrer mode. I felt myself wanting to have a Jack Nicholson in *A Few Good Men* moment. I wanted to bellow at my dad that he couldn't handle the truth. But that wouldn't be fair, because he wasn't the only one.

"Hello?" My mom's voice sounded from the front door.

My dad and I stopped speaking and turned. "Hi," we said.

My mother stepped into the kitchen. "Oh, it smells great in here, Pat," she said. She gave my dad a kiss on his cheek and then came over to sit at the kitchen table.

"Potato and cauliflower curry," said my dad. "It'll cure what ails a body."

My mother didn't point out the other containers of curry in the freezer, either. She knows that my dad finds cooking relaxing. Considering that they're so close to the emotional and financial edge most of the time, they're also pretty tender with each other. They got over their difficulties surprisingly well. My sister didn't seem to have the same resilience.

"Well, this body needs a bath before dinner," she said.

Slowly, like a woman twice her age, my mom got up and walked out. For once, she didn't ask where Keira was or whether she'd come out of her room or done anything remotely normal during the day. Rule Number #1 of the

Pale Family: don't ask questions for which you don't want answers.

Maybe that rule is what pushed me to do what I did. Maybe my teenage rebellion finally kicked in. But I went to my room and logged on to Facebook. Then I rethought. I logged out and created a new, fake profile. I looked up Lisette DeVries. And I sent her a private message.

Thirteen Words[66]

66. You know how there's a chapter in *As I Lay Dying* that consists of only five words: "My mother is a fish"? Well, in the interest of pushing the envelope, footnote-wise, I offer you a chapter that contains only a single footnote. Hilarious, right?

Here is what I wrote to Lisette DeVries: *Do you really think you are aboriginal? Or are you just lying? Again.*

The second I sent it, I wanted to delete it. I settled for deleting my fake profile and prayed that the message would disappear with it.

For sure, not my finest moment.

Friday, October 5

Small Format Effort

On Friday morning, when I still hadn't confronted Lisette, at least not directly, Dusk called a meeting of the Commission.

"Let's evaluate. Assess," she said.

"Didn't we just do that at Tina's?" I said.

"I feel like we weren't thorough enough. It's time for written reports. I'd like to get a handle on this thing. Maybe do a bit of strategic planning," she said. Dusk has more of her parents in her than she likes to admit.[67]

"Shall we meet in the Boardroom?" asked Neil.

"Excellent suggestion," said Dusk.

"I'm pretty busy. Classes. Bathroom breaks," I said.

Dusk ignored me. "I'd like a full written report from each of you," she said. "To that end, I've stolen one of my mother's prescription pads. I'm afraid you can't write yourself

--- --- --- --- --- --- --- --- --- --- --- ---

67. Speaking of disapproving adults, you were pretty free with the green pen on my Q&A chapter. You used it with such vigor that part of me thinks you were reacting to more than just a chapter with minimal action. It's okay. Teachers are allowed to be not self-aware, just like everyone except me. I saw you and Mr. W. talking in the parking lot. It looked intense, but not in a bad way. Maybe you two are having troubles and you took it out on my chapter? It's fine. I'm used to being held to the highest standard at all times.

prescriptions because her office has moved to a computer printout system and voided these pads, but I think you'll both enjoy working in the small format. I know I always do."

At the time of this conversation we were stalled in Nancy, at the end of Neil's long, winding driveway.

Dusk poked me in the side. "You especially," she said. "Since small format kind of fits your effort."

"Hey!" said Neil. "Hey, now. That's not the spirit of the Commission. Norm may have been truth seeking in private over the last few days. We don't know. She might be able to fill up a whole prescription pad with her discoveries."

"Norm?" asked Dusk. "Anything to report on the Lisette DeVries front?"

Before I could answer, Neil's dad pulled up alongside us. He was on his way out. He'd recently, to Neil's profound relief, traded in his Big Bird–colored Hummer for a new Jaguar. The car was low-slung enough that I had a good view of his hair plugs when I rolled down my window and he leaned out to crane his head in order to look up at us.

"Normandy!" he boomed. Neil's dad is full-voiced and full-figured. It seemed to me that everything about him said self-indulgence. I looked at him and saw foie gras, full-fat French cheeses, and happy-ending massages. He was a little creepy, but I liked him anyway. Everyone likes him.

"How are you, gorgeous? You got my boy in that jalopy?"

"Yes, sir," I said.

That made Mr. Sutton grin. He has a great smile, just like Neil, only his teeth were covered in veneers so white, they hurt the eyes.

"How'd my boy get to have such gorgeous friends?"

Mr. Sutton has a favorite adjective. Guess what it is? Half the time he calls Neil gorgeous, too. He's actually found the exact perfect balance of skeeviness and charm.

"Dawn, honey? You in there?"

"Yes, Mr. Sutton."

"You want me to send a tow truck? I can give you kids a ride to school. Or we can get the tow driver to haul you over there. Arrive in style!"

"That's okay. She'll be ready to go in a minute. She just flooded."

"I've heard that before," said Mr. Sutton, managing to make it sound incredibly smutty.

"Oh, God," muttered Neil, hanging his head. I bumped him with my shoulder.

"We're good, Mr. Sutton," I said.

"Nice car," added Dusk.

"Sure you don't want a ride? It's cozy in here, girls."

"Dad!" said Neil. "Enough."

"Mr. Sensitive," said Mr. Sutton. "He doesn't get it from me. It's that school, isn't it? Turning you kids sensitive. How about I pay for all of you to go get business degrees?"

"Rowan!" said Neil, using his dad's first name.

Mr. Sutton made a big show of wincing, like he was in serious trouble.

"Okay, gorgeous," he said, apparently addressing all of us. "But if you're still here when I get home from my appointment, I'm taking you to school. Norm, you'll sit next to me."

Neil made another low groaning noise.

Mr. Sutton flashed me a too-white grin and the sleek, low car pulled away.

"He's going to the spa," said Neil. "He and his buddies

spend about three hours a day in that Japanese bathhouse place in Courtenay."

"Seriously?" said Dusk. "He drives an hour to go for a steam?"

"They golf first," said Neil. "Then they go to the bathhouse. Then they drive back here and go to the Cactus Club."

"Oy," said Dusk.

"I don't call him Sordid Sutton for nothing," said Neil.

"Love you," I said.

"Double," said Dusk.

And we all bumped shoulders and felt better.

Too soon, the moment was gone. It faded as I looked around at the immaculately landscaped property with its concrete driveway etched to look like bricks, trimmed trees and tasteful shrubs and closely barbered grass. The single-story house was sprawling and contemporary and stayed just barely on the right side of McMansion territory— ostentatious, but without things like fake Grecian columns. It had decent proportions. The luxury detailing was obvious, but not overdone.

"As I was saying, I'd like to meet and evaluate. We've got spare periods after lunch today. Please make your reports on the pads provided."

Dusk handed Neil and me each a pad of prescriptions from her mother's medical practice.

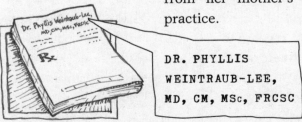

DR. PHYLLIS
WEINTRAUB-LEE,
MD, CM, MSc, FRCSC

"What do you want to know?" I asked.

"Excellent question," said Dusk, who is never afraid to sound condescending. "List the people whose truths we've explored. Then make note of any observations. Please remember to use codes for the names. We don't want this information falling into the wrong hands."

"What if some of our cases are still open?" asked Neil.

"Such is to be expected. The truth can take time. Just make a note of it. Maybe we'll do a spreadsheet."

Dusk recently took a best business practices for artists class, an elective, and she particularly enjoyed the spreadsheet unit. She thinks it might be part of her calling as an artist, though how spreadsheets fit with taxidermied shrews, I'm not sure.[68]

"Where are we meeting again?" I asked.

"The Boardroom," said Dusk. "I love the smell in there, even if it may be carcinogenic."

The Boardroom is what G. P. students call the climate-controlled storage room off the woodworking shop. Of course, because ours is a well-funded private art school, we have more kinds of specialty wood than most custom cabinet businesses. Not for G. P. Academy the standard birdhouse project. Our students make things like stools that defy gravity, miniature replicas of Graceland, complete with a dead wooden Elvis slumped on the toilet, and a rocking horse with the full text of D. H. Lawrence's "The Rocking-Horse Winner" carved into it.

The Boardroom smells excellent, but that was small

---

68. A fascination with a small format and precision, maybe?

consolation. I didn't want to make a report. My report, especially if I didn't include my deleted Facebook message, wouldn't even fill one-quarter of a prescription pad.

I started up Nancy and drove to school as slowly as possible.

Pockets of Sweet Lies

Here's a weak chapter opener for you: *Things were weird at school.*

What does weird mean in the context of a fine arts high school? Let me set the scene, even though it would be easier to write the following in the form of exposition.

Neil and Dusk and I got to school and disembarked. I got a closer look at his outfit. He had on slightly too-snug warm-up pants, not-leather sandals, and a Hawaiian dress shirt of the type worn by Dustin Hoffman in the bus scene in *Midnight Cowboy*, which is a 1970s movie starring Jon Voight as Joe Buck, a not-smart male prostitute, and Dustin Hoffman as Ratso Rizzo, Joe's tubercular and ineffective pimp. It's a sad film about deluded dreamers, but the fashion is completely excellent. Neil was going through a Ratso Rizzo phase, complete with slicked-back greasy hair and five o'clock shadow. When I looked at him I could practically hear the film's depressing harmonica theme music. He'd convinced Dusk and me also to dress in *Midnight Cowboy*–wear for the day. He said it would make us feel more authentic and gritty.[69]

- - - - - - - - - - - - - - - -

69. I'd never really aspired to feel gritty before, and dressing like a character in a movie isn't exactly the essence of personal authenticity, but there *was* something fun about it.

Dusk was dressed like Joe Buck in a beat-up buckskin jacket with fringes, an undersized black cowboy hat, and a kerchief. I'd worn a white suit.

We walked inside the school and then separated to go to our classes. Before I got to English class I decided to take a tour through the halls. I was stopped in the lobby by Tomas Beidecker. In another school Tomas would be a star on the football team. At G. P. Academy, he's a stone sculptor, which is the art school equivalent. Six foot two. Magnificent forearms. The whole bit.

"Hey, Normandy," he said.

He'd never spoken to me before, so I was taken aback. "Uh, hi, Tomas."

"Are you okay?" he asked.

"Yes!" I said, trying to draw my gaze away from his forearms.

"I like your white suit. Very Annie Lennox. My mom likes her."

"It's supposed to be Ratso Rizzo. Neil likes the movie." Then I realized Tomas probably knew as much about *Midnight Cowboy* as I did about Annie Lennox and it was best to stop talking immediately.

"So you're part of this truth thing that's going around?"

"Sort of."[70]

"I heard you asked Tyler Jones the truth."

"Well, not me."

"One of the other truthers?"

---

70. My dialogue in this scene was less than sparkling. This is a constant problem in scenes and in life.

"I can't comment."

"I'd like to know what you find out."

"We don't usually . . ."

"Just curious."

"Right. Okay."

"Later, Ratso."

Head reeling from the implications, I continued on my way. A few yards down the hall I was stopped by Aliya Said. She has the best hair at G. P. Academy, which is saying something. It's a veritable cloud of awesomeness, and at first I was so taken with it that I didn't hear what Aliya said (with apologies for the pun on her last name) to me. Her mouth was moving but I was just watching her hair.

"Normandy?" said Aliya.

"Yes?"

"So you're part of this truth thing?"

"I, uh," I said.

"I need you to talk to Jared.[71] I think he has the hots for Chelsea."

"That's not really what we—"

"The two of them are a little too socially networked, if you know what I mean. She's all over his Facebook and Twitter and Instagram and he's saying it's just online, but I don't buy it. I think it has an F2F component," said Aliya.

"It's just that—"

"I've asked him and asked him. He won't tell me. But

-- -- -- -- -- -- -- -- -- -- -- -- -- -- --

71. Her boyfriend.

he'll tell you. Because we all understand that what you're doing is important."

"Well, it's not—"

"Thanks, babe," said Aliya, walking off and taking her amazing hair with her.

As in a nightmare, I then saw other people who had been touched by the activities of the Truth Commission.

Mrs. Dekker stomped by, poncho billowing around her, a look of student loathing engraved on her face. I raised a hand in greeting but let it fall when Mrs. Dekker, with obvious effort, tried to unstick her expression into something approximating a smile.

Zinnia McFarland hurried past, holding some kind of sign. Her face was working with some vexing emotion.

"Are you okay?" I asked, for the hundredth time wishing we hadn't pried her open like a mollusk.

Zinnia shook her head and kept going.

I walked into the area that houses the art pods. Tyler Jones stood outside his private studio, his face pensive. When he spotted me he let his gaze linger. I had no idea what he was thinking or how he was feeling. I couldn't tell whether he was gay or straight or bisexual or asexual or post-sexual.

Then I passed an alcove in which Aimee was having a tête-à-tête with Neil, who must have been summoned on his way to class. Aimee was feeling up her own left breast and talking to him. Neil's hands were shoved deep in his shell pants pockets and he stared determinedly at the floor, only glancing up to catch my eye as I passed.

Then I looked into the Shed. Lisette was inside with the

other students. She had on an authentic Cowichan sweater, beaded moccasins, feathered earrings, a rawhide headband. I found myself sighing with relief and finally, I headed to class. The truth was almost everywhere, but there were still pockets of sweet lies left undisturbed.

Please Arrange Your Faces

The Boardroom, like every other supplies room at G. P., was well organized. Our teachers are actual artists, and despite their reputation for chaos, most artists keep their supplies and work spaces scrupulously tidy. It's the personal lives that get messy.

Dusk, Neil, and I sat cross-legged on the floor. Around us boards of varying types, lengths, and thicknesses were stacked neatly on shelves and clearly labeled.

"If there's an earthquake, we're in serious trouble," said Neil, casting a glance up at the shelves high over our heads.

"At least we'll be killed by high-quality, sustainably harvested lumber products," said Dusk. She consulted her prescription pad. "I'd like to call this meeting to order. Please arrange your faces into expressions of concentration."

Neil looked at his pad. "I was in math before this. It was quite demanding, so my notes might be sketchy."

"Hmmm," said Dusk, all pre-disapproving. "Carry on."

Neil touched the collar of his Hawaiian shirt and held the pad up to his face.

"I think prescription pads might cause doctor hand-writing," he said.

"Someone should do a study. Tell you what. I'll find out the truth about that," I said.

"Hush," said Dusk. "As the junior team member, it's best not to call attention to yourself."

I was a little offended. "Junior Team Member"? Well, I never! If Dusk doesn't stay true to her rebellion and become an artist, she's probably going to be a surgeon or a general in the military. Maybe even a surgeon general. She's definitely bossy enough.

"So far, I've asked the truth of two individuals," said Neil. "Aimee Danes and Tyler Jones. Of those two subjects, one told me the truth right away. One is still considering the question."

"Good," said Dusk. "Any other details you'd like to add?"

"Well," said Neil. "I'm beginning to think that sharing truth establishes a longer-lasting bond than I might previously have thought. Once you've asked someone the truth and they tell you, you can't just walk away. You're joined by the truth, whether you like it or not." As though to confirm this observation, Neil's cell phone buzzed. It might have been the low lighting in the Boardroom, but his face seemed to get a little paler.

Dusk didn't catch the exchange because she was flipping through her pad.

"Okay. I'll go next," she said. "I have asked two individuals the truth and it went exceedingly well both times. Mrs. Dekker, a secretary, responded well and honestly."

I wondered about the accuracy of that statement. Mrs. Dekker seemed like someone whose truth might change from day to day.

"Things went even better with Zinnia McFarland. She

not only told me her truth, she caused a truth riot that involved much of the school."

I thought of the expression on Zinnia's face when I'd seen her in the hallway earlier. She hadn't looked peaceful. I must have winced, because Dusk noticed.

"Do you have a comment, Normandy?"

"No. I'm good."

"Because of those successes, I've come up with several new candidates for us. But before we proceed, I'd like to review the participation of all group members."

Here was the peer pressure teachers were always on about. Only I thought I'd be hassled to smoke pot and drink and ride in cars with boys, not go around asking people their private business. Just my luck. Maybe if I took up smoking pot, boozing, and hooking up with random, inappropriate boys, my friends would back off.

I fanned the notes I wrote in class right before our meeting. I thought how I would like to do a series of drawings on medical prescription pads. Maybe make one of those flip stories where the character moves.

"Well, I have carefully observed the activities of the Commission."

Dusk drummed her fingers on the floor. Neil smiled encouragingly.

"And I've undertaken an investigation of a truth candidate. You know, by observing her. That sort of thing." I stopped. Then I jumped into the void.

"You know, sometimes I wonder if the three of us can do anything without being precious about it. I mean, just for once couldn't we use a piece of regular lined paper to write a report? Couldn't we wear hoodies and Uggs, drive Hondas, and eat Reese's Peanut Butter Cups? There are days when I have a hard time taking us seriously."

Neil and Dusk stared at me like I'd grown a horn out of my forehead.

"What?" said Dusk.

"Is it the *Midnight Cowboy* outfits?" asked Neil. "I just wanted to say how much it means to me that you guys are willing to honor the films I love. I was thinking next we could dress like *Cool Hand Luke*. Bring a bunch of boiled eggs to school."

Dusk fixed him with a glare. "Stop changing the subject."

"Sorry," said Neil.

"Normandy, continue your report," said Dusk. I continued my freefall into rebellion.

"I've decided that I don't want to confront Lisette. Her relationship with the truth is so . . . you know. Tenuous."

"Which is exactly why she needs us," said Dusk, pretend-reasonable. I could tell she was furious.

"But she seems happy being quasi-delusional."

"Our society's willingness to put up with and embrace falseness is killing us. We need to get real. Stop hiding behind false identities! Get off the Internet and into ourselves."

"George Orwell said that, in a time of deceit, telling the truth was a revolutionary act," added Neil, who was in the same English class as me and having his mind blown by *1984*. "What we're doing here is like thought crime in a world that encourages newspeak. It's radical."

I thought of Mr. Thomas's words.

"It's only a spiritual practice when you ask *yourself* the truth."

"Good p—" said Neil before Dusk cut him off.

"No one said this was a spiritual practice." Her perfectly proportioned face was set into a mask of stubbornness.

"I'm pretty sure we did. At least we implied it," I said.

"This is a social movement," said Dusk. "A revolution, like Neil said. I thought you understood that."

"I—"

"I think we should get something to eat. Come back to the Boardroom when the blood sugar is in better shape," said Neil.

"Can you please be quiet?" snapped Dusk.

"That's rude," I said before I even knew I intended to speak.

"*I'll* tell you what's rude. Pretending to be a part of our Commission and then shining us on. This initiative requires the full cooperation of every member for it to work."

Once again the words barged out of my mouth before I could organize them into a more diplomatic arrangement. "You're being a bully about this," I told her.

I heard a quick intake of breath from Neil.

"A bully?" demanded Dusk. "What are you? Some public service announcement? Also, that's doubly offensive because you know how I feel about bullies." It's true that Dusk has never been one to stand by when someone's being picked on. Unless she's the picker. She's got a bit of a blind spot in that regard.

"I'm sorry, but this feels like bullying."

"Well, I—" said Neil.

"How dare you!" cried Dusk.

"He never gets a word out. You're always cutting him off! It's always all about you!" I was yelling now, which came as a shock, since I haven't yelled since I was about four.

"I don't—" said Neil.

Dusk whirled on him. "Do I always interrupt you? Do you think I'm a bully?"

"I, uh—"

"I can't believe this!" she shouted. "The two of you being such assholes and ganging up on me like this!"

"Just because you don't get heard in your own house doesn't mean you can come to school and stomp all over us," I said.

"Oh, boy," whispered Neil, finally getting in a complete sentence.

"If I didn't talk, give a little direction, you two would just do nothing. Neil would paint pictures of women instead of having relationships with them. You'd just sit there trying to escape attention. Being as quiet as possible."

"I do not—" spluttered Neil and I together.

"My paintings are—" started Neil, but before I heard the rest of what he had to say, I stumbled to my feet.

"I don't need the truth or this Commission. We have no idea what other people's lives are like and asking the truth of every person in this school isn't going to make us empathetic people. Or interesting people or anything except snoops."

Neil made a low groaning noise.

I hesitated for a moment. "We need to mind our own business!"

"You need to *get* some business," said Dusk. "Until you have some, I don't want to talk to you."

"Come on," said Neil. "You guys. We're—"

"Over!" shouted Dusk. She crossed her thin arms in front of her and she leaned back.

I turned and ran directly into a furniture maker who was on his way into the Boardroom. He had on big earmuff headphones and screamed in surprise. I shoved him in the chest and ran for Nancy.

Goddamned truth.

Hole in My Life

If you've experienced moderate to extreme friendlessness, you'd think it would be easy to go back to it after a period of friend-having. Turns out, once you've had friends, there's no going back.

As soon as my heart stopped pounding, which happened about five minutes after Nancy stalled four blocks from our house, the hole in my life made itself apparent.

When you have friends with you, stalls are a time to relax and chat. When you're by yourself, stalls leave you alone with your gloom-laden thoughts and miserable feelings.

As I waited for Nancy's engine to recover, I found my emotions rearranging themselves. I might get a little internally judge-y, a little resentful, but I have never been a yeller or a particularly angry person.

I especially never wanted to be the angry one among my friends. That role had already been taken by Dusk. Neil was the joker and I was the diplomat. I also knew enough about Dusk to know that she's like her family, no matter how much she doesn't want to be. She wouldn't get over our first fight without a clear expression of regret from me in the form of a truth telling by way of apology.

I'd seen how her parents handled her explosions and

her smoldering rages. They waited until she calmed down and then made amends in a way she could understand. Her attendance at the Art Farm was their way of apologizing.

I had to find a truth target I could handle. Who, who, who . . . ?

My phone, a shitty flip that might as well puff out smoke signals as texts, burped. A text from Neil.

> You okay?

We use proper spelling and punctuation in our texts. Another form of quiet rebellion. Also, I insist on it, and my friends go along because writing is my thing. At least, I'd like it to be.

Slowly, using the non-text-friendly keys, I punched out a reply.

> This is bad. But I have an idea how to fix it.

> Message me later if you want to talk it over. I hate this.

> Me too.

It's interesting that neither of us went off on Dusk. She is who she is, and Neil and I have enough experience of tricky people that we know better than to try changing them. Also, we're not gossipy or mean, in spite of how our Commission might make us appear. I felt immediately better just hearing from Neil. At least he was still speaking to me.

Another text appeared.

> We'll get through this.

I turned the key, and Nancy's engine hacked and sputtered to life. I drove slowly home and formulated my plan.[72]

XXXXX

At home, I found Keira in the closet. Light leaked around the edges of the door frame.

"Keira?" I said.

"Working!" came her muffled reply.

"Me too," I muttered, too low for her to hear.

I sat at my small desk. I'll tell you what's difficult: to truly focus on anything other than embroidery when your sister's making magic happen in your closet. Stitching is like drawing mandalas. Meditative and precise. Structured. Writing often doesn't feel that way, but I gave it my best effort.

In the spirit of diplomacy and feather de-ruffling, I

--- --- --- --- --- --- --- --- ---

72. I really want to end this chapter here. I know most of what happens in this chapter is flashback, a bunch of thoughts, a list, and some text messages. This is not the stuff of narrative greatness, unless you are Marcel Proust, who, as you pointed out in your last set of comments, could write pages about a single cookie and make it great. I think we can agree that I am no Marcel Proust. Please note that I took *In Search of Lost Time* out of the library. I think I may have strained something just lifting it off the shelf. Imagine if he wrote about an entire cake or something! I know. I'll insert a scene break and then go for another partial scene. Sweet! I'm getting the hang of this structure thing!

wrote my plan on the tiny pages of the prescription pad.[73]

> TRUTH TO DOs
> 1. Ask two people the truth in a way that shows
>   fellow Commissioners my commitment
>   a)

I was going to have to come up with good ones or Dusk wouldn't budge. Truth seeking is simply not my forte. Doesn't "come natural," as those with bad grammar sometimes like to say.

I started again.

> Candidates for a Truthing Performed by
> Normandy Pale, Proud Member of the
> Truth Commission.
>
> 1. Brian Forbes
> 2. Prema Hardwick

"Norm?" Keira's voice was muffled inside the closet.
"Yes?"
"Want to talk later?"
I would rather die, thanks. "Sure."

73.

"That would be good. What are you doing?"

"Homework," I said.

"You needling?" she asked.

"Pretty soon."

"You want to come in here?"

"That's okay," I said, my skin crawling at the thought. Who knows what details would come sliding out of my sister if I got trapped in the closet with her?[74]

She said something I couldn't hear.

I used my lousy cell phone to take a picture of the prescription pad. After a deep breath, I messaged it to Dusk and to Neil. Then I sat back in my chair in my bedroom and ignored the sounds of my sister working away inside my closet. I put my stretched canvas under my lighted desk magnifier and started stitching.

--- --- --- --- --- --- --- --- --- --- ---

74. Here's a question: If I become a better writer, will my details become less blatantly symbolic? Will my life be more subtle? I mean seriously: ostriches, closets? These would be frowned on by the Annie Dillards of the world. Her symbols are always like wind and shit like that. Sorry for the swear.

Saturday, October 6

A Tall 'Scrip

Neil and I waited for Dusk in the parking lot at Pipers Lagoon Park. The rain was an insistent spittle that would continue off and on all winter until the clouds peeled away in their annual spring migration. Nancy's defrost system, like her heating and cooling systems, barely functioned, so the windows were fogged up. I traced a sad face in the condensation and then wiped it away with my sleeve.

"She didn't want a ride?" asked Neil.

I shook my head as I checked the cars around us. Some belonged to people who'd gone for an afternoon walk around the narrow spit with the ocean on one side and a saltwater lagoon with houses crowding the other. The spit terminated in a high rocky hump covered in grasses and arbutus trees and Garry oaks, which was home to a profusion of short-lived and rare native flowers in the early spring. Pipers is small but magnificent, and I find it fascinating how many people come here only to score drugs and meet the people with whom they are having affairs. I know this because Nancy has stalled in the lot many a time, giving me a ringside view of various illicit activities.

Dusk wasn't ready to ride in Nancy or to completely forgive me, so she was going to ride her bike to meet us. It wouldn't take long. Her house is a big, handsome place sided in red cedar with charcoal and light gray wood accents, and is the nicest one on the lagoon. It has attractive, environmentally appropriate landscaping, and four kayaks poised to launch when the water in the lagoon is high enough. Everything about the house and property screamed: *Two doctors plus high-achieving offspring live here!* The only offbeat detail was the coracle that perched like an ungainly plaything beside the kayak rack.

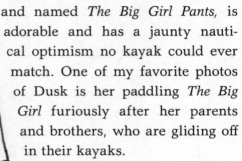

The crude little half-shell of a boat, which Dusk built and named *The Big Girl Pants,* is adorable and has a jaunty nautical optimism no kayak could ever match. One of my favorite photos of Dusk is her paddling *The Big Girl* furiously after her parents and brothers, who are gliding off in their kayaks.

"You nervous?" asked Neil.

"I guess."

"Dusk will be okay. She's just really into this."

"I know."

"I decided to start doing a podcast," he said. "You want to be on it?"

"What's your podcast about?" I asked.

"Making stuff," he said.

"That's cool."

"I hope so. Artists can be pretty boring to talk to. Some of us are nearly nonverbal. Also, we take ourselves too seriously."

"We do?"

Suddenly, Neil himself went serious, a rare enough event

that I paid close attention. "Of course. And I think that we should sometimes. Especially you, Norm. Just because you're—"

Dusk thumped on the passenger window, and Neil lost his train of thought.

Dusk had on a red tam. Worn with oatmeal sweater, leggings, flats, and a navy raincoat. If some European film-maker who had a thing for much-too-young girls saw her, he'd immediately offer her a lead role in a film about a crippled bureaucrat who collected kites in his spare time. Or maybe Wes Anderson would put her in his next movie about peculiar institutions such as boarding schools, sum-mer camps, or families.[75]

"You texted?" she said, looking unsmilingly at me.

"I did. I'm sorry. I apologize. I repent. I atone," I said.

"You use a lot of words, Grasshopper. Words are not enough."

"I know. Only the truth is enough."

Dusk inclined her tam-topped head. "You've written yourself a tall prescription," she said.

I resisted the natural urge to use a lot of words to explain myself.

"Have you seen this?" she asked Neil.

"Norm's list? I think it's awesome."

"Me too. But I've seen too much hesitation to really trust."

"I'm about this," I told her. "I'm part of this Commission."

-- -- -- -- -- -- -- -- -- -- -- -- --

75. I'm not even sure you're allowed to be an art student if you don't worship at the Anderson altar.

I had this overpowering urge to say something incredibly lame, like "I am a committed Commissioner!" but my fear of Dusk and my innate good sense prevailed.

"When will you start?" she asked.

"I'll start with Brian Forbes. As soon as possible."

"Excellent choice. Truth telling has the power to do a lot of good, I think. My guess is that after he comes clean, he'll go to rehab. Meet a girl who may or may not be a celebrity. He'll give talks at schools. Make a name for himself," said Dusk.

"Come clean," I said. "Good one." I saw her expression and wiped the smile from my face.

"It's no laughing matter."

But I agreed with her. I figured she'd outlined the usual trajectory for people who got honest about substance abuse issues and, unless everyone at school was wrong, Brian Forbes had developed himself a little drug problem over the summer. Actually, his slide started earlier than that. Last spring, he started skipping wrestling practice and losing weight and hanging around with iffies. His style changed. It was like seeing one of those advisory notices unfolding in real life. This fall, about two weeks after school started, Dusk elbowed me in English. Brian had finally showed up.

"Look at that," she said. "There is something way wrong with Brian."

That much was indisputable. His hair was long and stringy, and his muscles had turned into tendons. Normally, he was one of those slightly overblown guys, all popping energy and biceps, bouncing in and out of the welding shop. Over the summer, he'd turned into shadows.

He made me sad.

"He's looking pretty ragged. A little tense," Dusk added. We'd just started *As I Lay Dying* to kick us off on a yearlong list of what Mr. Wells called "dark readings." Most of the books were dystopians, but he'd thrown in a few realistic and experimental bummers as well.

"*As I Lay Dying* is enough to make anyone tense. Did you see this?" I held up the book, opened to the "My mother is a fish" chapter. "Imagine writing something like that and saying, 'Perfect. Let's end it there.' Who does that?"

"Somebody who doesn't want to spend all day writing long chapters," said Neil.

"Mr. Wells said Faulkner wrote it fast," said Dusk. "And he didn't revise."

"Shocker," I said.

Mr. Wells told us to please be quiet so he could finish telling us how Faulkner used to work in a post office, and his theory of how sorting mail affected Faulkner's handling of point of view. My theory was that working in a post office made Faulkner so bitter and depressed that he took it out on his readers by writing books that made no sense unless you had a teacher there to explain it to you.[76] Still, it was an interesting, if depressing, novel.[77]

"Are you sure you're up for this? What about Lisette?"

---

76. Mr. Wells is sort of cute when he's being authoritarian and teacher-ish. I can see what you see in him! Not that I see you seeing anything in him. Ahem. How is that going, by the way? I haven't seen you guys together lately. I know, I know: out-of-bounds footnote!

77. If I ever write a novel, I might do some experiments with point of view, even though I'm finding it hard to even figure out my own point of view.

Dusk's question pulled me out of my recollections of
Faulkner and Brian and September, which seemed months
past, rather than just a few weeks.

"I did ask Lisette. Sort of. But then I chickened out. I'll
take a run at her later. She just doesn't feel right."

"I'm glad you're joining us," said Dusk.

"Truce?" said Neil.

"And reconciliation," said Dusk.

Like the funny thing she is, she leaned her bike against
the passenger side of the truck, walked around the front,
and stuck her hand out at me.

We shook.

My best friend.

"To Brian Forbes," she said.

"To Brian Forbes," added Neil.

BTW

I'm aware that I have not mentioned my sister and her confession for several chapters. In the spirit of Mr. Faulkner, who, as noted in the previous chapter, didn't have to change so much as *one word* of his book (hint, hint), I offer you another really short chapter, because I'm just not ready to say more about her right now. I'll get to her story eventually. In the meantime:

My sister is a fish.

I'm becoming afraid of fish.

My Life Is an Issue in My Life

Because Monday was Thanksgiving, I couldn't set my truth seeking into motion until Tuesday. Nervous as I was about approaching Brian, I was still happy to be back in school. Anything was better than our painfully quiet house during a holiday. Of course, Keira didn't join us for turkey, and our small talk was all done in whispers and featured lots of long, awkward silences.

In class on Tuesday morning, I watched the door in English class and waited for Brian to show up. When he finally slid in, Mr. Wells was halfway through his opening remarks about M. T. Anderson's *Feed*, which was a welcome change from *As I Lay Dying*, even though it was also depressing. I think *Feed* may have the best opening line of any book ever written. "We went to the moon to have fun, but the moon turned out to completely suck." Sigh. Now that's an opener! I was distracted from fully appreciating Mr. Wells's commentary by my fervent wish that I hadn't volunteered to speak to Brian.[78] It was a task for a trained

----

78. That's not just me sucking up in preparation for Mr. Wells to be the second reader of this project. His remarks really were interesting.

counseling professional. I should not have volunteered.

Brian looked like he was in the grips of bad, bad cold. Eyes nearly blackened with fatigue, hollowed-out cheeks. His jeans hung on him the way they do when a person loses a lot of weight and doesn't have time to get new pants.

"Mr. Forbes," said Mr. Wells, pausing for effect. "I'm glad you decided to join us."[79]

Brian, who used to have a goofy, good-natured remark for everyone, just ducked his head as though trying to avoid blows and slipped into his seat in front of us.

Dusk caught my eye and nodded. I nodded back, because it seemed like the right thing to do.

On the other side of me, Neil also nodded. Again, I returned the favor.[80]

Then I tried to focus on Mr. Wells's lecture.[81]

When the bell rang for lunch, it was time for me to become a full member of the Commission. I got to my feet at the same time as Brian Forbes, and I was right behind

– – – – – – – – – – – – – – –

79. Interesting fact about Mr. Wells and something I'm sure I don't need to tell you, Ms. Fowler: he can say things that would sound snotty if another teacher said them but somehow coming from him they sound friendly and sincere. That is a pretty great quality.

80. I know you said that nodding is the cheapest and most pointless thing characters can do and that authors rely far too much on nodding and staring to convey meaning. But what about when people actually nod a lot? I can't pretend Dusk scratched her nose significantly or that Neil rubbed his temples. Sigh. Writing is hard. Especially true writing.

81. Which was excellent. ☺

him when he slipped out of the door. I could feel Dusk and Neil behind me.

As I followed, close but not right on his heels, I noticed people noticing us. Recognition dawned on their faces as they saw Brian, then me, then Dusk and Neil. A few nodded. One or two saluted. A boy in an engineer's cap gave me the "Live Long and Prosper" sign. A girl wearing a tutu and ballet slippers with a hockey jersey threw up a gang sign and thumped her chest. We passed Zinnia McFarland, who was slumped in a chair outside the guidance office, and we passed Aimee Danes who was surreptitiously feeling up her nose for a change of pace.

Brian Forbes walked through the crowds, head down, feet shuffling. Clouds of self-hatred seemed to trail behind him like a bus leaking exhaust.

I followed him outside. He walked past the Photoshoot Tree, skirted the parking lot, and headed for the playing fields. When I looked back, I saw that Dusk and Neil had been joined by three or four other people. I muttered a swear under my breath. Bad enough I was going to get all up in this guy's business. We didn't need an audience.

I caught Dusk's eye and gave my head a small shake. She and Neil slowed and Dusk held out a hand to stop the truth voyeurs.

Brian Forbes walked through the ball field and into the dugout. I hesitated. Did I really want to follow him in there? What drugs was he doing? Was he safe? I had never even spoken to the guy, and now I was going to do a one-woman intervention on him?

Deep breath. Stand tall. Switch into the present tense.[82]

The dugout is dark and colder than the day outside. Brian Forbes sits in the middle of the bench. He's lighting a cigarette. At least, I hope it's a cigarette. I'm not very druggy and I haven't gotten around to watching *Breaking Bad*.

"Hi, Brian," I say.

His head snaps up and I get the contradictory impression that I've surprised him and also that he's been waiting for me for a while now.

He doesn't speak. Instead, he takes a deep drag on his smoke.

"Good smoke?" I say, and wonder what someone like Brian Forbes thinks about when he sees me and Dusk and Neil and our candy cigarettes.

Brian narrows his eyes and gives me a half smile.

"Yeah. Sure. Like inhaling angel's sighs."

That stops me. Brian Forbes is quick.

I recover. "Sounds refreshing," I say. "Might have to try it."

"I wouldn't," he says.

Our intimacy feels weirdly immediate. Like I'm in Brian's head and he's in mine.

"You doing okay?" I ask.

"What's your name?" he says. "It's odd, right? Like Charles or something?"

----

82. I hope it's not too jarring. You said in class that using present tense is like making everything a little speedier and emphatic. It's the tense equivalent of shouting. This experience felt pretty emphatic to me.

"Normandy. Norm."

"It's cool when girls have dudes' names. Or when they're named after provinces. State names can sound a little porny."

I consider my response. Brian seems to like banter, so I need to come up with something witty. Witty-ish, anyway. "Alberta: sexy. Alabama: porny. I get it."

Brian leans farther back on the bench seat. My eyes adjust so I can see him better.

"I was wondering if I could ask you a question."

The low roof of the dugout presses in on us. I wonder if he knows there are people outside. Waiting to hear his truth.

"You don't have to answer."

Brian Forbes closes his eyes, which I have just realized are quite lovely and feathered with long lashes.

He doesn't respond, so I forge ahead. "Are you on drugs?" That sounds too harsh. I feel like one of those overly blunt people or like a drunk. Someone who has no filter. I'm embarrassed. I'm exhilarated. "I guess I'm asking whether substance abuse is an issue in your life."

Brian Forbes takes another drag on his smoke.

"My life is an issue in my life," he says. Because that's a sort of a Zen koan, I don't know how to respond. Luckily, he continues. "Why do you want to know?"

"Because my friends and I have this theory that the truth can heal. So we're asking people truths about things that other people already suspect."

"Oh, right. I heard about this."

"Yeah. It's . . . a thing."

"How's that going?" he says. "Asking people the truth?"

"It's good," I say, feeling that the interview has gotten offtrack. "I mean, some parts of it are."

"And some parts of it aren't," he finishes.

"My friends seem to enjoy it more than I do."

"How does it make you feel? Asking people the truth."

I consider. "Well, this is my first time. So, it's good. I mean, it's like unleashing something. Opening things up."

"Freeing?" he says.

"Yeah. I guess."

"Doing drugs is like that."

"Oh?" I remember from creative nonfiction class that, when interviewing, it's important not to interrupt. Silence can get people talking.

"You try it once. There's a rush, and all the barriers between you and other people, you and yourself, they're all gone. Everything is possible. You aren't alone anymore."

The description was exhilarating. Why *hadn't* I done much in the way of drugs?

"And then?"

"And then you want to have that feeling again. But it turns out there's like a half-life to getting high. The after-effects follow you around. Make the original situation, loneliness or whatever, worse. And it's never quite as good as that first time. Taking drugs turns out to be a shitload of work, once you get right down to it. I think the correct term is 'diminishing returns.'"

"I see."

"My guess is that the truth's like that. You ask somebody the truth. Feel like you've moved into a different dimension. But it doesn't end there. There are consequences to every action. Shadows."

Brian Forbes is freakishly articulate. He should be asking the questions. I've been standing like an intruder just inside the entrance for what feels like hours. I'm not sure where to put my hands, arms. I'm too aware of the cold concrete under my feet. I take a seat on the long bench, staying as close to the doorway as possible.

"That sounds right," I say. "In my limited experience."

Brian Forbes is sitting about five feet away from me. He turns his face and he is the oldest seventeen-year-old I've ever seen.

"What's supposed to happen now? I tell you I've got this problem that everybody already knows about. I sure as hell already know about it. What then?"

"I guess things change. At least, that's the idea."

"Yeah?"

"If you want them to."

"Therein lies the rub," he says, and somehow I know he's had this conversation before. "You going to tell me my options?" he says. "Treatment? Twelve Steps? Like that?"

"No. We don't give advice. We only ask and listen."

"Smart," says Brian. He drops his cigarette to the damp concrete floor and scuffs it out with his running shoe, which is falling apart and not in an ironic, experimental way. "It's after the truth comes out that the going gets tough."

Again, I have no response.

"Everyone at school knows," he muses. "Everyone at home. And it's up to me to make some changes. God, that is such a tiring thought."

"You can talk to me," I say. "Anytime. I want to help."

Brian Forbes levels his gaze at me. "You're Keira Pale's sister, right?"

The abrupt change in subject causes an obstruction in my airway.

"Yeah."

I wait for a comment about the sister in the Diana books. A comment about how I'm nothing like that pale starer or the hapless doughball, or how I'm just like her.

"If you want to ask someone the truth, you might want to start a little closer to home," he says.

"What?" I say. "What do you mean?"

But Brian doesn't answer. He's getting slowly to his feet, like some decrepit old-young man.

"I appreciate your interest in my situation," he says. He stands in front of where I sit like a block of cement on the wooden bench. He reaches out a hand to shake mine. I look at it. The moons of his nails are black.

I take his hand and it's cold, but his grip is gentle.

"You want my cell number?" I ask. Like I'm trying to pick him up.

"Maybe later," he says, and gives me a sideways smile. I suddenly understand how people fall in love with drug addicts.

And then he's shuffling out of the dugout and I'm left with more questions than I had before I asked Brian Forbes the truth. I sit in the dugout for a long time until Neil comes in to get me.

We Don't Take Requests

The next day I was still vibrating from the thrill of my honest talk with Brian Forbes. It was intoxicating to be entirely direct with someone. Dusk and Neil were right: it felt revolutionary.

Between savoring the feeling that I'd cut through the formalities to have a meaningful interaction with a strange boy and luxuriating in the thought of all the positive things that were likely to come from it, like him getting clean and me opening up, I hardly had time to think about the tensions at home. Keira had returned from another three-day absence and, after retreating to her room for a while, had gone back to work in the closet. I was curious about how far she'd gotten with the new Chronicle. I hoped there wouldn't be too much in it about the Flounder. I also hoped Keira hadn't named the new book something humiliating like: *Diana Chronicles 4: The Less Talented Sister*. Ha. Ha. Okay, so that's not really funny. But after her last confession, she'd stopped coming into my room to talk about what had happened. Maybe our vague, one-sided chats had healed her enough that she would soon go back to CIAD. The thought made me feel light with hope.

Plus, I was officially hooked on the truth.

"Still feeling great, right?" said Dusk, the day after I spoke to Brian.

We were back in painting class. Ms. Choo was teaching us yet another advanced brushwork technique. We were paying yet again only partial attention.

"It was a rush. I'm still kind of processing."

"Truth is power," said Neil. "So I'm not that used to it."

"Oh, Neil," I said. "You have way more power than you give yourself credit for."

He blew me a kiss and I blew one back. Dusk, who doesn't do what she calls "appalling outbursts of affection," made a gagging noise.

"Oh, *Dusk*," said Neil and I together. Before we could tease her any more, the sound of raised voices came from the other side of the studio.

Sarah Vanderwall was whisper-yelling at her girlfriend, Kim Yee.

"I'm sorry, but it's the truth!" said Sarah.

"Screw you!" said Kim, her voice low but reaching every corner of the room. "I *do so* have a sophisticated color sense. It's just different than yours."

"Oh, yeah, you're a real A. Y. Jackson."[83]

"What is your problem? Why are you being such a bitch?" hissed Kim.

"Hey, you said you wanted to move past polite into truth. You said everyone at school is doing it. And of course you just *have* to be part of it because it's a trend."

---

83. A member of the Group of Seven.

"Me?" said Kim. "Look at your tattoo! It's the worst one in this school. And this school is filled with awful tattoos."

"Why do you have to keep bringing up Winnie? I thought we got past that. I told you Winnie and I never *did* anything. We just talked about it. Then she moved to Victoria!"

"I never even *mentioned* Winnie!" yelled Kim. "But it's clear that she's obviously on your mind pretty much constantly."

"Girls," said Ms. Choo. "What seems to be the problem?"

"What's *not* the problem?" huffed Sarah.

Then their voices dropped so we couldn't eavesdrop properly. As Ms. Choo led them out of the room for a cooldown chat, Dusk, Neil, and I glanced at one another and then at our brushstrokes.

Flare-ups like that had been happening with greater frequency all over G. P. Academy. Our classmates were open people, for the most part. They were ready to embrace any new movement. They liked to stir things up.

We'd had to tell people that we didn't take requests, that we never shared what we learned except with one another. Even so, people seemed to find out, partly because the subjects talked about it (in the cases of Aimee Danes and Zinnia McFarland). Tyler Jones remained in a holding pattern, truth-wise, and rarely left his studio pod, and I hadn't pursued Lisette.

Truth seeking was turning into a social movement with vague, fluctuating rules. The part of me that enjoyed a bit of control and some guidelines was made nervous by the lawless nature of what we'd started. The part of me that craved something authentic and unpredictable loved it. So did the part of me that wanted to look at magazine pictures of celebrity cellulite.

We didn't comment on Sarah and Kim, our school's power lesbian couple. They'd be fine. Everyone knew that fighting was how they kept things fresh.

"Have you seen or talked to Brian today?" asked Neil finally.

"No."

"He probably went into rehab," said Dusk, all breeziness. "That's what happens after people get honest with another person. You were a serious catalyst for good."

I nodded. It had sure felt that way. His words about making changes had lifted me up, even if his other comments hadn't.

"On Monday, Prema," said Neil. It wasn't a question.[84]

"Yeah. She's next."

"Then we'll all be even," said Neil. "I love it when things are even."

"You nervous?" Dusk asked me.

"No. I think it'll be okay. I mean, everyone knows about her."

"About *them*," said Neil.

"About them," agreed Dusk. "But you need to be careful with her. Don't push. There's a lot at stake."

"Of course," I said, wondering at this, the first sign of caution Dusk had shown.

Ms. Choo came slippering back into the room. She had on little slides that seemed to be made of paper, and strange

---

84. Hence the lack of a question mark.

pants with a crotch that hung down to her knees and a vest
with complicated folds. Ms. Choo was shaking her head.
She looked at my canvas and my abbreviated brushstrokes.
"You have to use momentum," she said, and gestured fluidly
to demonstrate. "Just so long as the brush doesn't get away
from you and cause a mess."

Oh, indeed.

Monday, October **15**

High Drama Above the Tree Line

Prema Hardwick is G. P.'s token superstar athlete.[85]

Some readers may wonder why a jock would go to Green Pastures Academy. Why attend a school where you get zero love for your outlier muscle-twitch capacities, when you could go to the Churchill or Dover and get all the special treatment and team jackets your heart could desire?[86] Surely, Prema Hardwick was smart enough to realize that the golden children at G. P. are the ones who get opinion pieces published in national news magazines and film shorts in festivals. (Our badminton team, three-legged racers, and hopscotch athletes aren't about to get a stadium built for them, *Friday Night Lights*–style. Not even an ironic one.)

The answer to why Prema attends G. P. Academy is this: she takes fabric arts seriously. I've seen some of her

-- -- -- -- -- -- -- -- -- -- -- -- --

85. My guess is that you see her a lot in your capacity as a guidance counselor, because she probably needs to talk about issues pertaining to excellence.

86. For those who are not currently taking advanced gym, muscle-fiber types are divided into two types: fast twitch and slow twitch. If you have superstar slow-twitch muscles you can run marathons and do other unpleasant-sounding activities. If you have top-notch fast-twitch muscles, you can go very fast for short distances, which also sounds unpleasant. That pretty much sums up what I know about muscle twitch.

quilts and yarn installations. She's a real asset to our traditional arts program, and I mean that in all seriousness, even though it sounds condescending. I am an excellent stitcher, but less skilled with some of the other crafts. For instance, my weaving project was a tragic episode in my art career. Dusk confiscated what she called my "Lump 'n' Threads" wall hanging for "crimes against eyes," and took it out to the school sustainability patch to keep weeds down and vermin fearful.

As almost everyone knows, because of all the local newspaper articles and radio announcements and whatnot, Prema and two of her BC Ski Team compadres qualified for the national cross-country ski team. People say she's destined to win an Olympic medal one day.

Flashback alert!

Dusk's family has a cabin on Mount Washington (as far as I can tell this is pretty much a requirement for a two-doctor family in the mid-Island region), and last winter her parents invited Neil and me for a weekend. During that visit Dr. and Dr. Weintraub-Lee insisted that Dusk show me how to skate ski.[87] They tried to make Neil learn, too, but he told them he was asthmatic, which he is not.

I borrowed Dusk's eleven-year-old brother's skate skis and followed her to the trails.

"Skate skiing is just like it sounds: half skating and half

---

87. If you know nothing about Nordic skiing, "classic" is the regular kind of two-track cross-country skiing. It's approximately as exciting as walking on a treadmill in an empty, windowless room. Skate skiing is different from classic skiing in the way that ice climbing, up sheer and unstable glaciers, is different from having naps in cozy daybeds.

skiing. You know how to do both, right?" assumed Dusk.

She shoved off and demonstrated the basic technique. We ended up on a trail that led around the side of the mountain and opened up to reveal the mighty Pacific Ocean sprawling far below through broken cloud cover. At least, that's what I *should* have seen. I couldn't appreciate the view because I was dying. The vapor trail I left in my wake made it look like I was carrying a boiling kettle somewhere on my person.

I collapsed at about the three-quarter mark and lay atop the crust of snow, waiting for the end. It took a good ten minutes for my heart to stop jackhammering in a fatal-seeming way. Dusk finally noticed I was no longer behind her, and by the time she doubled back to check on me, I was past caring about small matters such as life and death.

"You may need to radio down to the lodge and get some medical support staff and a defibrillator," I told her. I'd sweated through my tights and woolen jersey and the sweat had dried, gluing me to the snowbank. "My body may be frozen here until spring," I added. "It will actually be a relief. Anything's better than trying to skate ski any farther."

"Come on, get up," said Dusk with the bedside manner of a dingo. "You're fine."

She jammed her poles into the bank, leaned over, and helped me into a sitting position.

That's when we heard the *shooshing* noise that indicated that a good skate skier was approaching.

I watched in awe as Prema Hardwick flew by, poling and skating with the ease and grace of . . . well, an elite skate skier.

She was followed by two ultra-lean guys. All three of

them wore the colorful, boldly patterned, aerodynamic uni-
tards of the Mount Washington Ski Team.

Among the three of them, they had perhaps one-half
ounce of extra fat, which would probably be used up by the
time they got back to the lodge.

Prema smiled graciously at us as she passed and inclined
her head. She appeared entirely unaffected by the effort of
pushing herself up a mountain on a pair of Popsicle sticks.

"That's disgusting," I said when they were gone, which
took about two seconds.

Dusk laughed. "I think she's propelled along by the
drama of the triangle," she said.

"Triangle?"

"The captain of the Nordic team is Luke. He's twenty.
He loves her. Tony, her other teammate, also twenty, is in
love with her, too. The three of them spend every minute
together. It's a sordid-yet-compelling love triangle. High
drama above the tree line." Dusk slid her hands back into
the straps of her poles. "Everyone is holding their breath
waiting to see which guy she's going to choose. It has the
potential to destroy the team. It's a code red love situation
up here at Mount Washington."

"She's torn between two lovers," I said. "It's like *The
Hunger Games* but with Nordic skiers."

"In other words, it's nothing like *The Hunger Games*."

"Right," I agreed.

The thought of Prema's hyper-athletic love triangle was
enough to sustain me until we made it back to the lodge,
where we found Neil enjoying a large plate of fries and
gravy.

"Come on in!" he said. "The fries are fine!"

Once we were settled with hot chocolate and our own fries, we watched Prema and her suitors at the ski team table. The two boys leaned close each time she spoke. Then they caught sight of each other and quickly leaned out, like wooden pecking-hen toys. The whole lodge seemed filled with low-grade tension. Prema, for all her ferocious per-fection and outdoorsiness, seemed anxious, looking from Luke to Tony and back. Part of me wondered if she was trying to tell them apart. They were *extremely* similar—high cheekbones, sandy curly hair, eyes bugged out from a bad case of love.

"You getting a load of those three?" asked Neil.

"Yeah," I said.

"You and the rest of the world," he said, and swiped another fry through the gravy. "What, oh what, is going to happen?"

And that's where we left it. Prema Hardwick, superstar athlete on whose talents and affections rest the dreams of so many people. End of flashback.[88]

At the end of last year, she and both of her would-be lovers joined the National Ski Team. Meanwhile, her smile became less frequent and her jock-perkiness wilted.

- - - - - - - - - - - - - - -

88. Apologies for the lengthy flashback. As per your lecture, I tried to make it more compelling by writing it as a scene rather than summarizing the experience. I'm sure a BP-worthy flood of green ink will inform me if I'm wrong.

Every time we saw her, I whispered my standard line, "Torn between two lovers," and shook my head sadly.

Dusk said, "It's like Romeo and Juliet plus another guy."

"That would be Paris," I told her.

"I thought the problem in that story was the parents," she said. "Then again, I suppose I would think that."

Of the three of us, Dusk seemed the most genuinely worried about Prema. After all, Dusk spent a lot more time on the mountain than Neil and me. Two days after I talked to Brian and a little less than a year after I saw Prema in her natural element, I was ready to get to the bottom of her romantic tribulations. I decided to approach her during the period designated, but only occasionally used, for physical activity. I knew that Prema would be running laps. Ski season hadn't started yet, but Prema worked out about four times a day. When the weather allowed it, she did fartlek on the track. Fartlek[89] is this running technique where you run at your normal pace and then every so often, when the spirit moves you, you run as fast as you can. Then you return to your regular pace. It's pretty fun. Not as fun as saying the word *fartlek*, but what is, really?

"I'm sure she'll appreciate your interest," said Dusk. "She's probably just waiting for an excuse to talk about it."

"I agree," said Neil. "Norm, I think you should tell her that the neurologists have done studies and they've discovered that secrets are hard on the body. They affect health and athletic performance."

-- -- -- -- -- -- -- -- -- -- -- -- --

89. Which means "speed play" in Swedish.

Only a few days before, I would have replied that was a good reason for us to stay out of other people's business. If we ended up learning a bunch of secrets, our health could be negatively affected. But the boost I'd gotten from my meeting with Brian Forbes was still clear in my mind.

As we walked outside into the cool, clear October afternoon, already scented with wood smoke, Neil massaged my shoulders like I was heading into a boxing ring, which made me feel kind of dumb and kind of great at the same time.

"Just be yourself," he said.

When we were near the track, Dusk said, "Maybe I should do it."

I turned to her.

"I know her, and it feels wrong to . . . outsource it."

"You don't think I can handle it?" I said.

"I just feel responsible. If everything goes to hell, it's better if it's my fault." Dusk wasn't usually one to admit that anything could go wrong with one of her ideas. Her reaction wasn't making sense.

"My dad is so excited about the ski team," she continued. "He's planning to take the whole family to the nationals in Banff. He's even planning to take us to the Olympics if Prema or any of our skiers make it."

"But then isn't it better if one of *us* messes things up? Your parents already think we're morons," said Neil.

"They do not think you're morons. They just see you as low achievers. It's not the same. Anyway, my parents are used to me doing stupid, disappointing things. I don't want them to get mad at you guys. If anyone's going to be responsible for dashing their dreams, it should be me."

"Would you like a shoulder massage?" Neil asked her.

"No, Neil. I do not want a shoulder massage. You and Norm can do bodywork on each other while I get this thing done."

"We don't have to—" I started, but Dusk was already striding off.

Soon, she'd reached the area of track on which Prema, lean and dark-complected, was stretching. Dusk began to do a pale imitation of the same stretches, and when Prema began running, Dusk hustled along behind. She looked extra unathletic because she wore men's brogues, a pair of lace pantaloons, and an oversized Celine Dion T-shirt.

Prema was apparently so depressed and distracted by her romantic difficulties that she didn't notice or didn't care that she had company. Her warm-up pace was similar to that of a coursing greyhound. Dusk was able to keep her in sight, but only barely. Then Prema found her next gear and began covering ground like a barn swallow.

When Dusk reached the spot where Neil and I stood, long after Prema had sprinted by, her brogues sounded like they were filled with concrete.

She slowed, then stopped, her hands on her knees.

"Go! Go!" said Neil.

I took Dusk's place on the track and hurried after Prema, who by this time had gone around at least twice.

I ran as fast as I could, but Prema was doing something else entirely. "Looking good out there," said Neil when I panted my way back within earshot. Dusk said she thought she needed to barf and that she'd give me encouragement later.

I realized that I was going to tear something if I didn't stop or slow down. Also, I had no idea why we were racing after Prema Hardwick.

"Can't we just wait until she finishes?" I gasped.

"It wouldn't be fair. We have to meet her in her natural environment," said Dusk.

"Oh, God," said Neil.

He stepped gingerly onto the track in his dark blue suit. He began to trot gingerly along the track, looking like a man chasing after his handkerchief on a windy day.

"Our boy is exercising," she said. "In a suit."

"I'm so proud," I agreed.

We stood with our arms around each other as we watched Neil trot his way uncertainly around the track while Prema hurtled by him again and again as though it was one-hundredth rather than a quarter mile. His burgundy tie flapped out behind him.

"How much do you love him?" I asked Dusk.

"As much as my own breath," she said.

"Me too," I said.

He made it all the way around, but just barely. Dusk limped onto the track to replace him. Fortunately for our newly formed shin splints, Prema finally slowed to a human jog and then stopped and began stretching on the bleachers.

Out of respect, Neil and I backed away as Dusk walked up to her. We saw her say something. Prema turned to stare at Dusk and we could hear the fateful words: "Mind your own business." Then Prema walked away.

"Not good," I said.

"Definitely not worth the exercise," said Neil.

Just the Three of Us

We still felt shaken the next day. Prema wasn't the first person not to tell us the truth, but she was the first one to get upset that we'd asked. Dusk, in particular, was unsettled when I picked her up for school.

"I could hardly sleep last night," she said. "My dad will have a coronary if he finds out I did something to ruin the team dynamic."

"Wasn't that the point of asking her which boy she likes best?" I asked. "To sort out the dynamic?"

"Yeah, I guess. But it's obviously working the way it is."

I sort of liked seeing Dusk being neurotic. Usually, I was the indecisive one.

When we arrived at school, Neil and I patted her on the hand and told her she'd tried her best, and Prema and her two men would probably continue to skate ski like the wind. Dusk slumped off to make tiny trailer furniture in her tabletop installation class.

Neil went off to European art history and I decided to skip social studies and head into the library for a bit of a read and maybe a short writing session. I'd just opened my notebook when I felt someone standing over me.

It was Prema Hardwick.

My heart rate picked up and I wondered if it was because I felt anxious from guilt or from excitement.

"You guys were following me yesterday," she said.

Our whole mandate was truth so I suppressed the urge to lie. "Yeah."

"Because of your Truth Club?"

"Commission," I said. "We've formed a Truth Commission."

"This place," said Prema, disgusted. "It just never ends. Can't anyone just . . . just be *normal*?"

"I'm not sure art school is the place to go looking for normal."

Prema radiated wiry strength. I have this theory that all elite athletes are beautiful thanks to fitness and focus, but mostly from figuring out what they're really good at. Just like the best writers often have amazing faces and great musicians are transformed by their talent, even if they're meek little people in plain sweaters.[90]

Her eyes were large and, like Brian Forbes, she had long dark lashes, which were probably good for keeping snowflakes out of her eyes when she was racing. She wore no makeup. There was no excess to her at all, which you can't say about many people.

"Here's what I have to say to anyone who wants to know," she said. Again, no niceties. No taking a stick to the

---

90. Bad paragraph. I need to work on it. I know what I'm trying to say but it's not really coming across. God, writing is hard. Sometimes I worry that I'll never get good enough to earn an extraordinary writer face.

bushes and beating around. "Tony and Luke are amazing. I love them both. And I'm going to keep loving them both. Our relationship is no one else's concern. The three of us are going all the way."

I felt my jaw drop and she seemed to realize what she'd said.

"With our skiing," she added.

There was a pause while we both digested her words.

"Are you going to tell everyone?" she asked.

"No. We just ask people their truth. We don't talk about it."

"You know something?" said Prema, pulling a chair over to my cubicle and sitting down with the unfamiliar movements of someone who doesn't like to be still.

She crossed one skinny-jean-clad leg over the other like she was really getting into this relaxation thing. "I feel better. It's funny. I know everyone wonders about us. I wonder about us, too. But I also don't. I love both of them and we'll figure it out eventually. In the meantime, our feelings for each other make us train harder, race harder."

"That's good," I said. "There have been successful threesomes throughout history," I added. As I spoke, I realized I should have done some research before saying that.

She made a wry face at me. I didn't blame her.

"What about you guys?" she said.

"Us guys?"

"You and Dusk and the guy with the outfits."

"Neil?" I said.

"Yeah. What about the three of you? Are you going to ask yourselves the same question? Because I think you should, if truth is your thing."

"I, uh, well," I said articulately.

"Tell Dusk I'm sorry I got upset at her. I don't like people in my business. Also, you are all such bad runners. You know how it hurts a person with perfect pitch when they hear a tone-deaf person? Well, watching you and your friends do athletics is like that for me."

"Oh," I said.

"Yeah. I definitely feel better after talking about this," said Prema. "Now I have to decide whether to tell Luke and Tony. I'm ready to acknowledge our truth, but I don't know about them."

"Be careful," I said, much too late.

"Don't forget about asking yourself the truth. You know what they say. 'Cast the stone out of your own moat before you go looking at glass houses.' It's pretty clear how *he* feels," she added, getting up from what was probably her longest voluntary sit in about three years.

"What?" I tried to figure out the meaning of her mangled malaprop-cliché combination. Then the last line hit me. "It is?"

She gave me another variation of her *Are you serious?* face before she walked away.

The Space Between

Neil and Dusk had stuff to do after school, so I drove home by myself and thought about what Prema had said. *It's pretty clear how* he *feels.*

What was she talking about? Part of me knew, and part of me pushed the knowledge away. Okay. This is a work of creative nonfiction. It's predicated on accuracy.

I know that Neil has an unstated romantic love for Dusk. You can see it in his paintings of her. As I may have noted a time or two,[91] he's a huge fan of beautiful women. He loves them all. But the girls he picks to be his muses are special. He's made more paintings of Dusk than of anyone else, including film stars of the 1960s and 1970s such as Jane Fonda and Kim Novak, and prematurely deceased rock stars such as Janis Joplin and Amy Winehouse. The paintings all have un-illuminating titles: *Gone-1*, *Gone 2-2*, etc. What does this focus mean? Love.

Neil loves me, too, but not the same way he loves Dusk. She loves him, but not the way I do.

We all love each other.

Complicatedly.

---

91. A few too many times, if your editorial comments are to be believed.

Apparently, this sort of thing seems romantic to a huge segment of the reading and film-going public.[92] Nothing about it seems romantic to me. I find it creepy and indicative of delusionality on the part of the less-loved point of the triangle. Allow me to explain. Unless you have one of those disorders that make it hard for you to interpret social cues or facial expressions, you should have a clue if someone likes your friend more than you. People aren't good at hiding their feelings.

I recognize that if you're in a love triangle, the fact that your love object likes your friend more than he/she likes you doesn't mean that you won't like him. Or her. Man, this is harder to write than I would have thought! Gendered pronouns make everything so awkward. I might need to work this out in a footnote so as not to expose the gentle reader to harsh mental confusion and poor word order.

Let me clarify.

Just because Neil likes-likes Dusk doesn't mean that I can stop myself from like-liking Neil.[93] I can, however, act with some modicum of dignity and not acknowledge my feelings. My personal rule for emotional and mental self-preservation: "I will not openly love any person who cannot love me back the same way." Why shouldn't you be into someone who is not into you? Because it's undignified

--- --- --- --- --- --- --- --- --- --- --- --- ---

92. *Gone with the Wind, The Hunger Games, Twilight, Bridget Jones's Diary.* And every single one of them would be better without a love triangle. Maybe I'm just prejudiced. And also a touch bitter.

93. I'm on the verge of throwing up. I may not be able to finish this project due to how badly I'm writing it right now.

and sad. There is already too much that is sad and undignified in my life. I refuse to add more to that smelly bucket,
and so I spend as little time thinking about my feelings
as possible. Nor will I talk about them to my guidance
counseling/creative writing teacher.[94] I will pretend I do
not have those feelings and eventually they will die from
neglect.

So there.

I understand where Prema Hardwick is coming from
and can relate to her attitude.

There is nothing to be gained by trying to change reality.

I know this.

Completely.

And yet.

And. Yet.

As I drove I considered her words: *It's pretty clear how
he feels.*

Was it obvious? Something about her words made a small
flag of hope rise up and flap around in my brain like a sparrow
trapped in someone's kitchen. Did other people see something
I didn't? Had Prema Hardwick with her elite athletic eyes seen
Neil staring at me the way he stared at Dusk? Had I misread
his cues thanks to my damaged self-esteem (courtesy of my
sister's portrayal of me in the Diana Chronicles)? Was such a
thing possible?

I tried to usher the hope out of my brain but couldn't
find an open window.

----

94. Except, apparently, *ad nauseam* in my work of creative nonfiction.

Maybe I was wrong. At minimum, I needed to find out how he felt.

No! That was an awful thought. If I asked how *he* felt, then he'd know how *I* felt. If I even mentioned the tensions among the three of us, our friendship would change forever. Acknowledgment of the truth would ruin everything.

I considered how cavalier we'd been about asking Prema. The nerve of us and our Truth Commission.

And then I thought that this sort of mental ping-pong was what the other two points of Prema's triangle, Luke and Tony, probably felt *all the time*! No wonder they skied so fast.

I found that I was shaking my head as I drove, which was probably unsettling for the other commuters.

At least I wasn't talking to myself.

When I finally pulled up to our house, I was exhausted.

Unfortunately, our house is the last place a person who is overtired should go, especially since my sister's Crown Vic was parked outside. What if Keira wanted to tell me more about her inappropriate relationship with her teacher? A person needs to have her denial shields up and her emotional baffles set on maximum before stepping inside chez Pale. So I immediately reversed and turned back toward town.

Nancy stalled once across from the Kin Hut on Departure Bay Road, and again just up the hill behind the Brooks Landing Mall.

I pulled halfway into a blocked-off entrance to the parking lot and waited for the truck to recover. Nancy's interior smells of a potent combination of old truck, lunch boxes, a hint of degraded plastics, plus a whiff of despair. Maybe it's just the odor of many art students. Who knows?

Considerations about the specific smells inside my hand-me-down truck were a welcome change from my obsessive contemplation of Neil and me and Dusk and were interrupted only when I noticed a boy lurking near the mall.

Hoodie up, shoulders hunched. It was Brian Forbes! He hadn't been to school since our talk, and I'd been hoping that Dusk was right, that he'd maybe gone home and confessed his problem to his parents and then gone into rehab and had begun a triumphant journey to wellness and cautionary school talks.

Standing uncertainly on the sidewalk between Shanghai City Restaurant and Oliver's Pet Supplies, however, he didn't look particularly triumphant. He looked all kinds of shady.

Of all those the Commission had approached, he was the only one who hadn't contacted us after. Aimee talked to Neil and so did Tyler Jones, even if Tyler hadn't coughed up his truth yet. Prema gave me the goods after her initial refusal to cooperate. Mrs. Dekker and Zinnia talked to Dusk. I wanted my truth bond with Brian to hold!

Spotting him was a sign. I would ask him how he how he was doing, post-truth.

I looked into the rearview before I opened the door. Nancy was sticking into the road a little bit, but it was a thirty-kilometer-an-hour zone, so she wasn't likely to get hit. Brian, turtled deep into his hoodie, didn't notice me.

As I was approaching, a young guy came out of a dark glass door to my right. I slowed. Brian walked to meet him. They shook hands and when they did so, I thought I saw something small pass between them. I stopped walking.

Brian and the other boy exchanged a few words and then went their separate ways. The other boy headed around to the front of the mall, and Brian walked through the parking lot and across Departure Bay Road. Then he disappeared into Beach Estates Park, the many-staired and extensively boardwalked path that winds its way onto the beach facing the Departure Bay Ferry Terminal.

I'd only been in the park a few times. It gave the impression of deep shade and rushing water. To be honest, the whole vibe was a little wet and rape-y to me.

I followed Brian Forbes down the first set of stairs before the part of my brain in charge of self-preservation could stop me. I was immediately plunged into the kind of day shade you find only in a rain forest. Brown foaming water rushed out of a huge pipe just below street level and fell in a violent waterfall to the riverbed below. The noise of the street above disappeared in the roar of the runoff.

The railing on the first set of stairs was new and strong but covered in graffiti tags and incoherent and badly spelled insults. *Jo-Jo Blowz Dicks* and *Krystal C Suks It* were illustrated with crude drawings.[95]

As I moved down into the park, the sense of being in a ravine increased. The banks rose steeply on either side. I made myself walk a little faster, hoping to catch Brian before he made it too far. A wide waterfall cascaded down a

----

95. Which I will not attempt to reproduce here for the reason of not wanting to cause mental distress in my project supervisor or the gentle reader.

rock face, and the next thing I knew I was nearly running. Then I yelled Brian's name but I couldn't hear myself over the water.

I ran down metal grate stairs and across a wooden bridge covered in wire mesh and I called Brian's name again as I rounded a corner and nearly collided with two people who stood in the path with a fawn-colored pit bull. I screamed and the dog lunged and the man strained to keep hold of the leash. The woman said something uncomplimentary about kids and I muttered, "Sorry," and stepped carefully around them and ran on.

The path straightened and I stopped. On the other side of the river, the bank had begun to collapse, uprooting dozens of trees. They'd been dragged out of the river and stacked in a disorganized heap on the crumbling hillside. The city had put up a sign, strangely permanent-looking, announcing that the project to reinforce the bank had run out of money.

It occurred to me that whoever had designed Beach Estates Park had done so with an eye to making it as menacing as possible.

I told myself to take note of the environment. To not be one of those annoying people found in horror movies who hears a noise in a basement and immediately goes down there without so much as a flashlight or a quick call to the local police. I slowed my pace to a fast walk.

Maybe it was beautiful in the park, and my nerves were too jangled to notice. That would be a shame.

Brian had to be in front of me. The sides of the ravine were too steep for him to have climbed out. Was he crouched under one of the bridges?

The light grew brighter, and I saw wide, flat sky ahead where the park opened out to the beach opposite the ferry terminal.

My steps slowed.

It occurred to me that I was acting like a crazy woman. Brian probably lived in the neighborhood on the other side of the park. He was simply on his way home, and I was going to have to walk back alone.

I decided to sit on the beach for a few minutes before doing so. Prepare my nerves. Look at the steel structures of the terminal and try to draw them later. Contemplate the nature of rocks and sand. Dream up new ways to describe the scent of the ocean. Salt, dead oysters, ferry.

The small bridge that led out of the park and onto the beach was surrounded by tall, rough grasses. The river had turned into a burbling creek. The light was non-foreboding and my heart remembered how much I love the ocean and our island. When I walked onto the beach and over a row of driftwood logs, I saw Brian sitting on a log, as though he'd been waiting for me.

His hoodie was pulled up and cinched tight around his face. I felt ridiculously glad to see him.

"Hey," I said.

He turned and watched me come and made a noise like a laugh but that was not a laugh.

"Can I sit down?"

He nodded, and I settled down beside him.

It had stopped raining and the day was a clean and gray. "Saw you at Brooks Landing," I said.

Brian Forbes dug the heels of his tattered Chucks into

the sand. He made another snorting noise. "What is that noise?" I asked. Just to be companionable.

"You know, I'm not even sure. My mother really hates it."

"I was just wondering."

"Why are you watching me?"

"I'm not watching you."

"Oh, sorry. Let me be more specific. Why are you following me?"

I could feel the grit of sand and salt between my palms and the smooth log. "That's a legitimate question," I said. "I don't know the answer."

"I already told you the truth. Isn't that what you guys are after?"

"Could you call me Normandy?"

Another snort-laugh. That's really not a good description, because Brian's particular noise managed to pack so much despair into a single syllable, like a man hung from the ceiling who is being punched in the solar plexus.

"Okay, Normandy," he said.

"And can you take your hoodie off?"

"You're pretty demanding," he said.

It was the first time anyone had ever said that about me in my entire life.

He slid his hoodie back, and his short hair was messed up. He ran his hands over it once and then pulled out his cigarettes. He took a half-smoked one out of his pack. It smelled worse than a normal cigarette.

"That reeks," I said.

"Halfies always do. All the shit is activated already. Tastes terrible, too."

"That's got to be a bad sign."

"No doubt," he said. The flame from his lighter leaped as he sucked on the cigarette, a small daylight explosion.

"I saw you at Brooks Landing," I said, then realized I'd already said that.

His cheeks hollowed as he puffed out a long stream of smoke. "Yeah?"

"Were you buying drugs?"

Snort.

"I saw that guy give you something."

"My man Mark."

"He's your dealer?"

"Fellow reluctant enthusiast."

Brian Forbes reached into the pouch of his sweatshirt and I watched, alarmed, sure he was going to show me a baggie full of something I'd only ever seen on HBO.

It was a business card.

I got this unseemly jolt of triumph at the sight of it.

"This is awesome, Brian," I said, sounding every inch the person who should be writing bad children's television.

And then, like I knew him much better than I did, I said, "I'm really proud of you."

He turned his head to look at me, his face suddenly softening. His neck was thin. "Don't get your hopes too high," he said. "I'm not."

I stared out at the ferry terminal. Lights shone through the small portholes, but I couldn't see anyone moving inside.

"About what I said before," said Brian. "The last time we had one of our little talks."

I went still.

"I'm sorry. It's not my business about what goes on in your house. With your family."

"Oh," I said.

"Forget I said anything. I should go. There's probably a drug test waiting for me at home. Peanut butter sandwich, glass of milk, and a piss test."

"Don't get them mixed up," I said. And the obviousness of my avoidance and the ease with which I could be turned away from the topic made me ashamed.

"Same to you," he said, pushing himself up.

"You going to use that card?"

"Jesus, if I close my eyes, I could pretend my mother was here."

"Sorry."

"You're a nice girl, Normandy Pale."

No one had ever said that to me before, either. I liked it.

"You're a good guy, Brian Forbes."

"But it's more complicated than that, isn't it?" he said.

It was my turn to make the snort-y noise. "Ain't that the truth."

We got up and smiled at each other. His eyes were lovely,

and I was reminded of a line in book I read once, that God exists in the spaces between people.[96] Maybe that's what the Truth Commission was. An attempt to find God in each other.

The dull day seemed to grow bright around us, and then Brian took his smile and walked away, and I already missed him.

---

96. The philosopher Martin Buber, *Ich und Du,* or *I and Thou.*

Teacher, Teacher

The sense of having found God in someone else only lasted until I got out of the park. In the blocked-off entrance to the back parking lot of the strip mall was . . . an empty piece of pavement that should have been covered up with my truck. Nancy had been towed.

I muttered a swear and started walking. I could have called my parents or Dusk or Neil, but I didn't feel like it. The walk took about forty-five minutes, and by the time I reached our house I felt better. Keira's Crown Vic was gone. Nancy would be fine in the impound. She'd spent the night there before. One good thing about having a peculiar and fragile family is that things that matter in a regular family, like having your vehicle towed, are considered inconsequential.

Having my small transgressions overlooked had always worked for me, but the past few days had made me bold. Direct. I'd looked truth up the nose a few times and it hadn't killed me or anyone else. Instead, it had given me a rush, shaken me up, unsettled and exhilarated me. I didn't think I could go back to tiptoeing. I wanted to stomp around our house like a Lord of the Dance troupe in an uncontrolled frenzy.

My dad was in the kitchen making vegetarian chili. *Quelle surprise!*

"Norm," he said. "You're late. What's going on? I didn't hear Nancy."

"Stalled," I said.

"Oh, that girl," said my dad. "Good thing she's a looker, or we wouldn't put up with her."

"Good thing," I agreed. "Chili tonight?"

"Yes, indeed!" he said. "Got this new recipe. Includes salsa, if you can believe it."

"That's amazing," I said even though it wasn't, particularly.

"You want to set the table?"

I went to the cupboard and pulled out four plates. Plain plates. Ones without our faces on them.

It occurred to me that setting a place for Keira was screwed up, so I put one back.

"Your sister's home." My dad paused to taste from a giant spoon containing what looked to be a single kernel of corn coated in chili sauce. "I think she's sleeping. Been burning the midnight kerosene at both ends," he said. "Set a place for her just in case she wakes up."

"Dad, can you even remember the last time Keira ate at the table with us?"

He turned back to the giant pot and didn't answer.

"When did she get home?" I asked.

He stared at the recipe book, which was one of the cheap ones without any of the photographs that make a recipe book worth having.

"Not sure, Normandy. I'm making chili." As though that had anything to do with anything. "Let's get things ready. Your mom will be home any minute. She had a hair appointment after work."

It was rare for my mom to do any kind of self-care,

and I knew he didn't want to ruin her afterglow.

But something had gotten into me, and I put out the three plates and then added three plain spoons and three plain butter knives and three water glasses.

My dad looked at the table settings, but didn't comment that we were short one place, or that I hadn't used any Dianaware.

I went to my room to get changed. I could tell Keira wasn't in the closet, because my room was absolutely still and calm and no light leaked out the narrow gap at the bottom of the door. My sister is one of those people who can change the entire atmosphere of a room just by her presence, even if that presence is tucked away in a closet.

My bed was neatly made and my desk was bare except for my magnifying glass clamped to the side of my desk like a clumsy bird of prey. My big laptop was closed. One wall was lined with neat plastic bins of embroidery thread, and photos of Dusk and Neil and me surrounded my old mirror. A handmade paper kimono I made last year hung above my bed, and one of Dusk's shadow box sculptures sat on a floating shelf on another wall.

A strange and restless defiance moved in me and I guess that's what made me open the closet door. As I'd expected, Keira wasn't inside. The shock was that her sketchbook *was*. I recoiled at the sight of it lying on top of her lap desk. Usually, my sister kept that book clutched to her chest like an attaché case containing the red button.[97]

----

97. I hope you appreciate the Cold War reference, Ms. Fowler! Do you think there still is a red button? What must it be like to carry that thing around?

I stared at it.

Like the coward I am, I edged to the door on her side of the space and listened. Total silence. I picked up the heavy pad and carried it into my room, my heart thudding in my chest.

The first pages were all drawings of the same man. Twenties, handsome face, disheveled hair, half smile. Dimples.

I felt like I'd stolen her diary. I guess I sort of had.

In one image, he stood at the front of what appeared to be a classroom. Keira had drawn tiny handwriting on the whiteboard. The man was in midsentence. The drawing was hasty but full of urgent accuracy. Keira's strengths as an artist are many, but she's particularly good at people.

Some pages were covered in three or four portraits of the man's face. Each one made me want to look deep inside him. A full-page illustration showed him at a desk, head down, reading.

She'd captured his face in so many iterations that he seemed almost alive and moving from image to image. Then came the extreme close-up. It was done in ink and the perspective was off.

I realized why. His face was shown from below, putting the viewer beneath him. The man was almost unrecognizable, his face twisted.

"What the . . ." I whispered as I stared at the drawing.

It was the work of a superb illustrator, and something about it was terrible. It was the face every woman is afraid to see.

With a growing dread I turned the next page and saw a drawing that made me go even colder.

This one showed the man falling from a great height. His face, tiny now, was still twisted, but this time with fear.

What the hell *were* these?

Keira's stories always started in the drawing pads. But this wasn't a story. It was a series of increasingly disturbing portraits of the man who had assaulted her.

I checked the front of the pad. Maybe this wasn't the right one. But I'd seen her carrying it around the house. The top corner was folded and frayed.

Slowly, I carried it back to the closet and placed it on her lap desk in the exact position I'd found it, backed out of the closet, and shut the door.

XXXXX

When my dad called, I went to dinner. He'd reset the table for four, with full Dianaware: tablecloth *and* place mats, cutlery, salt- and pepper shakers, plates. I ate the vegetarian chili. The salsa was a nice touch.

Keira didn't join us. My mom's hair shone in the bright kitchen lights.

When we were done, I cleaned up.

I sat and did embroidery under my magnifier for a few hours, and then I went to bed. My eyes, tired from staring at stitches, were drooping when Keira opened the closet door.

"I forgot my drawing pad," she said.

My breath grew ragged and shallow.

I didn't know whether to be relieved or upset when she came out of the closet and climbed onto my bed. "Can you switch on the light?" she whispered.

It occurred to me that she didn't need a light to lie on my bed and tell me things I wasn't sure I wanted to hear. But I turned the lamp on anyway.

"Did you look?" she asked simply.

"Yes."

"So you know."

Did I know? I guessed I did.

"Those pictures, they're of your teacher. The one you went hiking with."

"Jackson Reid."

I waited.

"I thought he liked me," she said. "But when we went to the hiking cabin, he . . ."

"I'm so sorry," I said.

I could feel small jerking movements on the huge mattress, and I thought she might be crying. Her face was buried in the hood of her sleeping bag and hidden in the shadows. Just the shine of her eyes reached me.

"l feel so stupid," she said after she'd gotten control of her voice.

Seeing my sister, so odd and oblivious to normal human interactions, hurt like this was too much for me and I started to cry, too. Unlike Keira, I couldn't do it quietly. My sobs were loud and wet and messy and I kept wiping my sopping eyes with the sleeve of my long T-shirt and the blanket.

"Have you told anyone?" I asked, knowing that she hadn't. She hadn't even mentioned the affair, if that's what it was, before it took a violent turn.

"I was just so shocked. I never expected him to . . . do that."

That set me off again. I felt kind of stupid that I was crying harder than she was, but I couldn't stop myself. All the tension of the past few months was coming out, whether I liked it or not.

"Are you going to tell anyone?" I asked when I had regained a tiny sliver of control.

"No!" Her voice was vehement. "It would ruin me. I'd always be that girl who got raped by her teacher. I'm already strange."

I would have protested that she wasn't strange. That no one would think the fact that she'd been assaulted was her fault. But my sister *was* strange. And she was famous. Whether they blamed her or not, people would be fascinated.

"What about a teacher? You could talk to someone at G. P. Our new guidance counselor is really good."[98]

Keira snorted. "I don't think so. This is a little beyond the Art Farm's capabilities."

----

98. That would be you, Ms. Fowler.

The image of the final drawing in the book rose in my mind like a specter. I wanted to ask about it. But I didn't. I didn't. I couldn't.

I could feel my face working as I considered what to do and what to say. I knew I looked ugly in that moment. I knew she was watching me. Nothing was ever simple with my sister watching.

"Just telling you about it has helped. Drawing and talking. Those things are good medicine. You're good medicine, Norm," she said. And I felt that old thrill. My sister trusted me. She'd told me about the affair. Now she'd told me about the terrible thing that had happened. About the worst betrayal possible. Her trust had to mean something. But I wasn't sure I could handle it.

Then, astonishingly, my sister fell asleep on my bed.

A Classic Story

Why did I call Sylvia? I guess because when I woke up to find Keira gone, my brain immediately started looking for someplace to put the load of bad news she'd left with me the night before. I was in no way equipped to deal with something this serious. What if he did it again to someone else? I had a duty to report it. Sylvia was an experienced and worldly person. She was used to dealing with problems, even really big ones. After all, she worked with artists. If anyone would know how to help my sister, it would be her.

People might wonder why I didn't tell my parents. All I can do is repeat that they are not truth handlers or reality dealers.

I texted Neil and Dusk and told them I was going to be late and they should drive themselves to school. I managed to wait until 8:30 a.m. and then I called Sylvia. Her assistant answered. He sounded like he spent the first few minutes of the morning sucking on helium balloons.

"I'm calling for Sylvia," I said.

"She's in a meeting right now. Who may I say is calling, please?"

"Normandy Pale."

"Oh," he said, unmoved by that information.

"Keira Pale's sister."

Silence.

"One moment, please."

A shuffling sound. Then the same complaining cat voice came back on the line.

"Can I take a message?"

"If you could just tell her that Normandy called."

"Uh-huh. So that's Normandy Pale? Keira Pale's sister?"

I'd never called an agent before. I thought they were supposed to have efficient, powerhouse assistants. This one sounded like one of Mary Norton's Borrowers.

I confirmed the details and hung up. The phone rang when it was still in my hand.

"Normandy! You never call! You never write! It's so great to hear from you, honey. What's up this fine morning?"

"Other than the voice of your assistant?" I said, because I try and be clever when I speak to Sylvia. Sometimes I even pretend that she's my agent. God, I'm so sad sometimes.

"Kevin?" she said. "He's the grandnephew of the head of the agency. He's eleven. It's Nepotism Day or something, so he's being my assistant."

"Oh," I said. "I'd like to get in on that sometime." I was not entirely joking.

"Absolutely. When there's a Long-Distance Nepotism Day, you're the first person I'll call." I could hear her attention wander, the way it always did when she spoke more than a few sentences to me that weren't about my sister.

"Look, I don't want to be inappropriate or—"

"Never!" she interrupted. "Just let 'er rip."

"We're—I mean, I'm a little concerned about Keira," I said.

"Oh," she said, her voice rising until she sounded a bit like her eleven-year-old assistant.

"She goes out a lot," I started. "Since she came home from school."

As I spoke, I knew I was taking the long and winding road to get to the point. But I couldn't just blurt it out. Before I went any further, Sylvia cut in.

"Probably just enjoying her new place. I know you're used to having her around and that she likes to work in your shared closet? Isn't that right? God, I love that detail. It just blows people away. But you've got to give her space to change. Grow."

"New place?"

"And now that she's paid off your parents' house and made so many other changes in her life, it's natural that things will change. Dynamics shifting all over the place. I'm talking tectonic movement here."

"What?" I said, every inch the dimwit.

"Your parents didn't tell you?"

To say "what?" again would make me sound even dumber than I felt, so I squeaked out a reply in a voice so small not even a Borrower could have heard me.

"When Keira decided to sell the option to Diana, it all happened in a rush," continued Sylvia. "She was so excited to renew our agreement. We've worked together for so long. She felt bad about our little breakup. Then the first thing she planned to do was to go to the bank and surprise your folks by paying off the mortgage. She's wanted to do that for a while. Your parents have worked so hard to support her. And you've been a big support, too, obviously. The three of you have been such good sports about the stories. When I

think of them slaving away delivering the mail and oper-
ating a horse-drawn milk truck or whatever it is. God, it's
such a classic story."

"I—" I felt like a fish flapping on the deck of a boat.
What the hell was she talking about?

"How thrilled were your parents when she told them?"

Suddenly, it seemed important to play along. Pretend I
had the smallest clue what she was talking about. "They
were surprised," I said.

"Thanks to my persuasiveness the production company
was willing to send part of the money as soon as she signed.
Half of mid-six figures is no joke. Usually, it would take
much longer to get the money in hand. I was shocked the
mortgage on that place was still so high," she said. "And
your school must cost a fortune. No one's going to be going
to your dad to ask for financial-planning advice. Well, no
worries. You are all going to be well taken care of. Now
what was it you wanted to talk about?"

The distraction was fogging up her voice again.

"Nothing. I just wanted to . . . nothing."

"Normandy, honey. You tell that sister of yours to call
me as soon as the new book is ready for me to look at. I'm
going to time the announcement of the option deal to coin-
cide with the announcement of the pub date of her new
project. Wham, wham! At first I didn't want to delay the
option announcement, but now I see the possibilities. Keira
was smart to make us wait."

"Right," I said.

Then Sylvia hung up and left me wishing someone
would just bash me in the head and get it over with.

Grinding Middles

What did I do with the bizarre revelation that my sister, supposedly incapacitated after being assaulted by her teacher, had sometime in the past few weeks rehired her agent and become rich from selling an option for her comics? I did what any deeply ambivalent and confused person would do: I went back to bed. My parents had already left for work, and Nancy was still in impound. When Dusk and Neil texted to ask when I was coming to school, I said I was sick. And I was.

I lay in bed and listened to the sounds of the house. The fridge hummed off and on, the foundation creaked, birds scuttled around in the gutters. I tried not to think. When my dad got home after his shift, I stayed in bed until he knocked on my door to tell me dinner was ready.

Dinner seemed to be ready about four times a day.

My mom was home by that time, and I'd been in bed for so long, I felt like I barely knew how to speak or interact with other humans. My mom's new highlights glowed and her cheeks seemed flushed. Maybe Keira *had* given my parents some money. I couldn't ask *her,* because she hadn't come home.

"Keira still out?" I asked.

My parents exchanged a glance, as though they'd been talking about me.

"She's an adult, Normandy. She gets to set her own schedule," said my mother. She spoke as though I'd been lobbying hard to get my curfew extended. Which would be pretty pointless, since I didn't have a curfew and had never managed to come within shouting distance of needing one.

"Just wanted to know if she was home." I said this even though I knew the answer. I felt a need to establish some sort of baseline reality.

My dad blew on his chili. This one was a white-bean version. Quite adventurous for him.

"I think she may have gone out. She needs privacy, Norm. You know how hard she's been working on her project."

"Ah," I said. Something in that syllable set them off.

"Normandy!" said my parents together.

"You really need to lose the attitude," said my mother. I could practically see the highlights fade from her hair with the effort of each word. "Your sister's life has changed since college. She needs more independence. It's important not to interfere as she works her way through this next phase."

"What's with the glum face?" said my dad. "We're a family."

And since that was exactly the kind of crazy talk that was making me feel like I might be losing my mind, I decided to join in.

"It must be awesome to have so much disposable income now," I said.

My parents stared at me. My mother lowered her spoon to the place mat that, tragically, shows her as she appears in the Earth realm of the Diana comics.

"I mean, since Keira paid off the mortgage for the house," I said. My words dropped like stones into a murky pond.

"Normandy," said my mother. "Are you feeling all right?"

I didn't want to look at her. To see the lines of her face blurred by work and worry and denial.

"I think you're being unkind," said my mother. "You know that Keira wants to help out with the household when she's able. But this isn't the right time. She had a lot of expenses. Her college cost a small fortune. We couldn't help much."

"She got a full scholarship," I said.

"Just for tuition," said my dad.

"There were a lot of other expenses," said my mom.

"The new book's coming along slowly," said my dad. "The last thing she needs is more pressure."

"So you're saying that she *didn't* pay off the mortgage?"

My father laughed uncomfortably. "You've been doing too much needlepoint."

"Embroidery," I said. "There's a difference."

"Your sister's money is her own. We're the parents. We pay the bills," added my mother in a brittle voice. It was as clear as freshly Windexed glass that my mother and father lived in suspended animation. Did they hope their patience would pay off somehow? That their agreeing to be turned inside out for public consumption would somehow be rewarded? That Keira would eventually put them on easy street, as she kept hinting?

For the first time, I really thought about what it was like for my parents to have a kid like Keira. What it took for them to ignore the fact that she doesn't even like us. They weren't ready to deal with the reality of my sister, and they might never be ready.

"We'll get this sucker paid off when we win the lottery," said my father fake-jovially and also insanely, because he doesn't play the lottery because he needs all his spending money to buy discontinued cookbooks and help pay my tuition.

My parents looked so confused and distressed, I wished I hadn't said anything.

"I was just kidding," I said.

"That's a strange sort of joke," said my mother.

My dad laughed. "Well, Betty. It's what we get for producing two artists. Warped reality!"

"White beans are a nice change in this chili," said my mother.

I tried to imagine dropping the bombshells of Sylvia's news and my sister's confession on them. The thought was laughable. Or maybe it was cryable. Either way, it wasn't going to happen. Instead, I ate my chili, gave false answers to my parents' pro forma questions about my day, and went back to my room. As soon as I shut the door, I knew I had to get out of the house before Keira came home from wherever she was, before she walked into the closet to draw more disturbing pictures, before she crawled onto my bed to tell me more stories without beginnings and ends. Stories that were all grinding middles. My sister had lied to Sylvia about paying the mortgage. What other lies had she told? And why?

I did something I had never done before.

I called Neil. Just Neil.

Right away, he knew something was wrong.

"You okay?" he asked. "What can I do?"

"I need to talk about my family. To you. Only you."

There was a pause on the other end of the phone as he digested this. There are deep-cover CIA agents who talk more about their families than I do. Did.

"Whatever you need, Norm. I'll be there in twenty minutes," he said.

My parents didn't notice me leave.

Shinola

Fifteen minutes later, Neil pulled up in the shiny black sports car that didn't suit him. I'd been waiting in our carport, leaning up against the woodpile, half of which was a marvel of spatial ingenuity and engineering, with each rough-hewn block tucked optimally against the next. The other half was a haphazard heap waiting to collapse the next time a big truck rumbled by.[99]

I emerged from under the carport and bent down to get into Neil's Mazda, which smelled like genuine leather seats.

"This car is luxe," I said, feeling disembodied by the rearrangement of our pieces. We weren't on our way to pick up Dusk and, as a result, we were somehow strangers to each other.

Neil wore the Ratso Rizzo outfit of a red polo shirt with a white windowpane pattern and white pants.

"You're going to be cold," I said.

---

99. When she was still in high school, my sister read some Buddhist mantra about stacking wood, and spent the next two days stacking the first part of our woodpile. The blocks were so neatly and intricately arranged that neighbors actually stopped by to take pictures. We could never bear to burn her beautiful woodpile, so we just added to it. None of us is the wood stacker my sister was.

"Got the suit jacket back there." He indicated the seat behind us, then backed the car out of our potholed driveway.

I have already admitted in the pages of this work of creative nonfiction that I like-like one of my two best friends. And watching him handle the car his father gave him reminded me why. For all his lack of outdoorsy qualities, Neil drove like he'd been doing it for years, not months. Unshowy, competent. Hands big and easy on the wheel, slicked-back hair falling onto his forehead. He wasn't proud of the car he didn't buy. He wasn't ashamed of it, either. He just treated the car like a car.

I thought about the things he did and the things he loved, his paintings of beautiful girls and, like a total fool, I started to cry.

"Oh, no," he whispered. I had the heels of my hands pressed to my eyes so I wouldn't have to see his face.

I felt the car pull over and come to a stop. Then I felt him reach around me to pull my seat belt tight and click it into place.

"That's better," he said. And off we went again.

How could I not like-like him?

When I finally allowed my hands to drop from my eyes and the temporary blindness passed, I risked a glance at him.

The look he gave me was pure Neil. Thoughtful and kind, concerned. And something else.

"I'm sorry," I said. "I forgot to mention on the phone that I am cracking up."

"Hey," he said. "No apologies."

We were on Rock City Road, which wound between rock bluffs and new subdivisions. You had to be careful, because there were deer all over the place. The light was fading and they were hard to spot.

We drove to Hammond Bay Road, and then Neil made the tight turn onto Linley. At the entrance to the trailhead was space for two cars and we were the only ones there. Neil nosed the Mazda into the tall grass at the edge of the bank.

"Okay," he said. "Be free." And he unlatched my seat belt.

We laughed.

God, it was strange to be in that car with him. And thrilling.

"Prema talked to me. She likes both guys," I said.

"Okay." Neil waited, somehow knowing I had more to say.

"I have some other things to tell you," I said. "About my family."

He said simply, "I'm happy you picked me."

I told him about my sister. About her return from college. About the affair and the drawing I found. About what her teacher had done to her. I told him about the call to Sylvia and the money. When I was done, he watched me.

The car had a fancy stereo with a display that made green illumination crawl across our faces.

We were listening to some kind of electronic music turned down low and hypnotic.

"There's one more thing," I said.

"Okay." His voice was husky. My nose was full of new car and thrift store suit and a hint of the old-fashioned Wildroot hair tonic he favored. My heart pumped in time with the music, which is to say, fast and insistent.

I stared straight ahead as I spoke.

"I like you. And I know I shouldn't. But I do. I'm sorry."

Now I couldn't catch my breath and I didn't dare turn my head.

The pause went on and on.

"Are you serious?" he said.

His disappointment, if that's what it was, peeled back a layer of skin that was already raw to touch.

"I know you don't feel the same. It's okay," I said, so he wouldn't feel too bad about turning me down. I watched the digital waves on the stereo flutter and felt hollow-boned and feathered enough to fly. Light enough not to care where I landed.

"How do you know that?" he asked.

"You've got that thing about extremely beautiful girls."

"That's just art. Anyway, have you looked in a mirror lately?"

I did my best not to. Features were checked in isolation. My face was a thing to be avoided. Just in case.

Neil put his hand on my chin and he gently turned my face to his.

"When it comes to liking, you don't know shit from Shinola, Normandy Pale," he murmured. Then he kissed me.

The Passive Persons' Rubicon of Love

When you have two best friends and you make out with one of them, things have a way of changing, and changing fast.

My dad took me to get Nancy from the impound the next day. We went first thing in the morning and he paid the bill, grumbling good-naturedly about the cost of living with spacey artists. I was in a daze. I guess that's what happens to a person after her first kiss. Then I drove over to pick up Dusk.

She hopped in the truck and put down her medical bag. (I sincerely hope she doesn't use it to carry around shrew corpses.) She was resplendent in a purple satin jumpsuit and matching purple headband. On her feet were granny heels. Once she was seated comfortably, she turned to look at me. And look at me.

"Norm?" she said.

I could feel the flush start at my navel and begin to roll up my body and head like a red carpet unfurling.

"Norm!" she said.

I know that thus far in this work I have presented Dusk as a) self-centered and b) kind of mean. She is both. I won't lie. But she's also observant and generous and affectionate in the same way a cat is. She is, like anyone worth knowing, many things at once.

I stared out the windshield, which could have done with a rinse, but I had forgotten to refill the wiper fluid.

"Normandy Pale! What have you done?" said Dusk.

I knew she'd sense something was different, but not so quickly. Not so completely.

I drove us back out onto Departure Bay Road and we headed for Neil's. Everything was moving too fast, like my emotions and life had been put into an off-brand salad spinner. *Whir. Slip. Catch. Whir.*

"I'm sure you'll tell me when you're ready. But it better be soon. Never mind, Neil will get it out of you."

I drove.

"Is it Prema? Did she talk to you? What's going on? You look *different.*"

I had taken some care getting dressed this morning. Something about the events of the night before made me want to express myself, at least a little bit. Normally, as I've mentioned, unless I'm wearing an outfit to support one of my friends' obsessions (*Midnight Cowboy*, *Dog Day Afternoon*, famous Victorian-era taxidermists), I'm a jeans person.

Today, I'd put on leggings and a hand-dyed violet-colored sweatshirt that I bought last year at the Clothes Cult's Après Fashion Show trunk sale. It was barely even identifiable as a sweatshirt because the drape was so complicated and the color was so pretty. It had a big cowl neck and I'd cinched it tight with a glittery belt, also designed by a Clothes Cultist. I wore it with tall brown leather boots and felt criminally great.

"I look different because I'm dressed up," I said.

"No," said Dusk. "That's not it. What's going on with

you goes deeper than clothes. Did you learn something? A truth?"

This was my chance.

"Yes!" I blurted, grateful. "That's it. Prema talked."

"Why so rosy-faced and strange? Sure, I'm disappointed that she didn't tell me. But you ran nearly as far down that track with her as I did. That truth seeking was a team effort."

"Let's wait until Neil's here."

"That's my girl," said Dusk. "Efficiency in all things."

I could feel her continuing to stare at the side of my face. Dusk is very intense. When she stares at you, it's a bit like being the target of floodlights on a dark two lane at midnight.

"Hmmmm," she said.

To distract her, I reached for the stereo, which was the only new thing in the truck. Keira had had it installed behind the original tape deck, so as not to disturb the retro feel of Nancy's dashboard. My iPod cord sneaked out of the cassette slot, and I fiddled with the original volume knob, which did exactly nothing.

"Never mind that," said Dusk. "I'll handle the entertainment. You keep your attention on the road."

Then she became engaged in picking a new song and getting the volume just right. That took a while, because Dusk has conflicted taste in music and spends a lot of time being disappointed in various artists for any number of reasons from politics to their friends.

She settled on Grizzly Bear because she has a soft spot for bands from Brooklyn and plans to live there for the majority of her twenties. Also, she used to figure skate and they made that excellent video about the sad, disoriented skater.

As we pulled up to Neil's house, Nancy coughed and died. I coasted her to a stop about ten feet from where I would normally have pulled up.

Neil, who is always very good about being ready, walked out to meet us. Mr. Sutton, wearing a bathrobe that appeared to be trimmed with dead weasels, waved from the wide front doorway.

"Dear Lord, please let his bathrobe stay closed," muttered Dusk, and we smiled and waved back.

Neil opened the door and waited for Dusk to jump out so he could get in the middle.

"How are my gorgeous girls?" called Mr. Sutton, gesturing with his coffee mug. "How did my boy get so lucky?"

"Hi, Mr. Sutton!" said Dusk and I in unison.

When we were in our usual places, we had to wait about three minutes for Nancy's engine to recover. Disconcertingly, Mr. Sutton stayed posted in the front door, smiling and nodding at us, between sips of coffee. We took turns smiling back while trying to negotiate the changing dynamics inside the truck. Neil was no longer just Neil. He was this electric presence beside me. I could practically see a current running between us, and Dusk, no dummy, picked up on it.

She waved at Neil's dad and shot us a sidelong glance. Then a longer sidelong glance. Her face shifted as some recognition dawned.

"What the . . . ?"

Without taking her eyes off Mr. Sutton, she said, without moving her lips, "Start the truck, Norm."

"Nancy's not ready," I said, also without moving my mouth.

I was afraid to look at Neil, but I could picture his

expression. It would be the one he always used when stressed: staring into the middle distance at the level of his third eye, mouth twisted in fierce concentration. It was a facial arrangement that would have made most people look the opposite of smart. Somehow, it just made Neil look well intentioned.

The atmosphere in Nancy was so thick that even Mr. Sutton picked up on it. His smile faded and he leaned forward to get a better look at us.

I waved.

"Oh, my God," said Dusk. "What the hell is going on here?"

That was my cue to try the engine. It sputtered, ground, and coughed reluctantly into action. I threw the shift into reverse and we began to back up, the engine's whining high and concerned.

"Okay. I'm going to take a guess here. Norm, you told Neil what Prema said. And it's big. And you two didn't tell me."

The red carpet had rolled back up over my face. Neil continued to gaze fixedly into the middle distance like a third grader who'd been given an eleventh grader's math problem.

"No, that's not it," mused Dusk. "There's no truth Prema could have told you that would have made you two so . . . whatever you are right now."

I was aware to the millimeter of how close Neil was. We were scrupulous about not touching. It was probably more obvious than if he'd sat on my knee. He was in his lucky light blue suit. I loved him in that suit.

"No," said Dusk. "I'm trying to take this in. Is it possible?"

She leaned farther forward.

"Neil. Look at me," she demanded. "Let me see your face."

I kept my attention on the road, but I knew we were doomed. Neil could walk around with a brown paper grocery bag over a balaclava, and everyone would know how he was feeling.

"I see guilt," said Dusk. "I see blushing. Which makes two guilts and two blushings."

I flicked a glance over at my passengers and saw that Dusk's face was about four inches from Neil's. "And I feel something. Hmmmm. What is it? I think it might be . . . Oh, do *not tell me that you two finally hooked up!*" shouted Dusk.

"Oh, shit," I whispered.

"The sexual tension is so thick in here, I am practically getting pregnant," said Dusk.

I made a dismissive noise that was entirely lame.

"Tell me what happened."

"Dusk," said Neil. "We, uh . . ."

Now I found myself listening even more closely, if that was possible. I wondered if I would hear regret in his voice. I wondered if he'd changed his mind since the night before.

"Can this just wait until we get to school?" I asked. "I'm trying to drive."

I felt Dusk collapse back against the seat. "Fine," she said. "It's a lot to take in."

When Nancy wheezed to a stop in the school's gravel parking lot, we were left listening to the soul stylings of Anthony Hamilton singing "Mad." Appropriately, it's a song about lying and love. Coincidence? I think not. Life is so full of portents and signs and symbols that it's a wonder not everyone is a writer.

"This is an excellent song," said Neil finally.

"Yeah, yeah," said Dusk. "Are you two going to tell me or not?"

Again, I felt my spine stiffen. What would I hear in the spaces between Neil's words? As oversaturated as the moment was, it was impossible not to think about the color of the moments that would follow from it. How would we be changed by what came next.

"We didn't mean for this—" I started.

"I'm glad it happened," Neil cut in, "but I feel bad we didn't call you right away."

My rib cage seemed to expand in a way at once painful and perfect.

"Well, *obviously*," said Dusk. "Everyone knew you two would eventually cross the Passive Persons' Rubicon of Love, and it's too bad it took so long, but you have a duty to me, your best friend and supervisor, to keep me abreast of developments. Sorry to use the word *breast*. It will probably inflame the two of you."

"It's only been about twelve hours," said Neil. "We are still getting used to the idea."

And then he did something incredible. Incredibler?

He took my hand and kissed it. Then he took Dusk's hand and kissed it. And then he let hers go and kept mine, warm and safe, nestled inside his.

"I love you both. But not like Prema loves Luke and Tony. I'll let Norm tell that part."

"What?" said Dusk. "Oh, my God. You two have done a double holdback on me?"

"Sorry," I said. "Things got away from me. There's more . . ."

I thought about whether to tell her about my sister and what I did and didn't know. I thought about how kind Dusk was being, inside her narrow emotional ability, about Neil and me.

And then I decided that I would tell both of my best friends and fellow Truth Commissioners everything.

"Prema loves both of her men. And she's decided to keep both of them."

"Threesome?" breathed Dusk. "No!"

"Yes," I said. "She told me."

"Have you seen the three of them? The perfection of it? I mean, if you're into aerobic fitness, it doesn't get any better."

"Aerobic fitness isn't really my thing," I said. "But I'll take your word for it."

Neil squeezed my hand.

"Would you look at that," said Dusk, who misses nothing. "I should be icked out, but I feel all warm and maternal about you two. Maybe I should have a kid. Two kids. Not like *Flowers in the Attic* kids, but regular ones."

"Finish stuffing your shrew first," said Neil. "Then decide. Maybe the right shrew will be enough."

"I think you should stick with the shrew," I agreed. "Less work. Easier to look after."

"And better for the old GPA," said Dusk. "Not that I will give my parents the satisfaction of thinking about that."

"The other thing we need to talk about is, ah, my personal . . . situation."

"You mean with World's Finest Catch here?" said Dusk. That made Neil grin, which made me grin. We were all being so amazing in that moment. I loved us very much.

"It's about my sister," I said.

Dusk stopped smiling.

If the first rule of Fight Club was to not talk about Fight Club, the first rule of being friends with me was not talking about my sister. Dusk and Neil had picked up on that instinctively. They'd grazed the situation lightly once or twice when we first started hanging out, but after that they'd never mentioned Keira again. They'd never asked me what it felt like to be indirectly famous (infamous) as a result of my sister's comics. They'd never asked what Keira was like or what it was like to live in our home. They'd spent our entire friendship respecting my privacy. That's why I'm pretty sure Dusk stopped breathing when I told her how Keira'd come home from college and started telling me about her teacher. I told Dusk everything I'd told Neil the night before.

The bell rang. I kept talking. The bell rang again. I talked. The first song on the playlist came back on.

When I finished, the three of us sat in exhausted silence.

"Huh," said Dusk. "I'm not sure what to feel outraged about first."

"Place mats," I said. "Eating off my own face. Let's start there."

Then we all cracked up. We laughed until we cried. We held hands.

"At the risk of sounding like Prema and her boys, I feel so much better now that it's all out in the open," I said.

"We'll help any way we can," said Neil. "Or we'll just support you, if that's what you want."

"Truth Commission, at your service," said Dusk.

The answer came to me.

"First order of business. I want to see my sister's new place. I want to know what she bought with her money."

And just like that, the truth changed everything.

But Officer, We're Art Students

Truth aftermaths continued to unfurl all over school like trees coming into leaf. Mrs. Dekker telegraphed her moods with her choice of outfits: if she had on her poncho—beware; if she was in her sundress—draw near. Aimee continued to text Neil every hour or two. She was so caught up in her relentless confessions, she didn't even notice me when she approached him in the hall to complain that he wasn't responding. Neil was holding my hand, so her oversight was egregious.

"Aimee? This is Normandy."

"Oh, hey," said Aimee, not looking at me. "Look, is everything okay with you? Since last night I've sent you at least five texts and I'm just getting this feeling like you're not that interested and I hope that's not true because frankly, I'm extremely interested and thinking about getting more work done and this is a demanding time for me right now and—"

She continued in this vein for a while. I tuned out and took back my hand so Neil could deal with her. I thought about what I should—scratch that—what *we* should do now that we were going to look into the situation with my sister. The *we-ness* of the plan gave me strength. If it had just been me, I would probably have kept my eyes shut and hoped things would just resolve themselves.

But now that Dusk and Neil were on board, I wouldn't be allowed to retreat.

I wrote down the To Dos in a fresh new notebook:

> 1. Figure out where Keira's new place is and why she hasn't told us about it.
> 2. Investigate the teacher who assaulted my sister and turned her life upside down.
> 3. Convince Keira to bring charges if that will help the healing process.
> 4. ~~When she is feeling more stable, tell her how I feel about being in her comics.~~
> 4a. ~~If that goes well, ask her to consider killing off my character.~~ [100]

In history class, where half the people were talking about treaties and the government's dirty dealings with First Nations, and the other half were drawing historically inaccurate pictures of voyageurs, cowboys, and aliens locked in mortal combat, I noticed Lisette DeVries joyously putting up her hand and correctly answering every question. Her knowledge of Canadian indigenous history was encyclopedic. And massively impressive. A twinge of regret about my Facebook message pinged through me, and I hoped again it hadn't gone through.

It was one thing to ask the truth of people who wanted to tell it. It was something else entirely to pry the truth out

---

100. You will notice, Ms. Fowler, that the last points are crossed out. That's because I was not ready to go there.

of liars, delusionals, and sweetly committed pretenders who weren't hurting anyone with their delusions.

The only time I really focused on the task at hand was in creative writing.[101] Ms. Fowler had us answer all these questions about the protagonist of the last story we wrote. We were supposed to know the following: Who is this character? What does she/he want? Why does she want it? How does she go about getting it? What gets in the way? Does she succeed or fail?

Needless to say, I had no idea how to answer the questions. Why did my character want to have a top-quality compost? Good question. I'm pretty sure the answer wasn't supposed to be "Because it would be cool." I wasn't even sure I could answer those questions about myself.

So I was intellectually engaged during that class, and I figured out that in my fiction I am embarrassingly transparent, psychologically speaking. Or fertile. Or a stinking

---

101. Sorry to be weirdly self-referential but this feels relevant. If you're a footnote skipper, this would be a good one to skip.

   Anyway, my story was about a girl who is trying to create a top-notch compost. It was sort of a horror story. In the story, too many people donate their scraps, and pretty soon the compost pile gets overwhelmed and nothing really breaks down. Instead, it starts to rot and stink. Then a strange man comes along and tells the girl that composts need straw and dirt and things like that. He also gives her a mysterious powder and tells her to sprinkle it on the pile. It's like "Jack and the Beanstalk," only with composting powder. She does so, and suddenly the compost pile becomes superefficient and hot. It's a solid mass of worms and they turn out soil so rich and powerful that people come from all over town to get a bucketful. But the compost needs to be fed constantly, and one day the man puts a hand in to turn over a large savoy cabbage, and the compost pulls him in. The end.

mess. Depends which way you look at it. And for some reason that felt okay.

When the bell rang, I met Dusk and Neil out front and we walked toward Nancy. The autumn air smelled of wood smoke. The leafless trees looked like charcoal etchings against the light gray sky. The three of us stopped when we saw an old Bronco pull into the parking lot. Luke and Tony, the two elite Nordic skiers, sat in the front. Prema ran out of the school, clutching a portfolio, a gym bag, and what appeared to be a small loom. She ran toward the Bronco, an expression of what can only be described as pure, two-boy-loving joy on her face. Luke, every bit as lean and agile as Prema, jumped out, threw open the back passenger door, took the loom and other things from her, put them inside. Then she *kissed Luke* (on the cheek, but still! Exciting!) and jumped into the front seat. He got in after her. He sat there while she *kissed Tony* (also on the cheek. I should admit for the purposes of accuracy that I can't tell Tony from Luke, but I am almost entirely certain that one of them was Tony and the other one was Luke). Then they drove off looking fit, competitive, and unstressed.

"Holy man," said Dusk.

"Truth Commission has set off a wave of whatever it's called when a woman has two husbands," said Neil.

We shook our heads in unison, looking a little polygynous ourselves.[102]

---

102. There are a surprising number of ways human love arrangements can be organized: polygamy, polyandry, polygyny, polyamory. . . . Lot of polys to choose from.

While Nancy's engine whirred and ground and gasped to life, Dusk asked Neil if there was any update from Tyler.

"He waved when I saw him heading to his pod this morning. Said he'd be in touch soon. Said he's been thinking."

"We don't want him *thinking*. We want him telling us the truth," said Dusk. "We want to know if a single female Truth Commissioner with a thing for old shoes has a shot."

"Even if he's outer far gay on the sexual continuum, I'm sure he'd consider it," said Neil reassuringly.

"Aw, thanks," said Dusk.

Their banter was soothing, but my nerve endings still felt electrified at the prospect of invading my sister's privacy. You'd think there was a shock collar around my neck the way every part of me cringed at the idea of doing something Keira wouldn't like.

Walking down Fear Street has never been a favorite activity of mine. I'm more of a noticing Fear Street and then ducking down Oblivion Avenue sort of person.

I didn't say any of this to Dusk and Neil. My guess is that they knew.

"So we're looking for her police car?" said Dusk.

"It's not actually a police car. It just looks like one. It's a white Crown Vic."

"Norm? Should we use another vehicle? Nancy's kind of distinctive," said Neil.

"Plus, there's the breakdown factor. Which is fun when we're heading for school, but if we're in hot pursuit or something, it could be a problem," added Dusk. "My car is one of several thousand Honda Civics in the north end alone. The top person at the CIA wouldn't be able to spot my car."

I drove us to Dusk's, and we switched into her car. My

passivity might not make me a very good character in fiction,[103] but it made me feel very warm and supported as a person. Having Dusk drive also left me free to watch other vehicles. We drove past my house. Keira's car wasn't in the driveway.

"So," said Dusk, as we headed downtown. "Where do famous graphic novelists hang out when they disappear?"

"Her agent said something about a new place," I said. And each word felt like a stabbing betrayal of my sister's privacy, and also like I was becoming pretty good with a knife.

"What kind of accommodations would she like?" asked Neil.

I thought. What kind of place *would* my sister like? She was a creature of retro vehicles, minimalist clothing, custom furniture, and closets. "I don't know," I said finally. Honestly. "It's hard to say."

"No problem," said Dusk, seeming to understand that it felt sad to admit that. "We'll just drive."

XXXXX

That afternoon we drove aimlessly around the Brooks Landing area, which doesn't seem that big until you start looking for a specific car parked somewhere in or around one of the many apartment buildings, town houses, and motels.

At first, Dusk just slowed as we passed the many

---

103. Good fictional characters are supposed to make things happen.

apartment buildings, most of which were three or four stories. They tended to be clustered near one another, so we
cruised the block like gangsters seeking drive-by opportunities. People on the sidewalk stared suspiciously. The
pedestrians were mostly women over sixty-five, so they
didn't seem like a threat.

"You know," said Neil. "Most of these places probably
have residents' parking in back."

"Or underground," mused Dusk.

I'd been thinking the same thing and hadn't mentioned
it. Why not? I guess there was part of me hanging back.
Ready to call it a day after a solidly cursory effort. I like to
think the ability to sometimes do things in a halfhearted
way is part of my charm. It's definitely part of what makes
me different from my sister.

"We're going to have to be more methodical," I said
reluctantly.

"We'll take turns," said Neil. "Dusk, you pull over near
the building. Norm and I will get out and check front and
back."

"Yeah," I said with no enthusiasm.

So we did that until someone called the police.

Turned out there were some limits to how honest we as
Truth Commissioners were willing to be.

The patrol car was parked behind Dusk's when Neil
and I emerged from the alley where we'd been checking the
parking lots of identical salmon-colored stucco buildings.

The officer, who stood between Dusk's Civic and his
vehicle, watched us emerge. His right hand was at his hip.
Not in an "I'm about to shoot you" way. More like a "Great.
What now?" way.

He was attempting to keep us all in sight at once, and the effort was costing him.

I froze. Was I supposed to put my hands over my head, or lie facedown on the crispy brown lawn? I felt an instant and absolute sympathy for anyone who had ever been arrested.

Neil, however, was unconcerned. His father is a wheeler-dealer, after all. Perhaps the ability to speak extemporaneously to just about anyone on just about any topic is genetic.

"Officer," he said. "How goes it this afternoon? Can we help you?"

The officer sighed and I calmed down enough to see past the uniform. He was probably in his mid- to late twenties, but had adopted the exhausted air of a seasoned detective who'd been working the hard streets of Chicago or Detroit for thirty-plus years and was counting the days until he could retire to his fishing cabin. The attitude was an odd fit with his R&B boy-band looks, complete with carefully shaped hair and brown skin as smooth as a cherub's butt.

"What's going on, kids?"

"We're just looking for someone," said Neil. "We can't remember where she lives, so we're checking cars."

"We've had three calls on you. Reports of kids behaving suspiciously."

Neil laughed. "Do we look suspicious?"

The cop tilted his head. He really should have been inflaming teenagers with his sultry crooner-ness, rather than rousting them. "Yeah. You kind of do," he said.

Dusk got out of the car, and the cop held up a hand to indicate she should get back inside. But before he did so, he did the requisite double take. Nothing new there. No amount[104] of peculiar fashion could hide the beauty of the Dusk, not even a shiny purple jumpsuit.

"Please stay in the car," he told her. When she got back in, he continued to stare at the place where she'd been, as though she'd left behind an afterimage.

The cop shook his head briefly. "Yes," he repeated. "You do look suspicious."

I thought we looked like art students, but to the untrained eye we probably looked like people who had been abducted by aliens on their way to prom in 1985 and spit out again in 2012.

"I promise you, Officer," said Neil. "We are as pure as the driven snow."

I wondered if it was a good idea to mention snow, because that is well known to be a code name for cocaine and maybe it would get the cop even more suspicious.

"Names?" asked the officer, who'd moved to stand by the driver's-side window.

"Dawn Weintraub-Lee," said Dusk.

"Neil Sutton," said Neil.

"Normandy Pale."

"I'd like to take a look in your car," said the cop. "You two stay where I can see you."

----

104. Correct use of "amount"? God, it really feels like the only time one can safely use that word is when writing about sums. Too bad.

He glanced at Dusk and then into the front and back-seats. Our portfolios and bags were piled in the backseat.

"I'm going to need to take a look in those," he said.

I could only see the back of Dusk's head, but I could guess the expression on her face.

"Officer, we're art students," said Neil.

"Oh, yeah? You go to Green Pastures?" he asked.

"That's right," said Neil, becoming animated. "Do you know about it?" Like all socially gifted people, he's always looking for shared experiences and knowledge.

"I have a nephew who goes there," said the officer.

"We probably know him!" Neil was so pleased, you'd have thought we were having this conversation on the out-skirts of Iceland's most remote village rather than one mile from Green Pastures.

"You can open those up and I'll just have a look." He stood back while I leaned in and opened the portfolios and project boxes.

"What's your name, Officer?" asked Neil. "If you don't mind my asking."

"Jones," said the cop, tapping his name badge.

"Are you Tyler Jones's uncle?" Dusk exclaimed.

The officer had obviously concluded that we were not members of the Mexican Sinaloa Cartel and so it was safe to give us a bit of personal information.

"My sister's kid. He's a great artist." Officer Jones shone his flashlight into the bags, pausing on one of my embroi-deries, stretched on the frame.

"What's this?" he asked.

"You can pick it up if you want," I said.

He lifted it out. "Wow. This is made by sewing?"

"Stitching," I said.

"That's unbelievable. The detail. You'd never think you could make something so realistic with thread."

He put the frame down, and shone the light into Dusk's workbox, which she'd pulled out of her medical bag. Inside were some of the tiny furniture and accessories for the taxidermied shrew's mobile home. There was a tiny flat-screen TV showing a soap opera, a minuscule can of Raid, a mini tray of Shake 'n Bake chicken, and a light blue sectional sofa.

"What's all this?"

"It's stuff I'm fabricating for a tabletop installation," said Dusk.

Don't mention the dead shrews, I silently urged her. *Do not mention the shrews.*

She didn't. I'm not sure what the law enforcement perspective is on small-scale taxidermy, but I didn't want to find out.

He picked up a tiny book that was going to sit on the shrew's glass-topped coffee table.

"Go ahead," said Dusk. "It's a photo album." She helpfully handed him a magnifying glass.

His movements were almost reverential as he pulled it out. The album is one of my favorite of Dusk's creations. It's three by one and a half inches, with scaled snapshots of shrews inside acetate sheets.

He brought the book close to his face and then held the magnifying glass over it.

"Huh," he said, and shook his head as he put the photo album back in its slot in her workbox. "Are those rats?"

"Shrews," said Dusk.

He had her unfurl her flexible knife case and shook his head again at the scalpels and other instruments. I guess there's no law against taxidermy tools.

"So you make embroidery," he said, looking at me. "And you make really small things." Pointing at Dusk. "What about you?" he asked Neil.

"Neil makes paintings," I put in. "Plus, he's interested in film. And podcasting."

"Norm's an amazing writer, too," added Dusk.

Officer Jones seemed to remember himself. "No drugs in here? No stolen goods?"

"No, sir," said Neil. "Just art."

The officer gave his head another shake, seemingly overtaken by wonder. "So is this the kind of thing Tyler's doing?" he asked. "He never talks about what he does at school."

"Tyler's very talented," said Dusk.

"And closed mouthed," said Neil.

"Our whole family's artistic," said the cop. "If G. P. Academy had been around when I was a kid maybe I'd have gone there. I love watercolors."

"You know what would be cool?" said Dusk to the officer. "A watercolor series focused on crime. You know, watercolors of jail cells. Watercolors of cop bars. Like Edward Hopper–type stuff, but harsher."

"I prefer Andrew Wyeth," said Neil. "Ms. Choo is going to teach us dry-brush techniques later this term."

"Wyeth would have made badass crime paintings," said Dusk.

It was such a good idea that we were all nodding by the time she finished speaking, the officer most vigorously of all. "Yeah. Nontraditional subjects. I've felt ready to move out of flowers and trees for a while now."

"Oh, my God, it would be so cool," said Dusk.

Office Jones looked like he wanted nothing more than to sit cross-legged on the lawn of the apartment building and talk about art. But something brought him back to his responsibilities. Perhaps it was a glance down at his shiny black shoes.

"Okay. Well, I think you better find another way to find your friend. You can't keep creeping all over private property and staring into people's vehicles."

That hadn't been exactly what we were doing, but I didn't want to say that because the officer was a frustrated watercolorist and probably a bit sensitive and tortured. Maybe I could tell the truth. It was getting to be such a habit.

"We're actually looking for my sister," I said.

That got his attention.

"She has been, uh, going missing. I think she might be in an apartment around here."

"An apartment," he repeated. "That's all you've got to go on?"

"It's kind of a complicated story," said Neil, and I could sense him feeling protective of me.

"Is that right?" Now the cop sounded like he'd never even seen a watercolor, much less painted one.

"My sister's always been very . . . private. Since she got back from college, she's started disappearing. I'm just kind of worried about her."

Neil looked at me. Dusk, who'd gotten out of the car while the cop was examining the art, looked at me. And I thought, *Screw it.*

"My sister's name is Keira Pale. She's a graphic novelist. You might have heard of her."

Something passed across Officer Jones's face.

Even people in this town who don't read comic books or graphic novels know my sister. Along with the jazz singer Diana Krall, she's the most famous person the place has produced. So far.

"She might have bought an apartment. Or a house. We don't know. I just want to be sure she's okay."

Neil and Dusk nodded.

Again, something moved behind the cop's eyes, and I felt my stomach clench in response.

For a long moment, he seemed to consider. Then he said, "Why don't you give me your number. If I hear anything, I'll call."

"Are you allowed to do that?"

"I'm not making any promises. Just tell me how to get in touch with you."

"Okay." Neil handed me the prescription pad and I wrote down my cell phone number and handed it to the cop, who frowned.

"Really? A scrip pad? Really?" he said.

"It's okay. It's discontinued," said Dusk.

He sighed. "I'm Ed Jones."

We introduced ourselves again, this time by first names only.

"Does that school of yours hold classes for older folks? Like night school?"

"Sure," I said. "Or we can talk to our watercolor instructor. See where else she teaches."

"Also, you're not older," said Dusk. "At least not much."

"Thank you. I appreciate that. All right then. Good luck to you all. And stop sneaking around." He smiled at us like he couldn't help himself.

"Thanks," we said.

We stood on the sidewalk and waved as he got in his patrol car and drove away.

"He knows something," I said. "About Keira."

Neil and Dusk nodded.

"So how do we find out what it is?" asked Dusk.

"We told him the truth. Now we just have to wait."

"If he doesn't do those crime watercolors, I'm going to have to do them, Wyeth-style," said Neil as we got back in Dusk's little Civic.

Mouth Breathing Is an Interest of Mine

After Dusk dropped me off, I decided that I'd go crazy if I had to sit around waiting for Officer Jones to call or for my sister to show up so we could tail her. In the meantime, I could investigate her teacher. Waiting for her to seek help or report him herself wasn't working.

I logged on to my Facebook and sent a message to Roberta Brown Heller II, she of the snarly attitude.

A little number one appeared above my Messages box.

> Hey, Pretend Sister. What a surprise to hear from you again.

> I just want to ask you something. Straight out. Just gearing up . . .

> . . . ??

> Still waiting. Maybe you need to grease those gears. I have a lot to do.

> Well, I wasn't completely honest with you about my sister. About the surprise party.

> Wow. What a devastating shock.

I ignored her and continued. My hands shook a little as I typed, and I had to keep going back and fixing typos.

> The part about her being different since she returned from school is true. The thing is . . . she's been telling me some things. Extremely bad things. About something that happened there. I don't know who to talk to about it.

> At risk of sounding like an asshole, why don't you talk to your sister?

> That's just it. Our talks aren't really helping her. At least, I don't think they are. And she doesn't

It had taken me ages to summon the courage to say that much, and then I bumped the mouse and the incomplete message was sent.

"Shit," I muttered.

> She doesn't what?

> She doesn't answer questions. Usually.

> You've lost me. You're concerned about your sister because she's telling you things about her time here. But you can't ask her any questions about it? That's highlyly screwed up.

> Correction: *highly*

It's complicated.

> God help me. You need to get off Facebook immediately if you're using that phrase.

It was time to plunge in. Keira had sworn me not to tell, but I had to. For both our sakes. I let out a long, thin breath.

My sister told me a lot of disturbing things about a teacher. At your school. I'm just really concerned that what happened to her is going to happen to someone else.

There was a minute, two-minute, three-minute pause before the message blinked again.

It occurred to me that Facebook was about the least secure platform to have this conversation. This was way too volatile to get into specifics.

> Go on.

Look, can I call you? I'm not comfortable writing this here.

Another long pause from her.

> Okay.

Then Roberta Heller II messaged me her digits and I

took out my crappy pay-and-talk cell phone and prayed I had enough minutes to get through a short conversation. Then again, I also prayed that I didn't have enough minutes because I was starting to get scared again and wished I'd just minded my own business.

After I dialed and waited for the phone to ring on the other end, I thought I could hear the sunny, dirty sound of California in the slight static. Probably just my imagination.

Roberta picked up before the first ring finished.

"Talk," she said.

"It's Normandy Pale," I said.

"I know who you are. I've looked you up. I know that Keira has a sister called Normandy Pale. I've even seen some of your work on your school's website. Holy shit. I had no idea a person could do that with embroidery. Chuck Close's tapestries are the closest thing I can think of."

Predictably, I felt a flush of pleasure. You could seriously get me to do or say just about anything if you gave me a few compliments first.

"Your whole school seems pretty cool. I had no idea there were schools like that up there in Canada."

"We're lucky," I said because it was true.

"Artistic family," she said. "Do your parents make stuff, too?"

"My dad used to do World War dioramas and whatnot." She'd probably seen his work satirized in the Chronicles, but politely didn't mention it. "And apparently we had an uncle who was a carver."

"Huh," said Roberta.

"Anyway, I'm hoping that what we talk about here can remain private."

"You don't know me," said Roberta. "Why would you assume I'm trustworthy? Is it because you're Canadian? You clearly aren't from Texas. A girl from the Big Hair state would never make that mistake."

"You're from Texas?" I asked.

"Connecticut," she said.

Roberta Heller's rapid changes of topic reminded me of Dusk, and I felt strangely comforted.

"It's just a request."

"I can't promise anything. We've had some bad things happen around here in the recent months. It's only now starting to feel like we might be able to get past it."

"What kind of things?" I asked.

"You called me," said Roberta Heller II.

I heard my breath whistle through my nose and into the receiver.

"Are you a mouth breather?" asked Roberta. "Because that's an interest of mine. One of my housemates is a chronic mouth breather. It gives him a distinctive audible style."

"Not usually," I said. *Come on, phone,* I silently urged. *Run out of minutes already.*

"Okay. Enough pleasant chitchat and social warm-ups," said Roberta. "What's up? What's your sister been telling you about our edumacators here at CIAD?" She pronounced it "*See*-yad."

"My sister told me that a teacher at the school was bothering her."

"With worshipful feelings of adoration?" asked Roberta.

"No. Like being too intimate with her. Then he did . . . worse."

"Wait. Which teacher?" demanded Heller II.

Something stopped me from telling her his name. Just in case. Just in case what, I didn't know. "She just said that he was really young. And that they hung out and went hiking."

"No," she said. "That's not right." Now it was Roberta Heller II's turn to breathe windily into the receiver. "When we lost the two of them so close together, it was like . . . part of the program died. All that talent just: poof. Gone. But it was unrelated."

"What do you mean, 'lost the two of them'?" I took a deep breath. "My sister said he assaulted her. That they went hiking and he"—I couldn't bring myself to say the actual word. It was too irrevocable—"assaulted her."

The receiver went silent as though Heller II stopped breathing. "*What?* No. No. All you need to know about—"

The automatic pay-and-talk operator took that moment to interrupt the call.

"No," I said. "Look, I'll get some minutes and call you back." But the line was already dead.

This was an emergency. I would use our home phone. The excuse for a long-distance call to California would occur to me later.

I slipped out of my room and found my mom on the couch, quilt over the knees, feet up on the peeling fake leather ottoman, large mug of coffee at her side. I could tell she was on the line with my aunt who lives in Alberta, and that it would be a long one.

I would Skype Roberta Heller! Except that wouldn't work, because when Skype actually allowed me to log on (a rarity), it usually froze up about thirty seconds into the conversation.

Facebook.. I would let RH II know that I was just

running out to get some minutes on my phone and I would call her back.

With a heart going like bongos, I hustled back into my room and opened Facebook. There was a message.

> There is some mistake here. This doesn't make sense. I'm going to find something and send it to you. Let you draw your own conclusions.

My fingers flew as I thumped in a reply.

> Thanks. Please don't tell anyone I talked to you.

I sent the message and slowly closed my laptop.

Montecore, the Well-Intentioned Tiger

We spent a few hours looking for my sister on Saturday and Sunday, but we didn't find her and she didn't come home.

Persons who are in high school are not supposed to have multiple dramas unfolding in their lives at the same time. The results of the history test or the specific challenges of the math 11 curriculum are drama enough. Then there's the whole friend management and extracurricular scene. But that's never the whole story, is it? Well, maybe it is if you've got Tiger parents like Dusk's. They would happily shut down every aspect of her life that wasn't directly related to academic achievement. Dusk's particular temperament has turned her poor parents into Montecore.[105]

---

105. Montecore is the name of the white tiger who bit into Roy of Siegfried & Roy in Las Vegas. Apparently Roy wasn't feeling very well, and Montecore was a hardcore codependent and he decided to drag Roy offstage by the scruff of his neck. Only Roy didn't have a scruff and was badly injured. Hence the perils of Tiger parenting: not a good fit for every offspring. Almost makes me glad my parents are more like ostriches than tigers. Now that I think about it, a person could do worse than kangaroo parents. Never mind.

What I'm trying to say, in a painfully roundabout way, is that life is not always compatible with high school, even an art-focused high school, where all students are encouraged to (safely) explore as much of life as possible in order to bring more fuel to their art.

Even before I'd fully committed to the Truth Commission, my academic performance had been adversely affected by the demands of living with a superspecial snowflake, as well as by the demands of the Truth Commission's relentless pursuits of truth. I wasn't writing as much as usual, I was getting low marks on core subjects, and my embroidery series was not going well. Add a new investigation into Kiera's whereabouts, and my ability to cope started to slip away.[106]

If there's one thing we learn at Green Pastures, other than the fact that in some cases art can pay very well, it's that there is help available to us if we get overwhelmed. As art students, we are presumed to have few practical life skills and to be less stable overall. Casual observation would suggest that this is a safe assessment. My guess is that fully 20 to 25 percent of the student population at G. P. is in tears at any given time. The figure would be even higher at a high school for the performing arts. You know how singers and dancers are.

At G. P., students get upset over a) ambition outstripping ability; b) lack of sleep; c) sexual and drug experimentation

---

106. This was the point at which I went to your office and had that little meltdown. Sorry. And thanks. You are a very good guidance counselor as well as an outstanding teacher of writing.

done in an effort to prove oneself talented. Of course, sex and drugs done strictly as an artistic affectation are just as powerful as they are if you do them with the purpose of getting loaded. It's a painful lesson that must be learned by every art student who assumes that if they wear ironic hats, surely they should be able to have ironic sex and do ironic drugs. There's a reason the Truth Commission was born in an art school.

Anyway, after I went to see the excellently empathetic and kind counselor/creative writing teacher and she helped me get extensions on several projects and taught me some breathing exercises and other calming techniques,[107] she suggested that I might want to remember that all trouble is grist for a writer's mill, I felt better. We even chatted briefly about my writing something for my Spring Special Project[108] (instead of doing embroidery) and I told her a little bit about what was going on, but avoided giving any specifics. When our appointment was over, I emerged to find Zinnia and another student in the waiting room.

Ms. Fowler followed me out.

"Zinnia?" she said.

"Hi, Ms. F. I'm looking for a drop-in appointment. If you've got one."

"Of course. I can take you next. Just wait here."

Then Ms. Fowler and the other student, a freshman, disappeared into the office.

-- -- -- -- -- -- -- -- -- -- -- -- -- -- --

107. I will do my best to "unpeel" my tongue from the roof of my mouth.

108. Which turned into this here piece of creative nonfiction. Such an excellent idea on your part, Ms. Fowler!

"Hey," I said, having burned through all my eloquence during my appointment.

There is a white-noise machine in the office, so I knew Zinnia hadn't heard what we'd talked about, but it was embarrassing enough that I'd been in the guidance office.

I sat beside Zinnia in one of the fabric-covered chairs stained with the tears of a hundred distraught art students. The waiting room wasn't very big, but Ms. Fowler had made it pretty with lots of delicate paper mobiles and quotes and poems that weren't stupid but rather thoughtful and sensitive.

"Chairs are pretty comfortable," I said.

Zinnia nodded her head, which in profile looked enormous because she'd tucked her abundant hair and perhaps someone else's entire head into a crocheted hat.

"Are you here because of our questions?" I asked.

"You sped it up," she said. "I'd been avoiding the truth for a long time. Taking it on. My bra is not the reason my sister got bullied. And that bullshit with the webcam and the morons in her school isn't the whole story. She could have come to this school. But she didn't want to."

I nodded. Questions tumbled through my brain. How *was* a person supposed to figure out her sister? Learn to live with her, no matter what?

"Also, I didn't tell you guys the complete truth."

That got my attention.

"I told you most of the truth. But not all."

I waited.

"After the bullying thing, maybe even before, my sister was getting into some high-risk stuff."

I visualized the white noise tumbling out of the machine.

"Getting high. Hanging around with the wrong people. A few of the girls in her school were already mad at her. Something happened with some other girl's boyfriend. Stupid shit went down at parties. I wanted to blame everything on those people who picked on her. But the story is more complicated than that."

"So you're saying she was partly to blame?"

"No. See, that's not it, either. No one deserves what happened to my sister. But it's not all good and evil and straightforward like that. The situation was a mess. It's way easier when you have someone to blame. We want a victim and a villain and a simple story and for everyone to play their role."

I wasn't quite sure what Zinnia was telling me.

She saw my expression and continued. "Our brains put situations and people into categories because it's too much work to let things stay unclear. I know mine does. Messes are psychologically displeasing."

I nodded slowly. That much was true.

"I've been talking to my sister more since you guys asked me about what happened. Before that, we weren't talking at all. She hates my march. But she thought the riot was cool. She likes Edmonton. Likes living with my dad."

"That's good," I said.

"My art is so out of control right now," said Zinnia. "You wouldn't believe. Abstraction is the only thing that comes close to doing the job."

I felt sad at that, because Zinnia's hyperrealistic figurative work was so great.

"I love your stuff," I said.

She smiled and I thought that maybe her visits to the guidance counselor were working. Her face looked less pinched.

"I'm glad you and Dusk and Neil asked me the truth. You started a process that needed to happen. But you need to be careful with it. You know?"

Oh, did I know. I took a deep breath. "I asked myself some truths just recently. Then I asked some about my sister. And you're right. We need to be careful."

It was her turn to wait for me to continue.

I ran my hands along the edges of my big fake-leather portfolio. "My sister's not doing so great. I was the only one who knew. But I couldn't handle it. So now I'm asking for help. Because I don't know what else to do."

Zinnia nodded. "I wish I'd asked for help for me and my sister earlier. Can I do anything? For you?"

Sitting there in the white-noise waiting room with the paper mobiles twisting almost imperceptibly overhead, I sketched the outlines of the story. Told her that my sister had a trauma at school. That she kept disappearing. That we were looking for her new place. I described my sister's car.

Zinnia was a very active listener, nodding and agreeing. "My skater friends and I will look, too. But I won't tell any of the others whose car it is or why we're looking. They might know. Quite a few of them worship your sister."

Of course every skateboarder in town would worship her. So would every gamer and every illustrator and writer. As a cult comic-book artist, it was Keira's lot in life to be loved best by people who didn't know her.

"I think you're an amazing writer," said Zinnia. "That story you had in *Careless Whispers* last year shook me.[109] The illustrations rocked. Also, I love your stitching."

Warm feeling flooded me, and I let it.

"Sisters are hard," said Zinnia. "So are parents, friends, and teachers. Art's hard, and so is school. I'm just trying to be present for it all. Not to look away."

"Don't look away," I repeated softly, thinking that would make a good mantra for life.[110]

---

109. *Careless Whispers* is our school's literary and art journal. I wrote a modern retelling of "Catskin," which is one of my favorite fairy tales. It reminds me of those old John Hughes movies, only creepier and more violent.

110. Which reminds me, Ms. Fowler. I saw Mr. Wells in the store the other day. And he was with a woman. She had a bit of a wife look to her. Something about her pants. They were maternity fit. I don't know what's going on with you two. But I hope you weren't misled. I'm really sorry to do this in a footnote.

Discerning Pixels

When I met Neil and Dusk in the parking lot after school, there were other people there. Quite a few of them.

I slowed my pace, my keys dangling from my free hand, and tried to figure out what Aimee Danes, Zinnia McFarland, and Prema Hardwick were doing standing next to Nancy.

"We want to help," announced Aimee, to whom I'd never spoken directly.

"I'm missing a workout because I think this is important," said Prema.

I looked from Neil to Dusk and I couldn't decide whether to feel betrayed or not.

There was a shuffling noise behind me, and I saw Brian Forbes emerge from between two cars. He looked marginally better. Not been-through-rehab-and-reborn-into-a-clean-and-sober-lifestyle better, but like he'd at least eaten in the last day or so. I had a brief, disorienting moment of wondering when Mrs. Dekker or the gorgeous Tyler Jones would show up.

Brian nodded and smiled his sad, wry smile.

"Look, as a result of your very direct questions, we have a bond. Like it or not. And information has to flow both ways," said Aimee, who obviously had hidden depths that were going to make her a terrific reporter. "I know I've been leaning on Neil pretty heavily for the past while. I want to give back. If not to him, then to his girlfriend."

I was startled to hear myself described that way, and I felt stripped bare that all these people knew things about me. Private things about my life and my family. Then again, I was hardly in a position to protest.

"We don't know any specifics," said Prema. "We just know you're looking for a car. We're going to help you look. We won't say anything about it."

"You kept my secrets," added Zinnia. "Or you would have, if I hadn't told them to everyone during a public action."

"My secrets are staying safe with the professionals," said Brian. Which was funny, because his secrets were etched into every line of his face and in the set of his shoulders.

"I hope it's okay," said Dusk, for once cautious and considerate.

"It's fine," I said. "Thank you."

Neil described my sister's white Crown Victoria. "Has she come home yet?" he asked me.

For obvious reasons, I couldn't call and ask my dad if Keira had returned while I was at school. "I'll swing by and check."

"Call us when you know, and we'll start looking," said the truthers.

"Four of us can go in my car," said Aimee. Which was a good thing, because Zinnia rode a crappy bike and Brian's mode of transport was his feet. Prema might have had a car, but I'd never seen it because her two boyfriends usually chauffeured her around.

My mind boggled at what the four of them would talk

about as they cruised the mean streets of Nanaimo looking
for my sister's Crown Vic.

"Okay, well, thank you all very much," I said inadequately.

Then, suddenly, we were all doing these spontaneous
bonding handshakes: half gang members greeting each
other, half secret order of the Masons. Short grip, half hug
and some finger flapping. And here's an embarrassing thing:
my eyes welled up. I was turning into an easy weeper.

"You want me to drive?" Dusk asked. Brian and Prema
and Zinnia headed for Aimee's gleaming wine-colored
BMW, like lost members of *The Breakfast Club*.

I nodded.

She climbed in behind Nancy's steering wheel, and Neil
got in the middle and I sat in the passenger seat. Neil and I
didn't hold hands or snuggle, because sometimes you need
to lay off that stuff around your friends.

Dusk drove, and I stared out the window and tried not
to think. I'd spent what felt like my entire life not talking
about my sister. Not talking about how it felt to be portrayed
as an inconsequential, helpless blob in her comics, how it felt
to have to work around her moods and whims, how it felt
to admire her so much even though I kind of hated her at
the same time. I hadn't talked about how much of a struggle
it was to make sure nothing I did stressed out my overburdened parents, who always seemed poised on the razor's
edge between catastrophic disappointment and long-awaited
reward for their efforts. Now half the world knew there was
a problem at home. Well, half of *my* world anyway.

I'd betrayed my sister's confidence. Where was that
piece of knowledge going to fit into the strange stew of pride

and resentment and fear and insecurity that bubbled in me every time I thought of her? And how would she react when she found out? Maybe getting to the bottom of her situation would help us. We'd get closer. Be more honest with each other.

As though he could read my thoughts, Neil bumped my shoulder, which I interpreted to mean that everything would be fine.

My sister's car wasn't in the driveway. She hadn't been home for over a week. My parents were half-dead with anxiety, and still they never breathed a word about it to each other or to me.

Dusk kept Nancy idling. No easy feat.

"So now we go looking?" asked Dusk.

"I'm just going to go inside for a second," I said. "I need to check something."

Dusk turned off the engine and she and Neil settled in to wait.

There was no one home. Our modest house, with its short dark hallways, tired paint, uninspired furnishings (with the exception of the German art chair), rested.

I made my way to my bedroom and logged onto my laptop. Sure enough, there was a Facebook message from Roberta Heller II.

> I can't believe he did what she said he did, but read these and draw your own conclusions. Check these out.

This was followed by two links.

How did she know which teacher I meant? Also, I wasn't

ready to click through. Tracking down Keira was scary enough; I couldn't handle knowing the rest of the story right now.

Instead, I shut the computer and ran back outside, and Dusk drove us around in another fruitless search for three hours. Probably forty minutes was taken up with stalls, during which time we sat in companionable silence and no one asked any questions about how things got so screwed up in my family. Twice we spotted Aimee and the other truthers in her gleaming BMW. It made me feel like we were in a gang, but one that generated more confusion than profit.

We finally packed it in, and dropped off Neil at around seven p.m. He gave me a kiss before he got out, and Dusk said, "Awww." Then we went to Shoppers Drug Mart to buy some minutes for my phone, and then to her house.

"We'll get her next time," Dusk said as she turned off the ignition. Realizing that sounded a little aggressive, she amended, "I mean, we'll find her. Get this sorted out."

I tried to see past the tightly packed houses to the lagoon beyond, but could only make out slivers of gray evening sea between them.

"Are you still okay with all this? Do you believe that figuring out the truth will help?" Dusk's face was made all the more serious by its haunting symmetry in the car's interior light.

"I hope so," I said. "Not knowing hasn't worked out so great. Then again, I don't know what I'm supposed to do when we find out what's going on. Where she's been staying."

"You'll know when the time comes," she said.

"You sure?"

Dusk looked into my eyes like someone trying to discern pixels on a high-definition television. "You really haven't spent much time in the real, have you?" Not a dig, not a judgment. A statement of fact.

"That's not the Pale way," I said.

"Once you know what's true for you, it'll all get clearer."

Only with Dusk could I have a conversation that was so vague and yet so completely clear. I thought about what it must take for her to disappoint her family every day in order to pursue her art. In order to be herself. The effort had made her a little bitter and sharp-edged, but there was no phony in Dusk, just like there is no lying in Tony Montana. (*Scarface* is another of Neil's favorite movies. He's all about the down and dirty.) But the Weintraub-Lees were strong. They weren't going to fall apart if one of their three kids turned into an artist. Dusk would probably be the biggest, best, and most successful artist imaginable, and all would be forgiven.

Pushing against expectations in a family that was held together by shreds of hope and strands of willful blindness was different. Riskier.

"I hope so," I said.

Dusk blew me a kiss. "I'm glad about you and Neil. He's a catch."

I blew the kiss back. When she was safely in her house, I drove back to my own.

Willing the World Right Side Up

I finally clicked on the links Roberta Heller II sent and I felt the world flip upside down.

In Memory of Jackson Reid, Animator and Award-Winning Instructor

With heavy hearts the CIAD community said good-bye to one of its most talented and beloved instructors on Thursday. Jackson Reid passed away March 24 in a tragic hiking accident.

He joined the CIAD faculty in 2010 when he was twenty-six years old. He'd established himself as an artist through his contributions to film, television, and graphic novels, including the blockbuster film *Zeus and the Small Ones* and his cult comic series, *Silt Gets in My Eyes*. He brought that same spirit of passion and innovation to his work with students.

His celebration of life was held at the Comica Galleria and was attended by his family, friends, students, and many of the most influential people in the animation and entertainment world.

Good-bye, J. R. You will be missed.

I stared at the article, which had been published in CIAD's online student newspaper.

He'd *died*. In a hiking accident. The article was accompanied by a photo of a man with a broad smile. His was the face I'd seen in my sister's drawings. He sat on the steps of a building, surrounded by students. They were all grinning. Except one.

I peered more closely.

My sister was in the third row. Her face was impassive in the shadow cast by a tall guy sitting in front of her.

It took me a minute or two to realize that I was barely breathing. I thought of the last drawing in her book. The one of the man falling.

The conclusion was too awful to consider. It was too awful to avoid. Had the teacher, this Jackson Reid person, jumped off a cliff because he felt bad about what he'd done to my sister? Has she *pushed him*?

Then I remembered Roberta's message. *I can't believe he did what she said he did.*

I clicked on the second link.

It was a clip from a cable newscast. The announcer, a polished young Asian-American woman, spoke into the camera.

"Today students and faculty from the California Institute of Art and Design held a celebration of life for well-known artist Jackson Reid.

"Fans and industry leaders crowded CIAD's theatre to say good-bye to popular instructor and top animation artist Jackson Reid. Gordon Holbeck, head of Animation Nation, told the capacity crowd that Reid was one of the most talented animators in California. CIAD President Marjorie Philiponi spoke about Reid's commitment to teaching.

"Jackson Reid is survived by his husband, Todd Gursky, an agent at William Morris Endeavor; his sister, Lindy; and his parents."

A wedding photo flashed on-screen of two men in suits with their arms around each other. Blue sky. White party tents. Flowers. One was Jackson Reid. The other, presumably, was his husband.

The announcer went on to show clips of Jackson Reid's work from film and television and screen shots of his books.

I could barely focus. *Husband?*

I clicked the windows closed and shut my computer. Then I let myself slide onto the floor and sat with my back against my bed, willing the world to straighten.

Explain That to a Non-Pale

I'm aware it's not groundbreaking news, but allow me to badly paraphrase a little writer I like to call Leo Tolstoy: all happy families are the same (boring) and all unhappy families are unique (and best viewed from the safe distance of fiction).[111] I would give Mr. Tolstoy the assist and add that all deeply weird and secretive families are baffling to outsiders.

It's nearly impossible to explain to a non-Pale how it is that none of us ever said anything to Keira about the fact that her entire fortune rested on our backs, since she turned us into comic-book characters. We never objected, which is sort of the same as agreeing.

How do members of families survive any number of strange situations? Usually, someone in the family knows the truth, but doesn't say anything. Sometimes, everyone is aware that little Gina has a drug problem and can't be trusted not to sell all the home electronics, but they hope she'll just grow out of it. Sometimes Dad comes home from work and confesses he accidentally slept with a

---

111. See the first line of *Anna Karenina*.

nineteen-year-old checkout girl, and then Mom and Dad tell the kids they're probably going to split up because of the affair. The kids don't know what an affair is, so Mom and Dad explain it. But then Dad gets a job in a new grocery store and never sees the girl again, and Mom acts hard done-by for the rest of her life, and life goes on. Families work around the fact that sometimes members hate each other and only stick around for the free food and shelter. Families are *too* adaptable, if you ask me.

That said, there was no way I could make myself forget what Keira had told me about her teacher. Why would a happily married *gay* man rape her? I know sexual assault is an act of violence rather than lust, but he didn't sound like a violent guy. What about the picture she'd drawn of him falling? I felt sick at the thought of what that might mean.

The last time I felt that awful was the morning five years ago when I saw the first panel that featured Diana's sister, Flounder. The illustration of the girl who was me but not me. I'd rushed to the bathroom mirror and stared at myself. And just as quickly looked away, because the Flounder's main character trait is that she stares all the time.[112] If you've read the Chronicles, images of Flounder staring, fish-eyed, in close-up will be etched into your mind. Reflected in her dull, wet gaze is all manner of

----

112. It's truly a mark of Keira's skill that she turned the most overused and boring action performed by fictional characters (staring/looking) into something totally fascinating and hilarious.

unpleasant refracted reality. Were my eyes really that bulgy? Did they really look like they'd migrated from elsewhere on my head? Was my affect that flat? Could I seriously not protect myself from people who meant me harm, even if they were 100 percent overt about their terrible intentions?

In the first Chronicle, Diana describes Flounder as being "like the worst pet imaginable." Adjectives used include "dim-witted," "charmless," and "barely house-trained." Diana tells the reader that Flounder has no redeeming qualities of wit or talent or personality. She's just this annoyance that everyone else has to stop themselves from kicking at when she drags herself underfoot.

Worse, the secrets that I'd shared with my sister were all there in the first Chronicle. Betrayals by peers. Fears. The boy I thought was cute who didn't notice me. Small things. Precious things. They all looked ridiculous on the page. It was the worst betrayal possible. And no one said anything—not even my parents, who should have. But, as I said, it's hard to explain all this to a non-Pale.

I am lucky enough to live in a small island town and go to an art school where everyone is too busy doing their own art to worry about how I'm represented in someone else's. The odd student has tried to do some meta-type stuff: i.e., use me in their art, but it never went anywhere. My guess is that Dusk fixed their wagons.

But in the larger world, I will always have a taint of the Flounder about me. My parents and I will continue to be profiled against our will on fan sites. My relationship with the truth will always be, as Holden Caulfield might have put it, "touchy as hell."[113]

Who knows how long I would have stared at my computer screen, absorbed in these thoughts, if the phone hadn't jangled loudly.

"Is this Normandy?" I recognized Brian's voice.

"Yes."

"You might want to check out the new row houses on Fitzwilliam. Near Prideaux. I think we found it. I talked to a guy."

"Is this Brian?"

"Meet you there."

The phone went dead.

I called Neil, who called Dusk. They pulled up twenty minutes later, and Dusk gave me a hug when she got out. She pushed the Mazda's passenger seat forward in order to get in the back.

"No, you don't need to do that," I said lamely. "Your legs are longer." But I got in the front seat anyway.

I felt like my voice was being projected from above, and that the light around us was being manufactured by a team of technicians to make it as unreal as possible.

"You okay?" asked Neil, and his voice seemed to be making its way across a great distance.

"Go to Fitzwilliam. Near Prideaux," I said.

---

113. As I write this story, I keep thinking about unreliable narrators. Art is always problematic, from a truth perspective even in a supposedly true story. You're always leaving something out and choosing to put something else in. I'm starting to think that pure truth is impossible, and that all narrators and all people are at least a little unreliable.

The sense of manufactured reality persisted until we turned onto Fitzwilliam and I saw it: a row of smart, two-story town houses with a high-end contemporary feel, thanks to red corrugated-tin siding and large windows and clean lines.

I knew instinctively we were in the right place. The other buildings on the short block were older heritage homes, Craftsman-style bungalows, and the like. My sister's taste for old things begins and ends with vehicles and barns and bikes. She's never been a big fan of old houses.

Neil sensed it, too. He slowed down and pulled over.

"I'll go check for her car," said Dusk.

I sat rigid in the front seat and leaned forward to let her out.

"It's okay," said Neil, taking my hand.

We watched Dusk trot down the sidewalk and behind the six connected houses, where the off-street parking was located. She was back almost immediately.

"She's here. At least, her car is."

Silence for a long beat.

"Norm? What do you want to do?" asked Neil.

Oceanic noises roared in my ears.

My friends waited.

Then things snapped into focus, the roaring stopped, and I came back to myself.

"We'll watch until she leaves. Then we'll go inside and see what she's been up to."

Each of My Nerves Is Having Its Own Nervous Breakdown

We waited until 1:00 in the morning. Then Neil's dad and Dusk's parents insisted they get home. Aimee Danes showed up in her BMW and I got in. Brian Forbes was in the backseat.

He handed forward a bag of sour Jujubes without a word.

Aimee Danes and Brian Forbes were good company. They did a little light bantering, but didn't get annoying or pushy. Clearly, they were each used to pulling all-nighters.

"This stressing you out?" Aimee asked.

I shrugged. "Numb" was the best description for how I felt.

"Each of my nerves is having its own nervous break-down," said Brian. "But that's standard."

Dusk came back a couple of hours before dawn.[114] Neil sat beside her. We'd texted throughout the night, so I knew they'd been awake almost as long as us, but they looked much better than I felt. I was nearly cross-eyed with exhaustion.

Dusk was standing at the driver's-side door trying to

---

114. Sorry to have to put it like that, but it's what happened.

convince me to go home and sleep for a few hours when the noise of a car starting in the parking lot made us all turn to look.

My sister's Crown Vic makes a distinctive growling sound.

"That's her," I whispered.

Dusk crouched down out of sight.

I put my hood up and stared through slitted eyes at the white Crown Victoria as it moved slowly out of the back parking lot along the side of the building. Keira's curly head was barely visible over the steering wheel.

All this effort for someone who only weighs a hundred pounds, I thought nonsensically.

I knew Keira wouldn't recognize my friends' cars. I doubted she'd recognize their faces, either, especially if she'd been up all night writing and drawing.

When the car's taillights had disappeared around the corner, Dusk stood. Outside, the veil of night was fading almost imperceptibly.

"So?" she said.

"I'm going to check it out," I told them.

Number Six

Each of the units had a front entrance with a tiny street-level patio in front, and each had a back exit. The trick was to figure out which of the six row houses was my sister's. Lights had shone behind the blinds in three of the units during the night.

I walked past the tiny patios and assessed the furnishings and décor. One had neatly trimmed boxwoods in matching fake antique pots. One had a bentwood loveseat and prettily faded cushions. A plaque hung on Number Three's front door. It read: I LOVE MY BOSTON TERRIER. Number Four had a small wrought-iron table set out front with an ashtray on it. Number Five, which had lights visible behind the blinds, had a patio empty of decoration and furniture. That one was a possibility. Number Six, whose lights were also on, had nothing on the little patio, but there was a strange shape beside the front door.

I looked around to make sure no one was watching, opened the latch to Number Six's front gate, and let myself in. The knee-height object was a small statue of a semi-naked woman with branching horns like bony wings coming out of her head. Her hair looked like snakes and she was scaly and also beautiful.

I tried to move her but couldn't. She was too heavy.

This was my sister's unit.

It was 5:30 a.m. and I was about to do my first-ever break and enter.

I hurried back to the street, and my friends poured out of their cars.

"We have to get in," I said.

While the rest of us kept watch, Brian examined the lock.

"I hope there's no alarm," I said.

"Me too," he muttered. "That would do wonders for my relationship with my probation officer." He took a thin piece of metal from his pocket and got to work. I could hear our collective breathing fall into a rhythm.

After the door clicked open, he stood back to let me do the honors.

I grasped the handle and tried to collect myself.

"This is freaking me out," said Dusk.

She wasn't alone. The thought that my closet-dwelling sister had a second existence in a fancy new town house made a certain amount of sense. After all, she *was* into alternate universes.

"What if we walk right in on some strange family?" asked Neil.

"We'll tell them we're doing a school project," said Aimee blithely. "Art kids get up to the damnedest things."

"Like breaking into houses," said Neil.

"How'd you learn to do this?" I asked Brian, who'd picked the lock in under three minutes.

"Metal shop. I was doing these metal installations. Got

interested in locking mechanisms. My final project was going to be an exploded-view lock and directions for picking it. I might still do that. If I'm not in jail for breaking into this place."

Aimee punched him lightly in the shoulder.

I blew out a long breath and turned the handle.

No alarm sounded.

"Are we in the right place?" asked Neil.

I looked around. There was nothing in the main room. No furniture. No rugs. It was bone white and completely empty.

We were in the right place.

Double Avenger

Plain roll blinds covered the floor-to-ceiling windows and the interior lights were on. At the back of the main room was a kitchen lined with gleaming brushed-steel appliances. There was a granite countertop, a butcher-block island, and wooden cupboards. It was the kind of kitchen found in my friends' houses, only more expensive, artier. The counters were bare, except for a single plastic tub of vegan protein powder beside the double sink, next to an unopened bag of chia seeds and two empty kombucha bottles, proving that my sister wasn't original in all things. There were also two pill bottles. One was half full of gelatin capsules: ADDERALL. The other bottle was labeled DESOXYN. Next to them was a small plastic baggie with some brightly colored pills in it.

Brian looked over my shoulder. Pointed at the bottle of Desoxyn and whistled.

"That shit is seriously hard to get," he said.

I put the pills down.

We went quietly upstairs.

Other than art supplies, a couple of tall drafting chairs and storyboards leaning against the walls, and three large drafting tables with pages scattered across them, the top floor was empty.

I walked over to check out the art. Drawings and stories:

enough for another book, by the look of it. My eyes were drawn immediately to a panel featuring a close-up view of the bugged-out eyes of the Flounder. The sister character who was me and not me was crying. Her face was bruised, her lip cut, the damage rendered in my sister's distinctive and confident hand. I began to read. At first, my mind pushed back against the story, then it seemed to crumple in on itself.

The story was called *Diana: Double Avenger*. In it, the Earth version of Flounder is seduced by an unscrupulous art teacher who, in an effort to get close to Diana, tells the Flounder she's much more talented than she really is. In Vermeer, poor slug-like Flounder is brutally assaulted by a drawing master who coaxes her out into the garden maze. I couldn't quite figure out what the drawing master's motivation was. Money, presumably. Revenge on behalf of a competing family. Sheer wrong-mindedness. The plots of my sister's stories are always a little murky. The worst part was that the assault on the Flounder, which I suppose I should start calling by its proper name—rape—was clearly depicted. *Very* clearly.

You really haven't lived until you've seen several panels showing a misshapen fun-house version of yourself being sexually assaulted in multiple universes in illustrations destined to be seen by countless people.

I followed the panels, skipping quickly past the ones that tracked Diana's thoughts and feelings until I came to the ones in which she began to exact her revenge on Flounder's behalf. The story was so overblown and gothic that it was almost laughable—until I came to the panel that showed Diana pushing the Earth art teacher off a ladder on which he's standing in order to get something out of a cupboard. He sustains two sprained ankles. In Vermeer, Diana invites the drawing master to walk with her to the top of the palace. When they reach the highest point of the overwrought edifice, she pushes him over the side. He tumbles to his death. The drawing of his screaming face before he hits the battlements below was a masterpiece of perspective.

For the longest moment, I couldn't catch my breath.

The villainous art teacher didn't look like Jackson Reid, at least not the same way my parents and I looked like the thinly disguised versions of ourselves. My sister had that much sense of self-preservation. Only something about the man's eyes was similar.

I found myself wheezing. Sudden-onset asthma. Bronchial shutdown.

Behind me, Neil asked if I was okay.

"Stay out!" I said. No one could see these drawings. Read this story.

I couldn't quite process it or understand how the story laid out on the desks fit with the story she'd told me. She'd always drawn our real lives and blown them up to super-sad-sack proportions. She'd been merciless about depicting my bad birthday party. She'd been unsparing about my dad's ouster as the president of the Diorama Club and my mom's various and frequent non-coping moments. This story was different. It had nothing to do with our lives. It was fiction all the way through.

But people would think my rape was true, even though I've never even had sex.

I backed away from the pages, vision blurry.

I backed away until I reached Neil's arms.

"You can look," I told my friends.

Silently, they spread out to read the panels.

There were sharp intakes of breath and dismayed mutters.

When they were done, they came back to stand around me. Dusk was crying, which was almost as alarming as the art around us.

"What *is* this?" she said. "Did something happen to you?"

I shook my head. "No."

Neil pulled me closer.

"How can she do this?" asked Aimee. "It's so sick."

"I don't know what's going on. But I'm going to find out," I told them.

Then the five of us backed out of the room as if its contents were toxic. We went down the stairs and out the front door in stunned silence.

Of Unreliable Narrators

"We'll wait," said Neil when he put the car in park.

I knew it would upset Keira to see a strange car in the driveway if she happened to look outside and was going to ask them to park down the street.

Then I realized that I no longer cared what upset my sister.

I got out of the passenger seat, and Dusk got out of the back. She gave me one of her strong, skinny-girl hugs. Then, on lead soldier legs, I walked to our front door. All the vehicles were home. The entire Pale family waited inside.

When I entered the house, I saw my parents get up from the kitchen table at the same time.

"Normandy!" cried my mother. I realized I'd forgotten to tell her I'd be out all night. She wore her very worst track pants, and her hands were raw and red. If Keira got a look at her hands or her pants, they were sure to be featured in a close-up drawing.

"Norm," said my father, worry straining his studied jauntiness to the breaking point.

"Sorry," I said. "I forgot to call."

"Were you doing something for school?" said my mother, her voice filled with hope.

Before I could get bogged down in a conversation with my parents, I headed for my room and looked into the closet. Keira wasn't inside.

I turned and walked the short distance down the hall to Keira's room. The door was shut.

"She's sleeping," whispered my mom, coming up behind me. "She just got home. It's probably best to let her be. You know how tired she gets when she's working."

I didn't respond.

Instead, I tried the knob. Locked.

I rapped my knuckles, which felt like they belonged to someone else, against the hollow-core door.

"Normandy!" said my mother, shocked.

"I think you might both be overtired," said my father.

I knocked again, this time with the back of my fist.

"Keira," I said. "I need to talk to you."

"Really, Normandy!" My mother's normally wan voice was fierce.

"I have to talk to her."

She and my father said something about Keira's schedule, about her need to have flexible hours. I ignored them again and went back to my room. I went through the closet and into Keira's room. It was the first time I'd ever done that. It had always seemed like a door that only opened one way.

Keira was sitting up in bed. She showed only the mildest surprise to see me.

My sister's presence in the house, in the school, in this town is so outsized that the reality of her comes as a shock, even to those of us who live with her.[115]

She wore a plain dove-colored smock that hung on her thin shoulders and would have looked expensive and chic in her new town house, but which in our worst-of-the-1980s suburban house looked a bit Walker Evans-ish. I don't think the smock was actually sleepwear, but everything she owns could double for pj's.

Keira tilted her head at me, taking me in with her staring blue eyes. Flyaway swirls of dark brown hair were held off her face with a simple, white cotton scarf. A girl out of time. That was my sister. Could anybody really be that ethereal?

No, I thought. *No one could.*

"I need to talk to you," I said, and pushed into the room.

"Normandy!" said my mother from behind me. I turned and saw my parents standing at the entrance to my side of the closet. Unlike my sister, my parents never invaded my privacy, not even when they should have.

"Girls?" said my father.

I closed the closet door and faced Keira.

Her delicate features were ever so slightly pinched, as if an ill-scented wind had just passed.

— — — — — — — — — — — — —

115. Back when she was still doing publicity, interviewers compared her to variously a fairy, an angel, and one of those big-eyed children featured in cheap drug store art. Which is to say that she's short, slender, and has slightly oversized eyes that are a hint too far apart. Slight alien influence there. It could be said that my sister is a little Vermeer-ish around the edges.

My courage coughed once, sputtered, and began to fail.

I didn't need to do this. Keira required special handling. She'd never been confronted with . . . anything.

I thought of the art I had seen.

I thought of Neil and Dusk sitting in Neil's car, just outside.

Truth telling was messy, unpredictable. But avoiding it was worse.

"I found your house," I said.

Keira's lips, only slightly darker than her parchment facial skin, parted slightly. She licked them and put her bare feet on the floor.

"Oh?" she said.

"It's nice. High-end for this town."

"You want to sit down? I have this new record. It's French. We could listen to it."

My sister orders a lot of vinyl over the Internet—mostly European albums featuring old guys who croon in gravelly voices and young women who whisper. Self-conscious, pretentious records.

"It's barely seven in the morning," I said. As though there was some agreed-upon standard time at which a person ought to listen to old French guy records. My sister's room was white and spare as a monk's cell. Her bed was ostentatiously small and simple, topped with a plain white down duvet. No art on the wall, except a small, beautifully executed and framed drawing of a rabbit with a guilty look on its face.

An old padded chair covered in a fine white quilt sat in the corner. A white wooden armoire held her few expensive clothes and, presumably, the rest of her meager but expensive belongings. Of course, she didn't have a closet, either.

At least she's not a hoarder, I thought somewhat hysterically.

"Take the chair," she offered.

I did. I'd never sat in it before. Normally, I stood in Keira's doorway or on the other side of the closet. It was disorienting to be in her room, but the chair was very comfortable.

"We went into your house."

My sister, who'd begun to relax, stiffened and stood up again.

"We?" she said.

"We saw the art for your new book."

Her head jerked once to the side, like an invisible companion had just said something surprising.

"I saw all the stuff about me."

Keira did the head-tilt thing again, a confused canary. She touched her thumb to her chin. "Normandy," she said. "You do know that's a fictional story about a fictional character." Her voice was like a series of soft slaps to the face. I imagined doing something to make her speak up. Grabbing her by the neck, maybe. "I know you get a little sensitive about some aspects of my art. About my success," she said as gently as only someone who means you harm can do.

I marshaled a response. I'd been silent for so long. Too long.

And then it all came pouring out. "Keira, you use me— or at least an awful version of me—in your art. I get nothing for it. You've been telling me all these terrible stories about what happened to you at school. About your affair with your teacher. About how he raped you. Only it was all some twisted lie. Now you've put it all in your new book and made all the bad things happen to me."

Her fine lips curled. Her dimples showed. And yet some-how her face remained entirely humorless.

"As a fellow artist and as my sister, I expect you'd under-stand. It's like alchemy. No one knows how inspiration works. But source material is quite different from the imag-inative product."

"I know about Mr. Reid. About his husband. Did you hurt him?"

She reared back. "Of course not!" Then, without any hes-itation, she continued. "I can't believe you and your friends invaded my privacy like that. You looked at my work before it was ready. Do you have any idea how many people want an advance look at my stuff? This is a serious betrayal."

"What did you do to Mr. Reid?" I asked. I felt my fingers digging into my thighs.

My sister was so pale, she looked like an accessory in her own room.

When she turned to me, the smile and dimples were gone and her voice was glass.

"The new book wasn't coming," she said. "People were waiting. Getting impatient. I was bored with Vermeer. People said I'd peaked already. As an artist."

I waited.

"I haven't peaked, obviously. I'm only twenty. I just needed a kick start. Some inspiration." She let out a laugh so full of disdain, it made me wince. "Turns out I need you guys," she said, waving a thin hand. "My family. *You're* my material. And then I had a brain wave. I realized that I don't need to wait for you to do things. After all, I could *die* wait-ing for you to do something interesting. I'm a writer—I can make things up. For my stories."

"Is this because of Mom and Dad? The affair?"

"Don't be an idiot. That was nothing. Half the kids in the world have divorced parents. Or worse. Your mind is really mundane."

Keira stared toward at her bedroom window, covered in a hand-painted paper blind she'd made herself. "I think the new book is some of the best work I've done."

"Mr. Reid," I said. "What happened to him?"

"He fell," she said simply, as though telling me that she'd eaten the last cookie.

"What about all those things you told me?" I asked.

"I needed to see how you'd react."

I still didn't follow. Couldn't. "To what?"

"Don't be dim, Normandy. Sometimes you need to go above and beyond the basics of imagination. It's called 'research.'"

"Did he touch you?"

"Of course not. He was gay. He thought he understood my writer's block. He kept trying to talk to me about how I needed to 'move beyond my family in my work.'" Keira's voice was flat.

My sister was not accustomed to criticism.

"Everyone thought he was this animation genius and a saint and everything, just because he was a popular teacher."

My sister shrugged and looked over her shoulder in the direction of some voice that only she could hear.

"He thought *I* was having a breakdown. Urged me to get help. We went for a hike so we could 'talk it out.' I told him that walking was the only way I could think. He liked to be helpful. He had an interesting face. Really open."

"Did you push him?" I asked.

"Normandy, you've always been so reductive," said my sister, going from pretty to terrifying in the flutter of an eyelash. "He fell and I watched. I was too far away to catch him. Plus, I'm not very big." She said this with icy satisfaction.

"You didn't tell anyone?"

Keira sighed. "A section of the trail collapsed, and he went with it. I didn't want to get into a whole big deal about it. No one knew I was there. And it gave me a great idea for the new Chronicle. So I came home and got to work."

"And me?" I said.

"I told you the stories so I could watch your reaction. You've got *such* an interesting range of expressions. Even when I add all that flesh to your face. Is there anything more expressive than a human face?" She gave her head a little shake in wonder at human faces and all they could be made to tell. "If you keep working at your drawing, maybe someday you'll begin to see like an artist."

"And the money?" I said, my voice nearly gone. "Why did you tell Sylvia you wanted to pay off the mortgage?"

"I knew she'd like that. Also, they'd get me my money sooner if they thought I was being generous with it. You saw that town house—I had to have it. Nanaimo isn't exactly awash in cool places."

"So you're not going to help out Mom and Dad?"

Keira looked at me like I'd just said something insane. "Maybe Mom and Dad need to stop looking for handouts."

"The only reason they thought you were going to help them out was because you said you were. Then you didn't."

"It's not my fault our parents are failures," said Keira.

That was as much as I could handle. More, actually.

"Okay," I said. I got to my feet. I had an urge to run out of her room, with its atmosphere anesthetized by a lack of color.

I thought about asking her about the bottles of pills. But I didn't. I'd had my fill of her truth.

"Where are you going?"

"Out," I said.

She smoothed the fabric of her smock over her sides, then ran her hands over her bedding and nodded distractedly.

I let myself out of her room through the regular door, and found my parents in the kitchen.

"I think you need to know that Keira's new book is—"

"Normandy! You know how your sister doesn't like anyone to see her work before it's ready," said my mom.

"Come on now, girls," said my dad. "Let's be positive!"

"But she's—"

"Seriously, Normandy. It's unacceptable for you to interfere with your sister's work."

I had to try. Just once more.

"She showed me being attacked in her new book," I said. "And by 'attacked,' I mean sexually. She drew that in her new book that she's writing in her new town house that you don't even know about."

The silence that followed was the moment between the bomb blast and the debris raining to the ground.

My dad put both hands on the counter. He seemed to be using it to hold himself up.

My mother's jaw worked silently. Then she swallowed.

"I'm sure it's not that bad," she said finally. "You're misinterpreting." She gathered some steam and kept going. "And really, Normandy, what are you doing? Did your sister invite you to her new town house? I'm sure she just wants to surprise us with the news about her . . . purchase."

For a split second I saw the way my dad stared, open-mouthed, at my mother and I understood the terrible position he was in.

When he recovered, he said, "We're a family. We support each other. I'm sure your sister didn't mean to hurt your feelings."

My ears rang and I seemed to be watching the scene from somewhere outside my body. *Hurt my feelings?* How was that any less serious than hurting me physically? Talking to my parents was pointless. They couldn't hear, they wouldn't see. They sure as hell weren't going to negotiate some useful solution.

So I went to my bedroom, packed up my laptop, and put a few other things into the cheap suitcase I bought to accompany Keira to her publicity events before I realized that I was being put on display as the Flounder. I thought of all those years I'd worshipped my sister. Was she really such a great artist if she had to steal people's lives? Twist them and make them ugly?

I walked down the driveway and back to Neil and Dusk.

Aftermath, as Opposed to Afterword

If this was a fictional story, it would end with a happily ever after. The parents would come to their senses and put down their feet about the way the family was portrayed in the Chronicles and the sister would apologize and burn the new book and emotional justice would reign.

This is not a fictional story, even if it may not be the truest or most complete story ever told. Not because I lied or made things up, but because the more I write, the more I realize that when you tell a story, you shape the truth. What you leave in, what you leave out, every word and every emphasis changes the meaning. Writers create the truth, for better or worse. I've done my best to make this story as accurate as I can. And the truth is that nothing ended neatly. It didn't even end.

What happened is this.

I told my creative writing teacher about my sister's book. I didn't plan to. I had to submit my proposal for my Spring Special Project, and it wasn't ready. Ms. Fowler called me into her office and asked me what the holdup was. I told her. She called in the principal. You have to remember that my sister is Green Pastures' most famous alumna. I was impressed that they didn't just tell me to be quiet in the hope that Keira would give them the endowment she'd been hinting at for as long as she'd been talking about paying off my parents' mortgage.

They asked what I wanted to do. They asked what I

needed. They put me in touch with the school's lawyer. No one knew how to handle the situation. They didn't know if I had any rights. But Ms. Fowler and Principal Manhas stayed when I said I wanted to call Sylvia. I thought my sister's agent might be able to help.

I was wrong. We had a seriously non-funny, uncharming chat, and I got a lesson in how Sylvia earns her 15 percent.

Keira must have called her already, because for once Sylvia wasn't friendly. At all.

"It's Normandy," I told her, even though I'd already announced myself to her assistant.

"Yes?"

"It's about Keira's new book."

Silence.

"She can't publish it."

I could practically hear the ice crystals forming over the phone line.

"Normandy, I'm not sure what gave you the impression that you have any say in what Keira publishes."

This set me back on my heels, until I remembered I was now all truth, all the time when it came to my relationship with my sister. "I *do* think I have a say. For starters, Keira's been drawing and publishing pictures of me without my permission. And her new pictures have crossed a line. I'm not a public figure. I'm a private person. What she's doing is wrong." I looked down at the notes Ms. Fowler and Principal Manhas helped me prepare so I wouldn't go back to tongue-tied, intimidated silence. I cleared my throat. "I, uh," I said. Cleared my throat again and tried to hide the shaking in my hands.

"Normandy, I thought you were more sophisticated than

this. The Chronicles are fiction. Pure fantasy. They take place in an alternate universe, for God's sake."

"She's drawing me and my parents, and you know it. You've always known it and you've never cared as long as you got paid."

I cast a quick glance at Ms. Fowler, who nodded encouragingly.

Sylvia, whom I'd always thought of as the world's coolest city aunt, dropped her voice into a phone-harassment register. "Do you have *any idea* how much is riding on this project? It's two years late. Viceroy has paid mid-six-figures for it. The studio included it in the movie option with the other books based on a partial. This is no time for you to begin behaving like a child."

"I know that." I took a deep breath. "It's time for me to start acting like an adult. I don't want to be in any more of Keira's stories."

Sylvia made a hissing noise through her teeth.

"If Keira does publish that book, I'll tell everyone what she did. How she told me she'd been raped by her teacher. How she hinted that she had something to do with his death. All so she could see how I'd respond. And then she drew it all happening to me!"

As I spoke, I realized that I didn't know what any of this would mean. Keira's fans probably wouldn't care what she said to me or why. Her demented mind games would just add to her allure. Maybe the world thought she could represent me any way she wanted. Well, the world could suck it.

"You are being very selfish," said Sylvia finally. "Interfering with your sister's career in this way."

After that, the situation got even more unhinged. Let me

lay out the facts in the least exciting possible way. I don't want to influence anyone's opinion with my overly persuasive prose.

After presumably consulting with Keira, Sylvia arrived in town the next day to fix things. She gathered up my parents, and Ms. Fowler and Principal Manhas and I met them in his office.

"Kiera can't be here. She's too stressed by what's happened and has to focus on her deadline. I'm acting as her representative in this matter." Sylvia leveled her expensive eyewear at me. "Normandy, you're saying some pretty irresponsible things. These kinds of accusations could have long-term ramifications for your sister's career." She'd apparently decided that calling me selfish on the phone hadn't quite gotten the message across clearly enough. She wanted to have the same conversation all over again, this time with my shell-shocked parents sitting beside her.

"I told you I don't want to be in Keira's book," I said. "Especially not in *those* drawings."

"Now, Normandy," said Sylvia. "You know that's not you in those pages."

"I *know* it's not me. Flounder just *looks* like me. A *hideous* version of me."

"It's art," she said.

"It's stealing," I said, my head thumping. "And her new story is lies."

I looked at my parents. What could I say to get them to understand?

"Keira's taking pills," I blurted. "Drugs." That was how Brian had found out where Keira lived. They shared a dealer, who had mentioned the crazy artist girl in the almost-empty, new, high-end town house on Prideaux Street.

My mother stared at her knees. I think she was medicated herself. My dad offered up a smile best described as "cringing."

Sylvia was unmoved by this revelation. "If she's developed a little problem, we'll send her to rehab. *After* she finishes the new Chronicle. You're upset, Normandy. Tell me what we can do for you. I've already told your parents that Keira's going to look after the mortgage."

"That book can't be published. Not with me in it. It shows me getting *raped*."

My dad winced, and my mother looked quickly away.

"Whose parents *are* you?" I said, my voice cracking.

"Normandy," said my dad. "I'm sure this is all a misunderstanding. A misinterpretation. We want the best for both of you."

Sylvia smiled. Her veneered teeth looked like they belonged in the face of a cartoon shark. "The story is fiction. None of the characters are real. I've spoken to our lawyers, and they've assured me there are no legal grounds for anyone to interfere with the publication of this book. There is *a lot* riding on it. I think it's going to be the biggest one yet. Especially with the films."

I closed my eyes and felt the throb of blood moving through my brain. I imagined someone playing me on-screen. On countless screens. Or an animated me. I wasn't sure which was worse.

"No," I said simply.

"I'm not going to argue with you, because I know you're

going to be reasonable once you settle down."

"I'm going to contact Mr. Reid's husband."

"Keira wasn't even there with the teacher on the mountain the day he died. She was making the whole thing up," said Sylvia.

I shook my head to clear it. *Another* lie? I had no idea what to believe. If what Keira had told Sylvia was the truth, I didn't know whether to be relieved or disgusted. My sister had used Mr. Reid's accident just like she'd used us. On the plus side, she wasn't a murderer.

If what she'd told *me* was the truth . . . well, that meant my sister was a monster. In that moment, I decided that Keira had told her agent the truth. Because that's what I wanted to be true.

"I'm going to tell Mr. Reid's husband that Keira used what happened to Mr. Reid," I said after a long pause.

"Prove it," she replied.

I just barely stopped myself from screaming a swear word at the ceiling.

"I think that's enough for one day," said Ms. Fowler.

"Norm," said my dad, "things get confusing." He looked like he wished he was making chili. In spite of everything, my heart hurt for him. I thought of how brutal this was for me, even with all of the support I had. My friends, my teachers. He had my mom, who wasn't big on coping, and my sister, who wasn't big on caring about others. And he had me, who had never let on that I wasn't thriving under current management. My dad wasn't a bad person. He was just too tangled up to see a way out.

On that decisive note, the meeting broke up. I never

spoke directly to Sylvia again. I doubt I ever will. In the months since that meeting, I haven't spoken to directly to Keira, either. So many people gone so quickly.

What happened after that? I moved in with Neil and his dad. Dusk had asked if I wanted to stay with them, but we both knew that her parents weren't really easygoing, add-another-kid-to-the-mix people. The Suttons had a lot of extra room, and Neil's dad told me about twenty times how happy he was for me to stay with them as long as I needed to. "Forever, if you want!" he said.

As Sylvia had promised, my threats and complaints didn't change Viceroy's plans. They were going ahead with the new Chronicle.

So I did what I could to tell my truth. The same day the film option and the publication date for the new Chronicle were announced, I sat down for an interview with *Comic*, the comic arts and animation journal. I told the reporter what it was like to be the unwilling subject of my sister's stories. I talked about how those stories had changed our family and partially paralyzed all of us. I told her about the new Chronicle and said I thought Keira had slipped a few gears—the new book wasn't rooted in any kind of truth. Instead, my sister had played a vicious game with reality to get the images she needed in her mind.

The article blew up, by which I mean it caused a contro-versy. My sister didn't respond, at least not directly. Sylvia issued a carefully crafted press release full of faux regret at the comments of "certain misguided individuals." It speculated that recent revelations were a result of "ongoing rivalry" and that Keira was not responding directly in order to protect the privacy of her accuser. It was pretty much a masterwork of indirect character assassination.

Critics and artists weighed in, and there were follow-up articles online and on paper. People took sides. Keira's most serious fans accused me of being jealous and bitter. Some well-known writers of creative nonfiction said Keira had been reckless and irresponsible in her handling of other people's stories. Academics began to discuss our family relationship in their classes in the same breath as the conflict between Augusten Burroughs and his adoptive family.[116] Libertarians said people should be able to write and draw anyone and anything they liked.

Some artists thought Keira should be more sensitive and responsible in her storytelling. Some thought she should be allowed free rein.

It all would have been extremely interesting if I hadn't been in the middle of it.

My sister is famous enough and the story was juicy enough that it got picked up by the mainstream press. At least, they tried to pick it up. Reporters from *Vanity Fair* and *Esquire* and *Maclean's* and the *Globe and Mail* and the *New York Times* called and emailed, asking for interviews. Talk show producers called. But I'd said all I wanted to say, and Mr. Sutton and the school directed the reporters to the interview in *Comic*.

----

116. I only know this because a couple of them wrote to me to ask if I'd be willing to join their classes via Skype to talk about our issues. Terms such as "historiographic metafiction" and "fictional autobiography" and "genre slippage" led me to give the virtual visits a pass. Plus my computer's crap at Skype.

Keira didn't respond to any of the commentary. Her silence made me look worse, at least according to people who'd already made up their minds.

Then Viceroy pushed back the new Chronicle a season. Keira's fans got the idea that I'd delayed the new book and maybe endangered the movie, and I became the target of their Internet rage. I was the Yoko Ono of graphic novels. Flounder hate sites popped up. My name became synonymous with sisterly jealousy. I pretty much had to get off the Internet, because Keira's nutbag fans made my life a misery. Then people started to fight back.

It started, as most protests do, locally. In this case, at Green Pastures. Someone broke into the display case in front of the office and removed the first edition copies of the Diana Chronicles and a self-portrait my sister had given to the school. They were replaced with small figurines of Santa, the tooth fairy, and Pocahontas. Art school. What can I say?

A few weeks later, Neil directed me to one of the most vicious anti-Flounder sites, the one that had published my name, photo, and all publicly available information, including my old cell number and my parents' address. Someone had hacked the site and posted illustrations of the site's previously anonymous author, a guy in his twenties. He was shown in Flounder form. Turns out he didn't look good as a flounder, either.

No one at school took responsibility for the start of the Normandy Pale Defense Campaign, but I knew it was the work of Dusk and Neil, then of Aimee, Zinnia, Brian, and Prema. Later, I think a lot of the people in our school joined in. (And I'm told by Aimee, who monitors such things, that it has spread around the world. Team Keira vs. Team Normandy.) I was grateful, but I also know that I will never be totally free of my sister's stories. I can imagine her turning the whole saga into another Chronicle. And the whole controversy will flare up again when the movie is released.

But I'd come to terms with the situation, after a fashion. At risk of sounding like an extremely obvious self-help book, I have no control over what people say and think about me. I'd said my piece and been as honest as I could. I knew what was real and what was lies. Some people would love me and some would judge me based on false information. Life would go on. And, at the risk of sounding like another self-help book, I would take it one day at a time.

XXXXX

And what about the Truth Commission?

It won't surprise you to hear that, after everything that happened with my sister, Dusk, Neil, and I didn't have much appetite for formal truth seeking anymore. I feel like I should point out that a project like ours only worked because it took place in our particular school. In another environment, the truth would have been weaponized.

XXXXX

You know how in movies there's sometimes that part at the end when you learn about what happened to all the characters? I love that style of ending.

Here's what happened to our Truth Targets as of this writing:

- Aimee Danes continues to monitor her surgeries carefully. She has also begun to produce and star in an investigative webisode series. The first episode was about corruption in the skin products industry. It's already received 20,000 views. She's going to be a phenomenal TV reporter.

- Mrs. Dekker has a new dress to go with the yellow sundress. This one has long sleeves and is made of a purple knit material. She's still into ostriches.

- Zinnia McFarland continues to protest and make good art. She's going to art school in Berlin in September. Her relationship with her sister is improving. She remains an un-snazzy dresser.

- Prema Hardwick skis like the wind and has two boyfriends and doesn't care who knows it. We have high hopes for their Olympic prospects, especially Dr. Weintraub-Lee.

- Brian Forbes has disappeared. I hope he's in a long-term rehab, but I'm not sure. We all miss him. I might try to find him, if he wants to be found.

- Lisette DeVries has turned French, as in French Canadian, rather than Parisian French, as she

is at pains to point out. She has joined the
Parti Québécois and the school's French Club.
She walks around with a baguette sticking out
of her backpack most of the time.

- In April, Tyler Jones unveiled his Senior Year
  Major Project. Big three-dimensional copper,
  glass, and tin letters form the word TRUTH.
  Water pours into the top T, courses through an
  obstacle course, and then spills out of the H.
  There's a pond at the base of the H with some
  exotic plants growing out of it. Somehow, the
  water is propelled back up the installation and
  jets out the top and back over.

  He calls the piece *Truthfiltration*. In spite
  of how it sounds, it's really quite beautiful.
  The water changes color as it moves through
  the letters.

  No one knows whether he's gay or not. Almost everyone's still hoping he'll declare for
  their side. He's off to the Nova Scotia College
  of Art and Design in the fall. Maybe someone
  there will get to find out.

- His uncle, Officer Jones, is apparently working on a series of gritty watercolors about
  Nanaimo-style crime and law enforcement.
  He never did get in touch with me about
  Keira, but Aimee, who hears everything, told
  me that my sister had been a nuisance caller
  to the police station. Apparently, Keira used

to complain several times a night about her
neighbors making noise. I guess they weren't
as well trained as her family.

I know I presented my friends' families as being dys-
functional. Now that I'm living at Neil's house, I am pleased
to report that it's not true. Admittedly, Mr. Sutton is not
a tightly scheduled individual. He works about half an
hour a day and makes more money than most people do
in a month. This results in a lifestyle and fashion sense of
alarming leisure.

Mr. Sutton, as it turns out, is also a devoted father. He
checks Neil's homework with interest and gives feedback on
Neil's paintings. He and Neil watch movies, mostly from the
late 1960s and 1970s, constantly. At Mr. Sutton's suggestion,
we've been watching Kurosawa's *Rashomon*. It's about the
rape of a woman and the murder of her samurai husband
and it's told from four different perspectives. It's about truth
and how it's influenced by perception. It's also evidence that
there's a piece of art to help a person understand any situation, no matter how strange or traumatic. Like I said, Mr.
Sutton, though prone to loungewear, is an excellent father.
There is a reason that Neil is the world's best boyfriend. Not
long ago, Mr. Sutton helped me to understand some things
about Neil's art.

"You know, Norm," he said, spearing an olive out of his
martini one afternoon when Neil was staying late at school
to paint. "Neil's work is fascinating. But it's also sad to me."

I waited for him to explain. Part of me was, in spite
of everything, still a little jealous or at least curious about
Neil's art. He still hadn't painted me.

"His mother was so beautiful. But she was always leaving. From the time I met her until the day she left for good, a few months after Neil was born, she was slipping away from us. It's why I've never remarried. It's bad enough I have a kid who can't stop painting disappearing women. No need to add another layer of complication to it."

That's how Mr. Sutton talked. Openly, but not inappropriately.

It was interesting to watch him try to sort out how best to have me living with them. I basically had my own wing. My bedroom was located on the opposite side of the house from theirs. I had my own bathroom and sitting area and more space than I'd ever had before. I even had my own garden patio.

I had a walk-in closet. I kept my clothes in it.

Mr. Sutton handled my living with them by sitting us both down and telling us how he felt, and asking how we felt. And getting us to agree to a clearly outlined set of rules. Reality. What a breath of fresh air.

XXXXX

In December, I got a part-time job at the art supply store. I left Nancy at my parents' house and last month combined all my savings to buy my own car. It's a Pacer. We call him Ken. He's got his own kind of cachet and almost never stalls.

This spring we each finished our Special Projects.

Dusk finally taxidermied a shrew to her satisfaction. It died of natural causes and was found almost immediately. This is the key, apparently, to a successful mount, which is what taxidermists call preserving animals. Dusk dressed the shrew in a tiny acid-wash jumpsuit, gave it big hair, and installed it in a miniature single-wide mobile home.

Neil's paintings revealed themselves to be linked. The women got farther away in each one. The final painting was a close-up of Neil's face. If you looked, you could see a reflection of the same painting in his eye. There was no woman in it. I'm not completely sure what it means, and that's okay.

In addition to my embroideries, a version of this manuscript was displayed with a description written by Ms. Fowler. It was titled *Work of Creative Nonfiction by Normandy Pale*. No one was allowed to pick it up and read it. I wasn't quite ready for that.

Dusk's parents came to the end-of-year show. They were impressed with Neil's paintings, and apparently startled by the realism of my embroidery. Several times they commented how photographic it was. Most of all they were proud of *Taxiderming the Shrew*. Still, they couldn't stop themselves from pointing out several times that many accomplished artists are also doctors.

Dusk just shrugged.

My dad came to the show and looked proud and awkward. No one could say he doesn't try. He's giving Mr. Sutton money for my expenses, which Mr. Sutton is just putting away in a college fund for me.

My sister emailed a month or so ago and said she forgives me for telling those lies about her. I haven't written her back.

She's out of rehab and back in her town house. She splits her time between there and my parents' house. It makes me sad to realize that my talented sister has chosen to live such a small, mean life. I know how she's doing because my dad and I get together once a week for breakfast or lunch. We go to a different place every time, because I think it's good for him to try new things, and he agrees. We talk about real things, at least we try to. I know my dad didn't want any of this. He didn't go along with Keira's presentation of us so she would pay off the mortgage, or for some other selfish reason. He did it because, he says, he knows how she really feels.

"She loves us, Normandy. That's why she draws us."

"Do you really believe that?" I asked.

"I'm her parent, Normandy. I have to believe that."

I guess I can see how it would be too much to believe that your own kid sort of hates you.

The truth, especially for my father, is like an onion. You don't want to peel that sucker all at once or you might never stop crying.

My dad says he understands that I'm not ready to come home if Keira's going to be there. He says he appreciates my courage. He's thinking about taking an art class at night. Getting back into his model-making. I hope he does.

I haven't seen my mom, because she says it's too painful right now. She hasn't been going out much since she stopped working, which she stopped doing as soon as the mortgage got paid off. I asked my dad if Keira gave them any extra money. He said it wasn't important, which means she didn't. But my mom and I talk on the phone sometimes. If there were prizes awarded for awkward and depressing conversations, we'd need a special trophy case to hold our winnings.

XXXXX

So that's the story of the Truth Commission. Did the truth set me free? Hard to say. I'm struggling for a way to end this story that will sound profound. A sound bite or a memorable Wildean quote.[117] Nothing's coming. That's kind of the thing about the truth. It's never complete and it's rarely simple.[118]

Oh, and I just realized I've never really explained my embroidery project. The series is called *The Corrections*.[119] It is made up of four separate pieces meant to be displayed together as a single picture. Each shows a section of a family photo taken of us before the first Chronicle was published. When you look at them all together, they still don't make sense. The pieces don't fit perfectly together and don't tell the whole story.

Only the viewer can say if I succeeded.

With love and respect,

Normandy Pale

--- --- --- --- --- --- --- --- --- --- --- --- ---

117. Such as "Lying, the telling of beautiful untrue things, is the proper aim of Art" from "The Decay of Lying." I think we can agree that particular quote is not a good fit for this particular story.

118. Okay, I just paraphrased Wilde there.

   Also, I don't need to tell you that sometimes the truth is a turd, Ms. Fowler. I'm sorry about you and Mr. Wells. I've decided to remove some of these footnotes before the manuscript goes to Principal Manhas, who has agreed to be my second reader. I've decided that Mr. Wells needs to focus on other things, such as learning to be a little more truthful in his dealings with colleagues.

119. Shout-out to J-Franz!

I would like to thank the following people for helping me to finally tell the truth: Ms. Fowler, Dusk Weintraub-Lee, Neil Sutton, Mr. Rowan Sutton, Aimee Danes, Mrs. Blaire Dekker, Zinnia McFarland, Lisette DeVries, Brian Forbes, Prema Hardwick, Tyler Jones, Randy Thomas, Officer Edward Jones, Principal Manhas, and everyone at Green Pastures Academy of Art and Applied Design.

As for everyone else? Good effort.

ACKNOWLEDGMENTS

My undying thanks to:

My agent, Hilary McMahon, for everything and then some;

Honored test readers Andrew Gray, Bill Juby, Stephanie Dubinsky, and in the early stages, Jamie Sigmundson and Tai Deacon, for smart, funny, helpful feedback;

My colleague, Marni Stanley, for generously sharing her expertise and vast library of graphic novels;

Former student and current illustrator Trevor Cooper, for his astonishing artistic talent and general excellence;

Mat Snowie, for helping me make "promotional" videos and being a delightful mix of calm, creative, and competent;

My students at Vancouver Island University, who are more hilarious and interesting than your average;

VIU First Nations Studies professors Keith Smith, Laura Cranmer, and elder Ray Peters, for advice and suggestions;

All the fabulous folks at Penguin Canada, particularly my beloved Lynne Missen and Nicole Winstanley;

Everyone at Viking Children's Books, especially Ken Wright, Kim Ryan, Denise Cronin, Kate Renner, Janet Pascal, Abigail Powers, Susan Jeffers Cassel, Cara Petrus—

And super special mention to Sharyn November, only the best champion a writer could ask for. Her magnificent hair is the perfect accessory for such a startling and original mind;

My husband, James, and our puppy, Rodeo. I'm glad only one of you steals socks and barks, or this book would never have been completed;

And myself, for making these acknowledgments the most Academy Awards–ish ever.

SUSAN JUBY is the author of many novels for teenagers and adults. She is best known for *Alice, I Think*, the first of the Alice MacLeod trilogy, which was made into a successful television series. She is also the author of a memoir, *Nice Recovery*, and the adult comic novel *Home to Woefield* and its sequel, *Republic of Dirt: Return to Woefield*.

She is currently working on another book set at the Green Pastures Academy of Art and Applied Design.

Susan Juby lives with her husband and their dog in Nanaimo, B.C., Canada, the setting of many of her books (including this one). Her website is www.susanjuby.com, and she Tweets at @thejuby.

TREVOR COOPER is a graduate of Vancouver Island University's visual art program and a former student in Susan Juby's writing classes. He lives in Nanaimo, where he draws pictures in a studio in the attic above his parents' house.

His website is www.trevcoop.com.